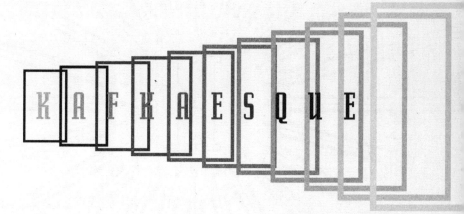

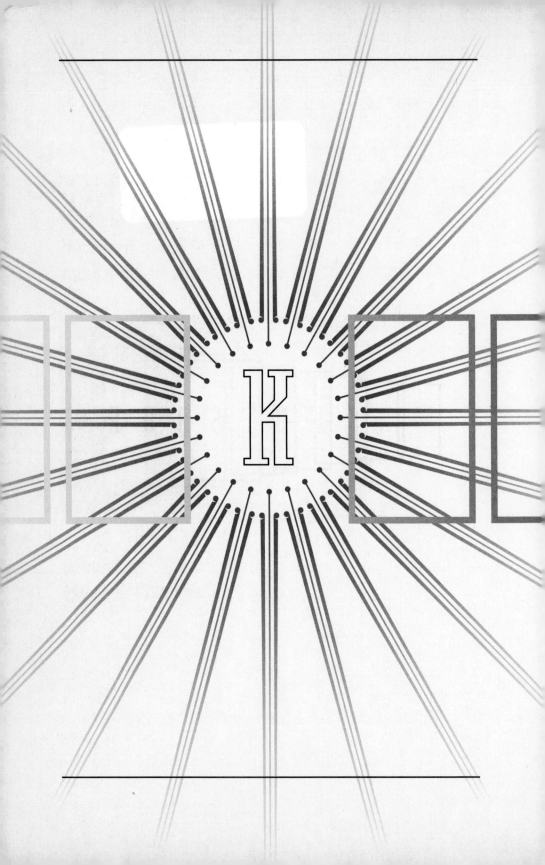

KAFKAESQUE

Stories inspired
by **Franz Kafka**

Edited by **John Kessel**
and **James Patrick Kelly**

TACHYON

Cover design by Josh Beatman
Interior design by John Coulthart

Tachyon Publications
1459 18th Street #139
San Francisco, CA 94107
(415) 285-5615
WWW.TACHYONPUBLICATIONS.COM
TACHYON@TACHYONPUBLICATIONS.COM

Series Editor: Jacob Weisman
Project Editor: Jill Roberts

ISBN 13: 978-1-61696-049-0
ISBN 10: 1-61696-049-3

Printed in the United States
of America by Worzalla
First Edition: 2011
9 8 7 6 5 4 3 2 1

To
Carol Emshwiller
on the occasion of her ninetieth birthday

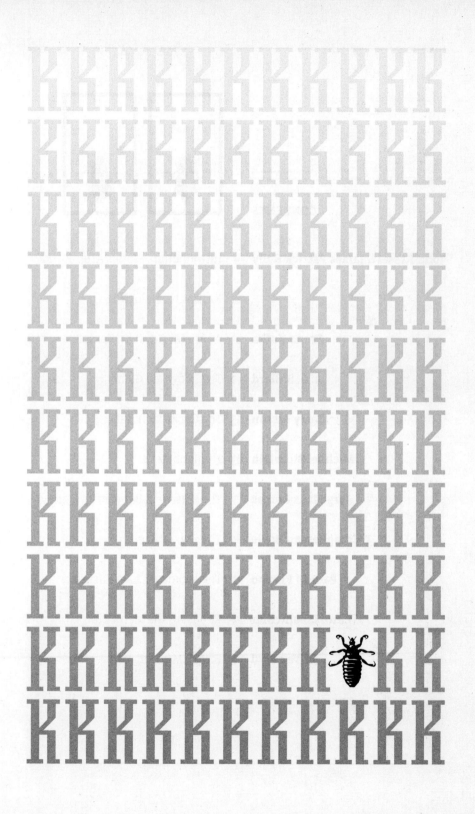

CONTENTS

Stories After Kafka

John Kessel and **James Patrick Kelly**

DB: You said, "When one reads Whitman, one is Whitman," and I was wondering, when you translated Kafka did you feel at any time that you were Kafka in any sense?

Borges: Well, I felt that I owed so much to Kafka that I really didn't need to exist.
—Jorge Luis Borges, interview with Daniel Bourne of *Artful Dodge*, April 25, 1980

THE ADJECTIVE

IN THE TOURIST shops of Prague, along with T-shirts announcing "Prague Drinking Squad," you may buy other shirts bearing the image of Franz Kafka. There are many varieties. Wearing your Kafka shirt you may visit the Kafka museum and at least two of the several apartments where Kafka lived. Afterward, in the Café Kafka, you may enjoy a latte, add sugar to it from a packet that has Kafka's face on it, and light your cigarette from a box of Kafka matches.

Stratford-on-Avon and Hannibal, Missouri, have promoted writers as their native sons, but we suspect that no writer who ended his life as obscurely as Kafka has had his reputation expand so far, so quickly into the popular consciousness. It is a remarkable metamorphosis. Imagery from Kafka's fiction is everywhere in our culture, from popular movies to editorial cartoons, and people who have never read a word of his fiction will describe their tribulations with the Department of Motor Vehicles as "Kafkaesque."

What does it mean when a writer's name becomes an adjective? From a certain perspective, this would seem to be any artist's ultimate symbol of success. After all, the number of writers who have been elevated to adjectival status in common parlance is vanishingly small. Shakespeare is one. Who else? *Twainian* sounds ridiculous. *Hemingwayesque*? No. English majors have coined *Chekovian* and *Shavian* and *Joycean* but the circulation of these specialized terms is limited. Kafkaesque, on the other hand, has an entry in the Merriam-Webster dictionary:

> of, relating to, or suggestive of Franz Kafka or his writings; *especially:* having a nightmarishly complex, bizarre, or illogical quality <*Kafkaesque* bureaucratic delays>

Kafka's influence happened, in literary time, very quickly. Before World War II his work was known in German, and the translations of *The Castle* and *The Trial* by Willa and Edwin Muir in the 1930s had received some attention, but not enough to establish a broad reputation. After the war, no writer seemed more relevant than Kafka. As Michael Hofmann has suggested: "It is as though Holocaust, Communism, Existentialism and Cold War all had to happen to validate a handful of texts written in the first quarter of the twentieth century."[1]

Franz Kafka died in 1924, in obscurity to the large world, having published a handful of odd stories in central European literary venues. It is true that in bohemian literary circles of Prague, and perhaps to some readers in Berlin, Munich, and Vienna, Kafka had established a small reputation. Yet even so astute a reader as Jorge Luis Borges, living in Switzerland at the time, was unimpressed by a Kafka story he read in one of these magazines:

> I shall never forget the first time I read Kafka in a certain self-consciously "modern" publication around 1917. The editors, who were not wholly devoid of talent, had dedicated themselves to inventing texts that were notable for their lack of punctuation, capital letters, and rhyme as well as for their alarming simulation

---

1 Michael Hofmann, "Introduction" to *Metamorphosis and Other Stories* (New York: Penguin, 2007), vii.

of metaphor, abuse of portmanteau words, and other experiments perhaps typical of all young people. Amidst all this boisterous print, a short text signed by Franz Kafka seemed to me—in spite of my youthful docility as a reader—extraordinarily insipid. Now, in my old age, I dare at last to own up to a case of unforgivable literary insensitivity; I was offered a revelation, and I passed it by.[2]

Yet while the wide acceptance and understanding of the adjective Kafkaesque is evidence of Franz Kafka's enduring influence on our culture, it is also a kind of a prison in which the writer and his work are confined. It is, in essence, Kafkaesque.

The person on the street, if she knows Kafka at all, will immediately associate him with the bizarre and impersonal bureaucracies of the novels *The Trial* and *The Castle* and perhaps with one touchstone story, "The Metamorphosis." Of course, Kafka famously asked that the manuscripts of those unfinished novels be destroyed at his death. Of his best known story he wrote in his diary: "Great antipathy to 'The Metamorphosis.' Unreadable ending. Imperfect almost to its marrow."[3] Would he then regret the work he is known for?

This question fits into the simplistic narrative into which some have wedged Kafka the man. Our hypothetical person in the street, if she knows anything of Kafka's biography, may well be under the impression that Kafka did not wish to become one of the best known authors of all time. Even as he rebukes his friend and editor Max Brod from the grave for publishing the unfinished masterpieces—despite the specific instructions in his will—certain readers can feel superior to the reclusive wretch, since his judgment of his own work was so obviously wrong.

If you accept the myth that has grown up around the man, then this book would seem to be a crime against Kafka's memory. What would he have made of the stories that follow? Other writers trampling across his tortured mindscapes, playing with his nightmare metaphors? Evoking laughter from the writings of this most solemn of pessimists?

---

2 Jorge Luis Borges, "Foreword" to *Kafka: Stories 1904–1924*, trans by J. A. Underwood, (New York: Little Brown & Co, 2001).
3 Kafka, Franz, *Diaries 1910–1923*, ed. Max Brod, trans by Joseph Kresh and Martin Greenberg (New York: Schocken Books, 1969), 253.

We are in mind of an anecdote that Max Brod, Kafka's best friend, tells of a reading Kafka gave. "We friends of his laughed quite immoderately when he first let us hear the first chapter of *The Trial*. And he himself laughed so much that there were moments when he couldn't read any further. Astonishing enough, when you think of the fearful earnestness of this chapter. But that is how it is."[4] We treasure the image of the allegedly somber author laughing helplessly along with the rest of his pals at the existential fix into which he had thrust his hapless protagonist. We like to think that, whatever he might have thought of the stories that follow, Franz Kafka would enjoy the joke literary history has played on him. And us.

THE MAN

"And the personal mark of each writer consists in his having his own special way of concealing his flaws."
—Frank Kafka, letter to his publisher, Ernst Rowohlt, August 14, 1912[5]

While it's possible to cast a straightforward Kafka chronology, understanding what the events of his short life meant to him has ever been elusive. He was a man who struggled with his many contradictions. Kafka was born in 1883 into an assimilated middle-class Jewish family in Prague, the third largest city of the Austro-Hungarian Empire. He had five siblings, two younger brothers who died in infancy and three sisters who survived him, only to perish in Hitler's camps during the Second World War. He was a member of the dominant German-speaking minority, just three percent of the population of Prague at the time, but he was also fluent in Czech. As a young man, he was athletic, taller than average, fond of swimming, rowing, and bicycling. Yet for much of his life he was also a hypochondriac: it was not until 1917 that he was diagnosed with the tuberculosis that would kill him at the

---

4 Max Brod, *The Biography of Franz Kafka*, trans by G. Humphreys Roberts (London: Secker and Warburg, 1947), 139.
5 Franz Kafka, quoted in *Franz Kafka: A Writer's Life*, Joachim Unseld, trans by Paul F. Dvorak (Riverside, CA: Ariadne Press, 1994), 67.

Kafkaesque

age of forty. He trained in university as a lawyer and eventually found a comfortable position in the state-run Workers' Accident Insurance Institute investigating claims. Although he chafed at the work, he also excelled at it. The great advantage of his public sector job was that he put in just a six-hour day, leaving time for writing, his lifelong passion. "My job is unbearable to me because it conflicts with my only desire and my only calling, which is literature. Since I am nothing but literature and can and want to be nothing else, my job will never take possession of me, it may however shatter me completely."[6]

Since he lived with his parents for much of his life, he was able to maintain an affluent lifestyle on his bureaucrat's salary until World War I. He dressed well, frequented cafes, and had an active social life. His literary friends were members of the avant-garde. Max Brod, the closest of this circle, was a well-published and highly regarded writer who tirelessly promoted his friend. In fact, before Kafka had published a word, Brod was mentioning him as one of the contemporary masters of German literature.

While Kafka was unable to finish the novels that helped make his posthumous reputation—these being edited by Brod, his literary executor— he did enjoy success as a writer of stories. He published seven short books in his lifetime, which included such masterpieces as "The Judgment," "The Stoker," "In the Penal Colony," "The Metamorphosis," "The Great Wall of China," "A Report to an Academy," "A Country Doctor," "A Message from the Emperor," "A Hunger Artist," and "First Sorrow." As he was dying he was working on the galleys for a collection called *A Hunger Artist* which included a new story, "Josephine the Singer, or the Mouse Folk." He was by no means an unknown; indeed, editors wrote to him soliciting submissions and at the start of his career he shared a prestigious writing award with the well-known playwright Carl Sternheim.

Of the many contradictions in Kafka's life, three stand out for the modern reader.

Although Kafka had many relationships with women, almost all of them were troubled. He was engaged to be married three times, twice

---

6 Franz Kafka, *Diaries 1910–1923*, ed. Max Brod, trans by Joseph Kresh and Martin Greenberg, (New York: Schocken Books, 1975), 230.

to Felice Bauer (the first engagement was broken off in part because he made advances to her best friend, Grete Bloch) and once to Julie Whoryzek. He fell in love with his Czech translator Milena Jesenská, who was unhappily married, but, for reasons that remain unclear, he could not bring himself to commit to her. He lived in the last year of his life with Dora Dymant, a young teacher and seamstress fifteen years his junior. He had other relationships and brief liaisons in his younger days. We know that he frequented brothels; his papers include pornography. "Sex keeps gnawing at me, hounds me day and night, I should have to conquer fear and shame and probably sorrow too to satisfy it; yet on the other hand I am certain that I should take advantage with no feeling of fear or sorrow or shame, of the first opportunity to present itself quickly, close at hand and willingly."[7] Because sex was always a fraught matter for him, he was never able to reconcile his sexual desires with the impulse to marry—or at least to settle down. "I regarded marriage and children as one of the desirable things on earth in a certain sense, but I could not possibly marry."[8]

Kafka was a student of Yiddish literature, and in his youth championed Yiddish theatre, much to the puzzlement of some of his literary friends. He was sympathetic to Zionism and yet there are no overt allusions to Jews or Jewishness in his fiction. "What have I in common with the Jews?" he wrote. "I have hardly anything in common with myself, and should stand very quietly in a corner, content that I can breathe."[9] But there are many things "missing" in Kafka's fiction—often a sense of place, or of time or of historicity—because these did nothing to advance his artistic goals. Kafka was not a realist and we ought not look to the work to understand his problematic relationship to Judaism. Of course, contemporary questions about Kafka's Jewishness are informed by tragedies that occurred after his death. Not only did his sisters perish in concentration camps, but Milena did as well. The Gestapo seized twenty notebooks and thirty-five letters that Kafka had left to Dora Dymant.

7 Franz Kafka, *Diaries 1910–1923*, ed. Max Brod, trans by Joseph Kresh and Martin Greenberg, (New York: Schocken Books, 1975), 400.

8 Franz Kafka, *Letters to Friends, Family and Editors*, ed. Max Brod, trans by Richard and Clara Winston (New York: Schocken Books), 216.

9 Franz Kafka, *Diaries 1910–1923*, ed. Max Brod, trans by Joseph Kresh and Martin Greenberg (New York: Schocken Books, 1975), 252.

Kafkaesque

Max Brod was forced to flee to Jerusalem with an even larger collection of Kafka's papers. Do the terrible realities of the Holocaust affect how we read the work? Undoubtedly, but this is a problem for us, and not for Kafka. Similarly, there are those who interpret *The Trial* and *The Castle* as predictions of the rise of totalitarian states like Hitler's Germany, Mussolini's Italy, and Stalin's Russia. Kafka, however, was not trying to prophesy some future world order but rather was attempting to engage imaginatively with a society he knew all too well.

Last there is the puzzle of Kafka's instructions to Max Brod to destroy his unpublished work. Brod claims that he told his friend plainly that he would do no such thing. After Kafka's death, Brod found two notes which explicitly stated that all his papers were to be burned unread. How was Brod then to have executed these requests if he was to burn them unread? And why didn't Kafka burn the papers himself, especially since he knew Brod was unlikely to do the deed? Even after his death, Kafka's contradictions remained unresolved. While we have no way to know his thinking in this matter, we do know that this was the request of a sick man whose financial fortunes had taken a radical turn for the worse. His modest pension from the Workers' Accident Insurance Institute was nearly worthless in the hyperinflation that plagued the defeated and disintegrating Austro-Hungarian Empire in the wake of World War I. It is clear that Kafka was a depressed and often anxious man, especially after he was diagnosed with tuberculosis. Never a risk taker, he suffered from feelings of inferiority that arose from the high standards to which he held himself as a writer. Frustrated that his reach continued to exceed his grasp, at the end of his life he struggled with despair.

There is an odd and, yes, *Kafkaesque* postscript to Brod's denial of Kafka's request. Brod brought many of Kafka's papers with him to Jerusalem in 1939. No one knows exactly what this cache contains although reputedly there are letters, diaries, and manuscripts. On his death in 1968, Brod left these papers to his secretary and presumed mistress, Esther Hoffe. But was she intended to be the executor or the beneficiary? Brod's will is ambiguous, since it also provides that his literary estate be given to a "public archive in Israel or abroad." In any event, Hoffe retained possession of the Kafka papers until her death in 2007, at which time they passed to her daughters in accordance with her will. Possession of these papers is the subject of a lawsuit in Israel, unresolved as we write this. It is likely, however, that in the near future, Kafka readers and scholars will have access to a trove of Kafka's previously unseen writing. Meanwhile, the Kafka Project at San Diego State University continues the search for the missing collection confiscated by the Gestapo from Dora Dymant.

THE WORK

> "The tremendous world I have inside my head. But how to free myself and free it without being torn to pieces. And a thousand times rather be torn to pieces than to retain it in me or to bury it. That, indeed, is why I am here, that is quite clear to me."
> —Franz Kafka, diary entry, June 21, 1913[10]

A strength of Kafka's work is that it stands in marked contrast to the prevailing standards of value in the literary world of the first two-thirds of the twentieth century. Kafka was an unapologetic allegorist in a time when allegory was shunned as old-fashioned and embarrassing. Though he wrote among and associated with writers who were to a greater or lesser degree consciously identified as Expressionists, though he was alive and working at the same time that Tristan Tzara and Marcel Duchamp created Dadaism, and though he was claimed by the Surrealists, Kafka was not an Expressionist, Dadaist, or Surrealist.

"A Hunger Artist" starts with a bald assertion in contradiction to reality: "In the last decades interest in hunger artists has declined a great deal." What is a hunger artist? The narrator takes the stance that we are at least passingly familiar with the theatrical tradition of hunger artists, and he proceeds to elaborate, letting us in on the details of that old practice since we are unlikely to have witnessed such a performance ourselves.

The rest of the story is the elaboration of that premise, examining all of its implications, making it real, turning it over, using it to allegorize

---

10 Franz Kafka, *Diaries 1910–1923*, ed. Max Brod, trans by Joseph Kresh and Martin Greenberg (New York: Schocken Books, 1965), 288.

our world and human behavior. Though a realist writer might acknowledge that his story set in the mundane world might have allegorical readings, the trend in the first half of the twentieth century was to flee allegory for either the documentation of the external world, or documentation of individual psychology—usually both. Even experimentalists like Joyce and Woolf, despite streams of consciousness or wild flights of imagery, assume that fiction is about what *is*, the surface of events and things and people. Hemingway and Faulkner, despite their rhetorical flights, likewise insist upon the reality of their worlds.

Kafka is not interested in documenting the manners and mores of any particular place; he is not interested in probing the psyche of individual characters. Joyce spent his life after leaving Ireland creating Dublin and its inhabitants in their specificity and individuality, their language, places, habits, strengths, and weaknesses. For the most part Kafka's characters don't even have names, and the worlds they inhabit are iconic rather than documentary. Though he spent most of his life in Prague, there is little sense of Prague, or any other specific place, in his work.

We are not interested in the hunger artist's biography. To even ask this question is to reveal its absurdity. Neither do we ask the biography of Melville's Bartleby or Jesus's Good Samaritan or the butcher in Chuang Tsu's poem about "Prince Wen Hui's Cook." We don't wonder about the hunger artist's childhood, his ethnic background, the place where he lives, the names of the towns and cities where he performs, the political climate, his interpersonal relationships, his sex life, what year it is, and what language is being spoken. Kafka spends little time evoking persons or places, does not give us individual gestures or idiosyncrasies, does not appeal to our senses, does not make us feel and live in the worlds he creates. Though he may give us objects and actions that appear in the real world, he is not documenting reality. A cage, an impresario, some straw, a circus. Or an apartment, a traveling salesman, a sister Grete, an unnamed mother and father, a narrow bed, the photo of a woman wearing a muff, an apple. Or a penal colony, an explorer, a prisoner, an officer, a bizarre execution machine.

Yet the stories are not divorced from the world—in fact they are cogently relevant, even political, as radically political in their universality as Jesus's parables. There is a power of intellect behind every sentence. A doubleness. Reading Kafka, one is challenged to interpret every image, every action. One reads *through* the surface of a Kafka story to the meanings behind. There are layers upon layers, prismatic reflections of abstract meanings.

However, it would be a mistake to say that the meanings of Kafka's parables are clear. As the critic Walter Benjamin wrote: "Kafka had a rare ability for creating parables for himself. Yet his parables are never exhausted by what is explainable; on the contrary, he took all conceivable precautions against the interpretation of his writings. One has to find one's way in them circumspectly, cautiously and warily."[11]

STORIES AFTER KAFKA

It was not difficult for us to come up with a table of contents. Our happy dilemma was in choosing just eighteen stories from the abundance of those inspired by Kafka. We selected three kinds of stories for this collection:

> *Stories that derive from specific works of Kafka.* Carol Emshwiller's "Report to the Men's Club" puts the form of Kafka's "Report to an Academy" to feminist purposes. T. Coraghessan Boyle's "The Big Garage" takes *The Trial* to an automotive service center. "The Cockroach Hat" revisits the conceit of "The Metamorphosis." R. Crumb's offers a graphic adaptation of "A Hunger Artist."
>
> *Stories that use Franz Kafka as a character.* Some of these take the form of alternative histories, in which Kafka survived his illness and lived to come to America and establish a new career as in Paul Di Filippo's "The Jackdaw's Last Case," Philip Roth's "'I Always Wanted You to Admire My Fasting'; or, Looking at Kafka" and "Receding Horizon" by Jonathan Lethem and Carter Scholz. Others, such as Scholz's "The Amount to Carry," present a

---

11 Walter Benjamin, *Illuminations: Essays and Reflections,* ed. Hannah Arendt, trans by Henry Zohn (New York: Schocken Books, 1969), 187.

scenario that might have happened to the real Kafka, while Rudy Rucker presents a bizarre fantasia of multiple Kafkas in "The 57th Franz Kafka." And while there is but the merest hint the mysterious stranger in Tamar Yellin's "Kafka in Brontëland" may be Kafka reincarnated, he symbolizes Kafka to the narrator.

Stories that use the methods or materials of Kafka. We acknowledge that this category is subjective. In some of the stories Kafka's guiding hand is evident, while in others the writer may not have had Kafka directly in mind at all. J. G. Ballard's "The Drowned Giant" presents like a Kafka story: its nameless narrator, who comes from the unnamed city to the unlocated seashore to see the corpse of the huge man who has washed ashore there, can readily be seen as a brother to Kafka's protagonists. Eileen Gunn's "Stable Strategies for Middle Management" may have more to do with American bureaucratic culture, yet it operates in the shadow of "The Metamorphosis." Damon Knight's deadpan exposition of the fantastic in "The Handler" owes a debt to Kafka's signature effects. Jeffrey Ford's metafictional "Bright Morning" exorcises Kafka's ghost. Michael Blumlein's claustrophobic "Hymenoptera" recalls the economy of characterization in the short fiction. "The Rapid Advance of Sorrow" by Theodora Goss deftly showcases the modern uses of allegory. "The Lottery in Babylon" is but one of many stories in which Jorge Luis Borges acknowledges the master's influence.

In practice, these categories blend together, as "Jackdaw" crosses *Amerika* with American Sunday comics of the 1920s and '30s, and "Receding Horizon" fuses elements of Kafka's "The Judgment" with the plot of Capra's *It's a Wonderful Life*.

In their afterwords and excerpts from their public commentary, these authors have addressed the degree to which their work was directly or indirectly influenced by Kafka, giving us some insight into their intentions. But the burden of their comments, and the history of Kafka's influence on writers who came after him, is that influence is not something that may be simply circumscribed.

Borges in "Kafka and his Precursors" asserts that every writer creates his ancestors, inventing a tradition from works that previously might not have seemed to have any connection at all. We suggest that this process works forward in time as well as backward: that sufficiently vital work creates descendants out of works that otherwise might not seem related. These stories are, some of them, direct descendants of *The Trial* or "The Metamorphosis," or were created in a literary culture and atmosphere that Kafka's work helped to create, or in a world that regardless of the existence of Kafka, grew to have a space within it into which fiction resembling Kafka's might fit. Consider this anthology a case study in the ways in which a writer of sufficiently original sensibility, in the context of a world that changed, can fashion, if not a genre, a way of seeing things.

The reach of the concept of the Kafkaesque is a testimony to the power of a single mind to create a territory that, after the fact, can draw in the minds of others whether they are aware of him or not. That the work of a man who died as Kafka did, convinced that he had never fulfilled his promise, should produce ultimately so many works, and more than that a vision of the world that compels us to see his influence even where it may not exist, is as powerful a mystery as any of the startlements Franz Kafka wrote in Prague almost one hundred years ago.

Kafka Chronology

1883	Birth of Franz Kafka in Prague, July 3, son of Hermann and Julie.
1885	Birth of brother Georg, who dies at fifteen months.
1887	Birth of brother Heinrich, who dies at six months.
1889	Birth of sister, Gabriele.
1890	Birth of sister, Valerie.
1892	Birth of sister, Ottilie.
1889–1903	Early writing (lost).
1901–1906	Studies law in German-language section of Charles University, Prague.
1904–1905	Writes "Description of a Struggle."
1906	Law degree; begins work in Prague courts.
1908	Takes a position at the state-run Worker's Accident Insurance Institute; friendship with Max Brod.
1909	First publication: eight prose pieces under the title *Meditation*, in Munich journal *Hyperion*.
1910	Publication of five prose pieces in the newspaper *Bohemia*; begins keeping diary.
1911	Contact with Yiddish theater; friendship with Yiddish actor Yitzak Löwy.
1912	Meets Felice Bauer; writes "The Judgment" in a single night, September 22–23, "The Stoker" (first chapter of *Amerika*, also known as *The Man Who Disappeared*), and "The Metamorphosis"; publication of a collection, *Meditation*.
1913	Publication of "The Stoker."
1914	Engaged to Felice Bauer, writes "In the Penal Colony" and begins *The Trial*; World War I breaks out; engagement to Felice Bauer ends.
1915	"The Metamorphosis" published; awarded Fontane Prize for "The Stoker."
1916	"The Judgment" published; writes stories collected in *A Country Doctor*.
1917	Learns Hebrew; second engagement to Felice Bauer; tuberculosis diagnosed; health leave of absence from Workers' Accident Insurance

Institute; second engagement to Felice Bauer ends.

1919   Brief engagement to Julie Wohryzek; correspondence with Milena Jesenská; publication of "In the Penal Colony" and *A Country Doctor*; end of World War I.

1920   Relationship with Milena Jesenská, his Czech translator; takes health leave and stays at Matliary sanitarium.

1921   Attempts to return to work but forced to take further leave.

1922   Writes *The Castle*, "A Hunger Artist," and "Investigations of a Dog"; last meeting with Milena Jesenská; retires from Workers' Accident Insurance Institute.

1923   Relationship with Dora Dymant; moves to Berlin with Dora; sends the collection *A Hunger Artist* to publisher.

1924   Writes "Josephine the Singer, or the Mouse Folk"; returns to Prague; dies in sanitarium in Kierling on June 3; publication of *A Hunger Artist*. Milena writes in obituary, "His stories reflect the irony and prophetic vision of a man condemned to see the world with such blinding clarity that he found it unbearable and went to his death."

1925   Publication of *The Trial*, edited by Max Brod.

1926   Publication of *The Castle*, edited by Max Brod.

1927   Publication of *Amerika,* edited by Max Brod.

1930   First English translation of Kafka: *The Castle*.

1939   World War II begins; Max Brod flees Prague for Tel Aviv with Kafka papers, many unpublished.

1941–1943   Kafka's sisters die in concentration camps.

1944   Milena Jesenská dies in concentration camp.

1945   World War II ends.

1952   Dora Dymant dies.

1960   Felice Bauer dies.

1968   Max Brod dies; Kafka's papers transferred to his secretary Esther Hoffe.

2007   Esther Hoffe dies; lawsuit over Kafka's unpublished papers.

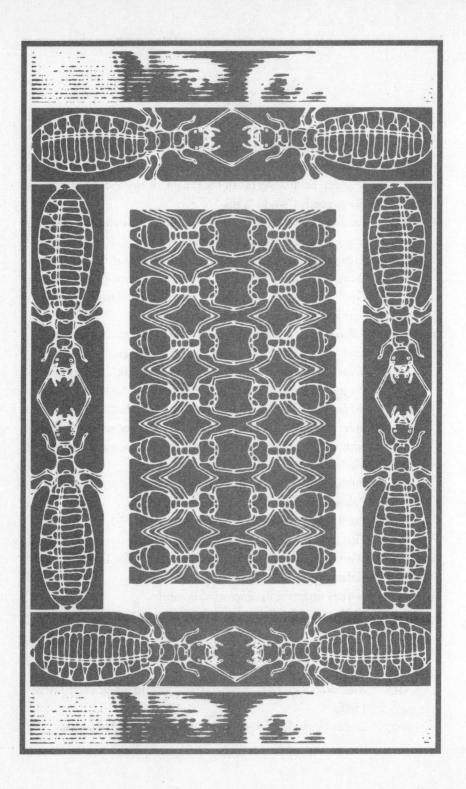

A Hunger Artist

Franz Kafka

Translated by John Kessel

In the last decades interest in hunger artists has declined a great deal. While once it was profitable to produce such major performances under one's own management, these days it is completely impossible. Those were different times. Back then the entire city devoted its attention to the hunger artist; from day to day of his fast attendance climbed; everyone wanted to see the hunger artist at least once daily. Later on there were subscribers who sat from dawn until dusk before the small barred cage, and at night viewings took place in torchlight in order to increase the effect. On beautiful days the cage would be carried into the open air, and then it was especially the children to whom the hunger artist would be shown. While for the grownups he was often just a joke that they took part in for fashion's sake, the children would look on in amazement with open mouths, holding each other by the hand for security as he sat, pale in black tights, with stark protruding ribs, spurning even a chair, on straw that had been scattered about. On occasion he would politely nod, his smile strained as he answered questions, or stretch his arm through the bars to let them feel how thin it was. But then he would sink again into himself, paying attention to nothing, not even the—for him—crucially important striking of the clock, the sole furniture of the cage, but only looking out with eyes almost closed, and now and then sipping from a tiny glass of water to moisten his lips.

In addition to the ever-changing spectators there were also permanent watchmen, elected by the public—usually butchers, strangely enough—always three at a time, whose task it was to observe the hunger artist day and night so that he did not obtain food in some secret way. This was however only a formality introduced to satisfy the public, because the initiates well knew that during the fast the hunger artist would never, under any circumstances, even under duress, eat the slightest thing: the honor of his art forbade it.

Of course not every observer could grasp this; sometimes there were nightly teams of watchers, very lax in their duties, who deliberately sat together in a distant corner and became engrossed in card games with the clear intention of allowing the hunger artist to take a little refreshment, which they believed he could bring out from some secret store. Nothing tormented the hunger artist more than such watchers: they made him miserable, they made his fasting terribly difficult. Sometimes during these nights he overcame his weakness and, for as long as he could, sang to show these people how unjust their suspicions were. But that didn't help; they only marveled at his ability to eat while singing. He much preferred those watchers who sat right up close to the bars, and who did not make do with the dim night lighting of the hall, but illuminated him with flashlights that his impresario had provided. The glare did not bother him at all; sleeping was out of the question anyway, and he could always doze a little no matter what the lighting or the hour, even in a crowded, noisy hall. He was very happy to spend a sleepless night with such watchers; he was ready to joke with them, to tell them stories about his nomadic life, then listen to their own stories in order to keep them awake, to demonstrate once again that he had nothing to eat in the cage, and that he fasted in a way that none of them could.

But he was happiest of all when the morning came and at his expense a lavish breakfast was brought, upon which they threw themselves with the appetite of healthy men after a wearying, sleepless night. There were people who sought to see in this breakfast an undue influence over the guards, but that went too far, and if you asked these doubters whether they would undertake the night watch for its own sake without breakfast, they disappeared—but still clung to their suspicions.

These suspicions were, however, an inevitable product of the nature of fasting. No one could spend all his days and nights guarding the hunger artist without a break, so no one could know from direct experience whether the fast had actually taken place continuously, without fail. Only the hunger artist himself could know this, so therefore he could be the only completely satisfied observer of his fast. But he was never satisfied, for yet another reason: perhaps it was not fasting that made him so very emaciated that many people, to their regret, had to stay away from his performances because they could not bear the sight of him; perhaps he was only so wasted away out of dissatisfaction with himself. He alone knew what no other initiate knew: how easy it was to fast. It was the easiest thing in the world.

He did not conceal this but no one believed him. At best they held him to be modest, but mostly they considered him addicted to praise, or simply a fake for whom fasting was indeed easy because he knew how to make it easy, and who then had the nerve to half admit it. He had to take all this, had gotten used to it over the years, but the injustice always gnawed at him. And yet never, after whatever period of fasting—one had to grant him this—had he ever left the cage of his own free will. His impresario had firmly set forty days as the maximum length for the fast. Beyond this he never let him go, not even in the big cities, and for very good reason. Judging from experience, for about forty days one could, through gradually increasing publicity, spur on a town's curiosity, but after that audiences lost interest and a significant decrease in response was noted. There were naturally in this regard small differences between different cities and countries, but as a rule, forty days was the maximum.

So on the fortieth day the door of the cage, decorated with flowers, was opened, an enthusiastic audience filled the amphitheater, a military band played, two doctors entered the cage to carry out the necessary examination of the hunger artist, the results were announced to the hall through a megaphone, and finally came two young women, happy they had been selected, to lead the hunger artist out of the cage and down a couple of steps to where, on a small table, a carefully selected meal for an invalid was served. And at this moment the hunger artist always resisted. Though he willingly laid his bony arms into the helpful, outstretched hands of the women bending over him, he would not stand up. Why stop now after forty days? He could have held out still longer, infinitely longer; why quit now, when he was doing his best, no, not even his best fasting? Why would they steal from him the fame of fasting on, to become not only the greatest hunger artist of all time—which he probably already was—but to surpass himself to the point of incomprehension, since he felt no limits to his ability to starve himself? Why had this crowd, which purported to admire him so much, so little patience with him; if he could stand fasting longer, why couldn't they? Also he was tired, and was sitting comfortably in the straw, yet now he was supposed to stand up straight and tall and go to the food, the very idea of which nauseated him—which he suppressed only with difficulty out of consideration for the ladies. And he looked up into the eyes of the young women, apparently so friendly, actually so cruel, and shook his head, which felt over-heavy upon his weakened neck.

And then what always happened, happened. The impresario came, silently—the music made speech impossible—lifted his arms above the hunger artist as if calling on heaven to look down on its handiwork here on the straw, this pitiable martyr, which the hunger artist certainly was, only in an entirely different sense. He seized the hunger artist around his narrow waist with convincingly exaggerated care, as if he were dealing with a fragile thing, and presented him—not without shaking him a little in secret, so that the hunger artist's legs and torso swayed uncontrollably back and forth—to the ladies, who had become deathly pale. At this point the hunger artist tolerated everything; his head lay on his breast as if it had rolled around and inexplicably come to rest there, his body was hollowed out, his legs were drawn together tightly at the knees in self-preservation, yet still scraped the floor, as if it were not real and they couldn't find the real one. The full weight of his body, although almost nothing, rested on one of the women, who seeking help, with fluttering breath—she had not imagined this honor to be like this—at first stretched her neck as much as possible, to keep at least her face from contact with the hunger artist. But then, as this did not work and her luckier companion did not come to her aid, but contented herself with tremblingly holding the hand of the hunger artist—this little bag of bones—she broke into tears, to the delighted laughter of the auditorium, and had to be replaced by an attendant who had long before been ready and waiting. Then came the food, a little of which the impresario forced into the hunger artist during his swoon-like sleep, accompanied by some funny patter designed to distract attention from his condition. After that a toast, which allegedly the hunger artist had whispered to the impresario, was raised to the public, the orchestra confirmed everything with a great fanfare, the crowd broke up, and no one had any reason to be dissatisfied with the show—no one, only the hunger artist, always only he.

So he lived with regular short breaks for many years, in seeming glory, honored by the world, but in spite of that usually in a dark mood, made only darker because no one took his trouble seriously. How should he be consoled? What else could he wish for? And if he occasionally encountered a good-natured person who felt sorry for him and tried to explain that his sadness was probably caused by his fasting, the hunger artist, especially when he had been fasting for a long time, might respond with an outburst of rage, and to everyone's alarm begin to rattle the bars of his cage like a wild animal. For such situations the impresario had a means of punishment he liked to use. He apologized for the hunger artist before the assembled onlookers, admitting that his conduct could only be excused because of the irritability caused by fasting, which well-fed people could not understand. In connection with this he then went on to speak about the hunger artist's equally unbelievable claim that he could fast much longer than he fasted now; he praised the high striving, the good will, the great self-denial that certainly were present in this boast, but sought to refute it simply by showing photographs—that were coincidentally for sale—of the hunger artist on the fortieth day of a fast, in bed, almost dead from exhaustion.

This twisting of the truth, though all too familiar to the hunger artist, was always freshly unnerving, and proved too much for him. The result of the premature end of his fast was here presented as its cause! To fight against this stupidity, against this world of stupidity, was impossible. Yet he always stood by the bars and eagerly and in good faith listened to the impresario—but once the photographs came out he let go, sank back into the straw with a sigh, and the reassured public could once more approach and peer at him.

When a few years later the witnesses to such scenes recalled them, they often could not understand themselves. Because in the interim the change mentioned earlier had taken place; it happened almost overnight; it might have had deeper causes, but who cared to discover them? At any rate, one day the pampered hunger artist saw himself deserted by the pleasure-seeking crowd, who preferred to go streaming off to other attractions. One last time the impresario raced with him through half of Europe to see whether here and there the old interest might be found again. All in vain: everywhere, as if by secret agreement, a downright aversion had developed to demonstrations of starving. Naturally this could not have come about so suddenly, and in retrospect they could recall some things, inadequately suppressed warnings, to which in the intoxication of success they had not paid enough attention, but now it was too late to do anything about it. Of course it was inevitable that fasting would become popular again, but for those living today this was no consolation. What should the hunger artist do now? He whom thousands had cheered could not show himself in booths at small fairs, and the hunger artist was not only too old but above all too fanatically devoted to fasting to take up another profession. So he said goodbye to the impresario, his comrade in an unparalleled career, and quickly hired himself out to a great circus; in order to protect his feelings, he did not even examine the terms of the contract.

A large circus, with its huge turnover of men and animals and equipment, can use anyone at any time, even a hunger artist, if of course his demands are appropriately modest. And anyhow, in this particular case it was not only the hunger artist himself who was engaged, but also his old, famous name. Indeed, since by the nature of this art increasing age did not mean decreasing skill, one could not even say that here an exhausted artist, no longer at the height of his ability, was seeking refuge in a quiet post in the circus. On the contrary, the hunger artist quite believably asserted that he could fast as well as ever; he even maintained that, if they let him have his way—and this he was promised without further ado—he could now, for the first time, legitimately astonish the world—a boast that, considering the temper of the times, which the hunger artist in the heat of the moment had easily forgotten, only made the experts smile.

Fundamentally, however, the hunger artist did not lose his sense of his true situation, and it went without saying that they would not place him with his cage as a main attraction in the middle of the ring, but outside in some readily accessible spot near the animal stalls. Large, colorfully painted signs framed the cage and announced what was to be seen there. When, during the breaks in the performance, the audience pushed out toward the stalls to view the animals, it was nearly unavoidable that they should pass by the hunger artist and pause. Perhaps they might have remained by his cage longer if the people pressing from behind in the narrow passage, who did not understand this delay on the way to the menagerie they were eager to see, had not made longer, quiet contemplation impossible. This was also the reason the hunger artist shuddered at the prospect of these visiting hours, despite the fact that he longed for them as his life's purpose. In the beginning he could hardly wait for the intermissions; delighted he had watched the crowd roll forward, but soon he became convinced—even the most stubborn, almost deliberate self-deception could not stand up to the experience—that most, as revealed again and again by their intentions, were nothing but visitors of the menagerie.

And this sight of them from a distance always remained the best. Because when they had come up to him, immediately there raged around him shouts and curses from two continuously re-forming groups, the first—to the hunger artist they soon became the more embarrassing— who wanted to look at him at their leisure, not out of understanding, but out of whim and stubbornness, and the second, who only demanded to get to the animal stalls. When this great mob was gone, then came the stragglers, and yet even these, who were no longer prevented from staying as long as they wanted, hurried with long strides, hardly glancing aside, to get to the animals in time. And it was an all too rare stroke of luck when a father with his children came, pointed his finger at the hunger artist, explained in detail what was going on here, and told of years gone by, when he had been at similar but incomparably more marvelous performances. The children, inadequately prepared by school and life, remained completely uncomprehending—what was fasting to them?—but still in the brightness of their searching eyes betrayed something of new, kinder times to come.

Perhaps, the hunger artist said to himself now and then, everything would get a little better if his cage were not so close to the animals. That made the people's choice too easy, not to mention that the stench of the stalls, the restlessness of the animals in the night, the hauling of raw hunks of meat past him for the carnivores, and their howls at feeding time, left him upset and continually depressed. But he dared not complain to the management; after all, it was to the animals that he owed the crowds of visitors, among whom here and there he might find one intended for him. And who knew where they would stick him if he reminded them of his existence, and with it the fact that he was, strictly speaking, only an obstacle on the way to the menagerie?

A small obstacle, certainly, an ever smaller obstacle. People realized how strange it was for a hunger artist to try to claim their attention nowadays, and with this realization the judgment on him was spoken. He might starve himself as successfully as only he could—and he did—but nothing could save him anymore; people went right by him. Try to explain the art of hunger! Those who don't feel it can't be made to understand. The bright signs became dirty and illegible; when people tore them down, no one thought to replace them; the small tablet indicating the number of days the fast had gone on, once carefully updated every day, for a long time now had remained always the same, because after the first weeks the staff had become tired of even this small job. And so the hunger artist fasted on, as he had once dreamed of doing, and succeeded effortlessly, as he had predicted back then, but no one counted the days; no one, not even the hunger artist himself knew how great his achievement already was, and his heart grew heavy. And when once in a while some idle passer-by stopped, made fun of the old number on the tablet and spoke about swindles, that was in its way the stupidest lie that indifference and innate malice could invent, for the hunger artist did not cheat—he labored honorably—but the world cheated him of his reward.

Still many more days went by, and they too came to an end. Finally an overseer noticed and asked the attendants why they let this perfectly useful cage with the rotting straw in it stand unused; no one knew why, until, prompted by the number board, one of them remembered the hunger artist. They stirred the straw with poles and discovered him there.

"You are still fasting?" asked the overseer. "When will you finally stop?"

"Forgive me, all of you," whispered the hunger artist, and only the overseer, who held his ear by the bars, understood him.

"Certainly," said the overseer, and tapped his finger against his forehead to indicate the condition of the hunger artist to the staff. "We forgive you."

"I always wanted you to admire my fasting," said the hunger artist.

"We do admire it," said the overseer obligingly.

"But you should not admire it," said the hunger artist.

"Well, then we don't admire it," said the overseer. "Why shouldn't we admire it?"

"Because I have to go hungry, I can't do anything else," said the hunger artist.

"Look at this guy," said the overseer. "Why can't you do anything else?"

"Because I—" said the hunger artist, lifting his head a little and, with pursed lips as if for a kiss, speaking directly into the overseer's ear, so that nothing would be lost, "—because I could not find the food that I liked. Had I found it, believe me, I would have made no fuss and stuffed myself just like you and everyone else."

Those were his last words, but in his broken eyes remained the fixed but no longer proud conviction that he continued to fast.

"Now straighten this place up!" said the overseer, and they buried the hunger artist along with the straw. Into the cage they put a young panther. Even to the dullest mind it was a palpable relief to see this wild animal throw himself around in the cage that had been barren for so long. He lacked nothing. Without thinking about it the keepers brought him the food that he liked; he did not even seem to miss his freedom; his noble body, equipped almost to bursting with everything it needed, seemed to carry freedom around with it; somewhere in his jaws it seemed to dwell, and the joy of being alive came with such fiery passion from his throat that it was not easy for the spectators to stand up to it. But they steeled themselves, crowded around the cage, and did not ever want to move away.

J.P.K.

A story that twists and squirms as it resists interpretation. Is the hunger artist a saint or a fool? Are we meant to feel sorry that he has been undervalued and forgotten, or was his art a sham? Does this story get an ironic reading or a sympathetic one?

J.K.

There are some similarities between this story and Herman Melville's "Bartleby the Scrivener." Like the hunger artist, Bartleby asserts himself through denial ("I would prefer not to") and dies of starvation—if not in a cage, then in prison. There is no evidence that Kafka ever read "Bartleby." Its grim vision of American office life, though it might have seemed all-too-familiar to Kafka, was not in keeping with his image of America as a land of possibility. One of Kafka's favorite books was Benjamin Franklin's *Autobiography*.

JOHN KESSEL: ON THE TRANSLATION OF "A HUNGER ARTIST"

For the most part I stuck as close to Kafka's language as I could, but I took some liberties. In particular I made two choices that most of Kafka's translators do not. Kafka's sentences are actually many separate sentences strung together with semicolons or commas; in many places I chose to break them. Similarly, I broke some of Kafka's long paragraphs into shorter ones.

What is lost by these choices is the cumulative force built by Kafka's stringing together clause after clause, each a development, elaboration, or qualification of the previous statement, so that the last words of a page-long paragraph carry the weight of everything piled up before them. What is gained, I hope, is the opportunity to pause occasionally to absorb these meanings. To put it in simple terms, sometimes Kafka's long sentences and paragraphs cause him to "step on" his best lines. For example, in the German text the statements, "He alone knew what no other initiate knew: how easy it was to fast. It was the easiest thing in the world" come after a long discourse on the extraordinary pains the hunger artist takes in his fasting. These lines fall in the middle of a paragraph. By breaking the paragraph after "the easiest thing in the world" I seek to give the paradox (fundamental to understanding the nature of the hunger artist) space to breathe.

In Kafka's text, the final exchanges between the hunger artist and the overseer take place in a single paragraph. In formatting them as conventional dialog, with alternating paragraphs, I sought to make clearer the "tennis match" quality of their speech, as the overseer asks practical questions that we as readers might ask, but in his condescension indicates the unbridgeable gulf between the audience and the artist.

I am indebted to previous translators Willa and Edwin Muir, Stanley Corngold, and Michael Hofmann, all of them more schooled in translation than I. My thanks are also owed to Dr. Ruth V. Gross of the North Carolina State University Department of Foreign Languages and Literatures, who read my text and offered suggestions. She is of course not responsible for errors of taste or judgment I may have made here.

I make no claim to have "corrected" any "errors" of earlier translators, and I take comfort from the fact that so great a writer and translator as Jorge Luis Borges says, "the notion of a 'definitive text' belongs to religion or perhaps merely to exhaustion."[1] For Borges the act of reading itself is a form of translation. It is not the purpose of a new version to supplant earlier ones: the justification of a new translation is that it gives the work a new voice, for new readers. I hope you find this one worthwhile.

1 Jorge Luis Borges, "Some Versions of Homer" (translated from the Spanish by Suzanne Jill Levine). *PMLA* Vol. 7, No. 5, Oct. 1992. p. 1136.

Kafkaesque

J. G. Ballard:

I think that Kafka writes a variety, a very serious variety, of horror fiction which is based on another major strand running through all fiction, and certainly through horror fiction—that is the threatening and impersonal world created by modern society. Kafka's heroes are always anonymous figures; usually their names are just initials. They're surrounded by enormous bureaucratic systems, by the huge industrial landscapes of the early twentieth century that were superimposed on the smaller cities of nineteenth-century Europe, and Kafka expresses the fears, the unconscious fears, that are built into the individual living in an enormous anonymous society.

—Ballard in discussion with Dr. Christopher Evans, BBC Radio 3, London, December 30, 1971

The Drowned Giant

J. G. Ballard

ON THE MORNING after the storm the body of a drowned giant was washed ashore on the beach five miles to the northwest of the city. The first news of its arrival was brought by a nearby farmer and subsequently confirmed by the local newspaper reporters and the police. Despite this the majority of people, myself among them, remained skeptical, but the return of more and more eyewitnesses attesting to the vast size of the giant was finally too much for our curiosity. The library where my colleagues and I were carrying out our research was almost deserted when we set off for the coast shortly after two o'clock, and throughout the day people continued to leave their offices and shops as accounts of the giant circulated around the city.

By the time we reached the dunes above the beach a substantial crowd had gathered, and we could see the body lying in the shallow water 200 yards away. At first the estimates of its size seemed greatly exaggerated. It was then at low tide, and almost all the giant's body was exposed, but he appeared to be a little larger than a basking shark. He lay on his back with his arms at his sides, in an attitude of repose, as if asleep on the mirror of wet sand, the reflection of his blanched skin fading as the water receded. In the clear sunlight his body glistened like the white plumage of a sea bird.

Puzzled by this spectacle, and dissatisfied with the matter-of-fact explanations of the crowd, my friends and I stepped down from the dunes onto the shingle. Everyone seemed reluctant to approach the giant, but half an hour later two fishermen in wading boots walked out across the sand. As their diminutive figures neared the recumbent body a sudden hubbub of conversation broke out among the spectators. The two men were completely dwarfed by the giant. Although his heels were partly submerged in the sand, the feet rose to at least twice the fishermen's height, and we immediately realized that this drowned leviathan had the mass and dimensions of the largest sperm whale.

Three fishing smacks had arrived on the scene and with keels raised remained a quarter of a mile offshore, the crews watching from the bows. Their discretion deterred the spectators on the shore from wading out across the sand. Impatiently everyone stepped down from the dunes and waited on the shingle slopes, eager for a closer view. Around the margins of the figure the sand had been washed away, forming a hollow, as if the giant had fallen out of the sky. The two fishermen were standing between the immense plinths of the feet, waving to us like tourists among the columns of some water-lapped temple on the Nile. For a moment I feared that the giant was merely asleep and might suddenly stir and clap his heels together, but his glazed eyes stared skyward, unaware of the minuscule replicas of himself between his feet.

The fishermen then began a circuit of the corpse, strolling past the long white flanks of the legs. After a pause to examine the fingers of the supine hand, they disappeared from sight between the arm and chest, then re-emerged to survey the head, shielding their eyes as they gazed up at its Grecian profile. The shallow forehead, straight high-bridged nose, and curling lips reminded me of a Roman copy of Praxiteles, and the elegantly formed cartouches of the nostrils emphasized the resemblance to sculpture.

Abruptly there was a shout from the crowd, and a hundred arms pointed toward the sea. With a start I saw that one of the fishermen had climbed onto the giant's chest and was now strolling about and signaling to the shore. There was a roar of surprise and triumph from the crowd, lost in a rushing avalanche of shingle as everyone surged forward across the sand.

As we approached the recumbent figure, which was lying in a pool of water the size of a field, our excited chatter fell away again, subdued by the huge physical dimensions of this dead colossus. He was stretched out at a slight angle to the shore, his legs carried nearer the beach, and this foreshortening had disguised his true length. Despite the two fishermen standing on his abdomen, the crowd formed itself into a wide circle, groups of people tentatively advancing toward the hands and feet.

My companions and I walked around the seaward side of the giant, whose hips and thorax towered above us like the hull of a stranded ship. His pearl-colored skin, distended by immersion in salt water, masked the contours of the enormous muscles and tendons. We passed below the left knee, which was flexed slightly, threads of damp seaweed clinging to its sides. Draped loosely across the midriff, and preserving a tenuous propriety, was a shawl of heavy open-weave material, bleached to a pale yellow by the water. A strong odor of brine came from the garment as it steamed in the sun, mingled with the sweet, potent scent of the giant's skin.

We stopped by his shoulder and gazed up at the motionless profile. The lips were parted slightly, the open eye cloudy and occluded, as if injected with some blue milky liquid, but the delicate arches of the nostrils and eyebrows invested the face with an ornate charm that belied the brutish power of the chest and shoulders. The ear was suspended in mid-air over our heads like a sculptured doorway. As I raised my hand to touch the pendulous lobe, someone appeared over the edge of the forehead and shouted down at me. Startled by this apparition, I stepped back, and then saw that a group of youths had climbed up onto the face and were jostling each other in and out of the orbits.

People were now clambering all over the giant, whose reclining arms provided a double stairway. From the palms they walked along the forearms to the elbows and then crawled over the distended belly of the biceps to the flat promenade of the pectoral muscles which covered the upper half of the smooth hairless chest. From here they climbed up onto the face, hand over hand along the lips and nose, or forayed down the abdomen to meet others who had straddled the ankles and were patrolling the twin columns of the thighs.

We continued our circuit through the crowd, and stopped to examine the outstretched right hand. A small pool of water lay in the palm, like the residue of another world, now being kicked away by people ascending the arm. I tried to read the palm-lines that grooved the skin, searching for some clue to the giant's character, but the distention of the tissues had almost obliterated them, carrying away all trace of the giant's identity and his last tragic predicament. The huge muscles and wristbones of the hand seemed to deny any sensitivity to their owner, but the delicate flexion of the fingers and the well-tended nails, each cut symmetrically to within six inches of the quick, argued refinement of temperament, illustrated in the Grecian features of the face, on which the townsfolk were now sitting like flies.

One youth was even standing, arms wavering at his side, on the very tip of the nose, shouting down at his companions, but the face of the giant still retained its massive composure.

Returning to the shore, we sat down on the shingle and watched the continuous stream of people arriving from the city. Some six or seven fishing boats had collected offshore, and their crews waded in through the shallow water for a closer look at this enormous storm catch. Later a party of police appeared and made a halfhearted attempt to cordon off the beach, but after walking up to the recumbent figure, any such thoughts left their minds, and they went off together with bemused backward glances.

An hour later there were a thousand people present on the beach, at least two hundred of them standing or sitting on the giant, crowded along the arms and legs or circulating in a ceaseless melee across his chest and stomach. A large gang of youths occupied the head, toppling each other off the cheeks and sliding down the smooth planes of the jaw. Two or three straddled the nose, and another crawled into one of the nostrils, from which he emitted barking noises like a demented dog.

That afternoon the police returned and cleared a way through the crowd for a party of scientific experts—authorities on gross anatomy and marine biology—from the university. The gang of youths and most of the people on the giant climbed down, leaving behind a few hardy spirits perched on the tips of the toes and on the forehead. The experts strode around the giant, heads nodding in vigorous consultation, preceded by the policemen who pushed back the press of spectators. When they reached the outstretched hand the senior officer offered to assist them up onto the palm, but the experts hastily demurred.

After they returned to the shore, the crowd once more climbed onto the giant, and was in full possession when we left at five o'clock, covering the arms and legs like a dense flock of gulls sitting on the corpse of a large fish.

I next visited the beach three days later. My friends at the library had returned to their work, and delegated to me the task of keeping the giant under observation and preparing a report. Perhaps they sensed my particular interest in the case, and it was certainly true that I was eager to return to the beach. There was nothing necrophilic about this, for to all intents the giant was still alive for me, indeed more alive than many of the people watching him. What I found so fascinating was partly his immense scale, the huge volumes of space occupied by his arms and legs, which seemed to confirm the identity of my own miniature limbs, but above all, the mere categorical fact of his existence. Whatever else in our lives might be open to doubt, the giant, dead or alive, existed in an absolute sense, providing a glimpse into a world of similar absolutes of which we spectators on the beach were such imperfect and puny copies.

When I arrived at the beach the crowd was considerably smaller, and some two or three hundred people sat on the shingle, picnicking and watching the groups of visitors who walked out across the sand. The successive tides had carried the giant nearer the shore, swinging his head and shoulders toward the beach, so that he seemed doubly to gain in size, his huge body dwarfing the fishing boats beached beside his feet. The uneven contours of the beach had pushed his spine into a slight arch, expanding his chest and tilling back the head, forcing him into a more expressly heroic posture. The combined effects of sea water and the tumefaction of the tissues had given the face a sleeker and less youthful look. Although the vast proportions of the features made it impossible to assess the age and character of the giant, on my previous visit his classically modeled mouth and nose suggested that he had been a young man of discreet and modest temper. Now, however, he appeared to be at least in early middle age. The puffy cheeks, thicker nose and temples, and narrowing eyes gave him a look of well-fed maturity that even now hinted at a growing corruption to come.

This accelerated postmortem development of the giant's character, as if the latent elements of his personality had gained sufficient momentum during his life to discharge themselves in a brief final resumé, continued to fascinate me. It marked the beginning of the giant's surrender to that all-demanding system of time in which the rest of humanity finds itself, and of which, like the million twisted ripples of a fragmented whirlpool, our finite lives are the concluding products. I took up my position on the shingle directly opposite the giant's head, from where I could see the new arrivals and the children clambering over the legs and arms.

Among the morning's visitors were a number of men in leather jackets and cloth caps, who peered up critically at the giant with a professional eye, pacing out his dimensions and making rough calculations in the sand with spars of driftwood. I assumed them to be from the public works department and other municipal bodies, no doubt wondering how to dispose of this monster.

Several rather more smartly attired individuals, circus proprietors and the like, also appeared on the scene, and strolled slowly around the giant, hands in pockets of their long overcoats, saying nothing to one another. Evidently its bulk was too great even for their matchless enterprise. After they had gone the children continued to run up and down the arms and legs, and the youths wrestled with each other over the supine face, the damp sand from their feet covering the white skin.

The following day I deliberately postponed my visit until the late afternoon, and when I arrived there were fewer than fifty or sixty people sitting on the shingle. The giant had been carried still closer to the shore, and was now little more than seventy-five yards away, his feet crushing the palisade of a rotting breakwater. The slope of the firmer sand tilted his body toward the sea, the bruised swollen face averted in an almost conscious gesture. I sat down on a large metal winch which had been shackled to a concrete caisson above the shingle, and looked down at the recumbent figure.

His blanched skin had now lost its pearly translucence and was spattered with dirty sand which replaced that washed away by the night tide. Clumps of seaweed filled the intervals between the fingers and a collection of litter and cuttlebones lay in the crevices below the hips and knees. But despite this, and the continuous thickening of his features, the giant still retained his magnificent Homeric stature. The enormous breadth of the shoulders, and the huge columns of the arms and legs, still carried the figure into another dimension, and the giant seemed a more authentic image of one of the drowned Argonauts or heroes of the *Odyssey* than the conventional portrait previously in my mind.

I stepped down onto the sand, and walked between the pools of water toward the giant. Two small boys were sitting in the well of the ear, and at the far end a solitary youth stood perched high on one of the toes, surveying me as I approached. As I had hoped when delaying my visit, no one else paid any attention to me, and the people on the shore remained huddled beneath their coats.

The giant's supine right hand was covered with broken shells and sand, in which a score of footprints were visible. The rounded bulk of the hip towered above me, cutting off all sight of the sea. The sweetly acrid odor I had noticed before was now more pungent, and through the opaque skin I could see the serpentine coils of congealed blood vessels. However repellent it seemed, this ceaseless metamorphosis, a macabre life-in-death, alone permitted me to set foot on the corpse.

Using the jutting thumb as a stair rail, I climbed up onto the palm and began my ascent. The skin was harder than I expected, barely yielding to my weight. Quickly I walked up the sloping forearm and the bulging balloon of the biceps. The face of the drowned giant loomed to my right, the cavernous nostrils and huge flanks of the cheeks like the cone of some freakish volcano.

Safely rounding the shoulder, I stepped out onto the broad promenade of the chest, across which the bony ridges of the rib cage lay like huge rafters. The white skin was dappled by the darkening bruises of countless footprints, in which the patterns of individual heel marks were clearly visible. Someone had built a small sand castle on the center of the sternum, and I climbed onto this partly demolished structure to get a better view of the face.

The two children had now scaled the ear and were pulling themselves into the right orbit, whose blue globe, completely occluded by some milk-colored fluid, gazed sightlessly past their miniature forms. Seen obliquely from below, the face was devoid of all grace and repose, the drawn mouth and raised chin propped up by gigantic slings of muscles resembling the torn prow of a colossal wreck. For the first time I became aware of the extremity of this last physical agony of the giant, no less painful for his unawareness of the collapsing musculature and tissues. The absolute isolation of the ruined figure, cast like an abandoned ship upon the empty shore, almost out of sound of the waves, transformed his face into a mask of exhaustion and helplessness.

As I stepped forward, my foot sank into a trough of soft tissue, and a gust of fetid gas blew through an aperture between the ribs. Retreating from the fouled air, which hung like a cloud over my head, I turned toward the sea to clear my lungs. To my surprise I saw the giant's left hand had been amputated.

I stared with shocked bewilderment at the blackening stump, while the solitary youth reclining on his aerial perch a hundred feet away surveyed me with a sanguinary eye.

This was only the first of a sequence of depredations. I spent the following two days in the library, for some reason reluctant to visit the shore, aware that I had probably witnessed the approaching end of a magnificent illusion. When I next crossed the dunes and set foot on the shingle, the giant was little more than twenty yards away, and with this close proximity to the rough pebbles all traces had vanished of the magic which once surrounded his distant wave-washed form. Despite his immense size, the bruises and dirt that covered his body made him appear merely human in scale, his vast dimensions only increasing his vulnerability.

His right hand and foot had been removed, dragged up the slope, and trundled away by cart. After questioning the small group of people huddled by the breakwater, I gathered that a fertilizer company and a cattle-food manufacturer were responsible.

The giant's remaining foot rose into the air, a steel hawser fixed to the large toe, evidently in preparation for the following day. The surrounding beach had been disturbed by a score of workmen, and deep ruts marked the ground where the hands and foot had been hauled away. A dark brackish fluid leaked from the stumps, and stained the sand and the white cones of the cuttlefish. As I walked down the shingle I noticed that a number of jocular slogans, swastikas, and other signs had been cut into the gray skin, as if the mutilation of this motionless colossus had released a sudden flood of repressed spite. The lobe of one of the ears was pierced by a spear of timber, and a small fire had burned out in the center of the chest, blackening the surrounding skin. The fine wood ash was still being scattered by the wind.

A foul smell enveloped the cadaver, the undisguisable signature of putrefaction, which had at last driven away the usual gathering of youths. I returned to the shingle and climbed up onto the winch. The giant's swollen cheeks had now almost closed his eyes, drawing the lips back in a monumental gape. The once straight Grecian nose had been twisted and flattened, stamped into the ballooning face by countless heels.

When I visited the beach the following day I found, almost with relief, that the head had been removed.

Some weeks elapsed before I made my next journey to the beach, and by then the human likeness I had noticed earlier had vanished again. On close inspection the recumbent thorax and abdomen were unmistakably manlike, but as each of the limbs was chopped off, first at the knee and elbow, and then at shoulder and thigh, the carcass resembled that of any headless sea animal—whale or whale shark. With this loss of identity, and the few traces of personality that had clung tenuously to the figure, the interest of the spectators expired, and the foreshore was deserted except for an elderly beachcomber and the watchman sitting in the doorway of the contractor's hut.

A loose wooden scaffolding had been erected around the carcass, from which a dozen ladders swung in the wind, and the surrounding sand was littered with coils of rope, long metal-handled knives, and grappling irons, the pebbles oily with blood and pieces of bone and skin.

I nodded to the watchman, who regarded me dourly over his brazier of burning coke. The whole area was pervaded by the pungent smell of huge squares of blubber being simmered in a vat behind the hut.

Both the thighbones had been removed, with the assistance of a small crane draped in the gauzelike fabric which had once covered the waist of the giant, and the open sockets gaped like barn doors. The upper arms, collarbones, and pudenda had likewise been dispatched. What remained of the skin over the thorax and abdomen had been marked out in parallel strips with a tarbrush, and the first five or six sections had been pared away from the midriff, revealing the great arch of the rib cage.

As I left, a flock of gulls wheeled down from the sky and alighted on the beach, picking at the stained sand with ferocious cries.

Several months later, when the news of his arrival had been generally forgotten, various pieces of the body of the dismembered giant began to reappear all over the city. Most of these were bones, which the fertilizer manufacturers had found too difficult to crush, and their massive size, and the huge tendons and discs of cartilage attached to their joints, immediately identified them. For some reason, these disembodied fragments seemed better to convey the essence of the giant's original magnificence than the bloated appendages that had been subsequently amputated. As I looked across the road at the premises of the largest wholesale merchants in the meat market, I recognized the two enormous thighbones on either side of the doorway. They lowered over the porters' heads like the threatening megaliths of some primitive druidical religion, and I had a sudden vision of the giant climbing to his knees upon these bare bones and striding away through the streets of the city, picking up the scattered fragments of himself on his return journey to the sea.

A few days later I saw the left humerus lying in the entrance to one of the shipyards. In the same week the mummified right hand was exhibited on a carnival float during the annual pageant of the guilds.

The lower jaw, typically, found its way to the museum of natural history. The remainder of the skull has disappeared, but is probably still lurking in the waste grounds or private gardens of the city—quite recently, while sailing down the river, I noticed two ribs of the giant forming a decorative arch in a waterside garden, possibly confused with the jawbones of a whale. A large square of tanned and tattooed skin, the size of an Indian blanket, forms a back cloth to the dolls and masks in a novelty shop near the amusement park, and I have no doubt that elsewhere in the city, in the hotels or golf clubs, the mummified nose or ears of the giant hang from the wall above a fireplace. As for the immense pizzle, this ends its days in the freak museum of a circus which travels up and down the northwest. This monumental apparatus, stunning in its proportions and sometime potency, occupies a complete booth to itself. The irony is that it is wrongly identified as that of a whale, and indeed most people, even those who first saw him cast up on the shore after the storm, now remember the giant, if at all, as a large sea beast.

The remainder of the skeleton, stripped of all flesh, still rests on the seashore, the clutter of bleached ribs like the timbers of a derelict ship. The contractor's hut, the crane and scaffolding have been removed, and the sand being driven into the bay along the coast has buried the pelvis and backbone. In the winter the high curved bones are deserted, battered by the breaking waves, but in the summer they provide an excellent perch for the sea-wearying gulls.

J.P.K.

It is usually a mistake to imagine that there is a controlling metaphor at the center of any Kafka story, and although it is tempting, it is probably wrong to assume we know exactly what the giant means here. That it dwarfs the humans in the story is obvious. Are we meant to feel regret or outrage that it is treated with such little respect? Perhaps. It is striking how carefully Ballard describes the giant. His painstaking observation is reminiscent of the care Kafka takes to describe the apparatus in "In the Penal Colony," both of which are destined to be destroyed.

J.K.

At the same time that the giant and its decay and dismemberment are described in such detail, with the reactions of the city's people exposing a range of human foibles, as in much of Kafka's work the narrator is a cipher. We don't know his name, his age, his life beyond the barest circumstances. But the image of the boys playing on the giant's face, with one of them hiding in his nostril and barking, commands our belief.

TERRY BISSON:

This story was written as a community service project, in lieu of jail, after a minor—excessively minor—dust-up in the local library. Since the incident involved Kafka (as indeed do most of its kind) I decided to unite the three most persistent themes in his work, Love, Death, and Misdirection, with my personal interest in canals, hats, and roller skates. Like Breughel's "Landscape with the Fall of Icarus," the narrative employs the Kafkaesque (which long predates Kafka himself) device of astonishing alterations misunderstood if noticed at all.

The Cockroach Hat

Terry Bisson

SAM GREGORY WOKE up one morning and found, to his dismay, that he had turned into a big cockroach. "Oh, no," he thought. He had some idea of what was happening because of the Kafka story. He hadn't exactly read it, but he had heard all about it back when he was in college. Sam's roommate, Cliffe with an E, had taken a course called Shape Shifters in Modern Lit, thinking it would be an easy A, like the video games he played in the Student Union, taking on all comers, or Eco-Alternatives for example. Instead, it required a paper, and Cliffe felt betrayed. Sam said I told you so (the wrong thing to say) and Cliffe suggested he shut the fuck up. That only made things worse and soon they weren't speaking at all. Several times, they almost came to blows.

Instead, they became the best of friends.

Here's how that happened: Cliffe's girl friend was a Conflict Resolution major, and she suggested they go bowling blindfolded (neither of them bowled) in an effort to change the subject through creative misdirection while she monitored the experiment for credit. They even rented the shoes. It might have worked, too, but she didn't know how to keep score, plus they had forgotten the blindfolds, so they played the pinball machine instead; there was just one, between the Men's and the Ladies', a leftover from some previous universe of bells and flippers.

"What I don't like about it," said Cliffe, "is that is it's just a metaphor instead of something real."

"What if it *was* real?" I asked. (I'm Sam) "What if it was me and I actually turned into a cockroach someday?"

"Then I would do everything I could to help you out," said Cliffe.

I was to remember that promise later when I actually did turn into a cockroach.

Meanwhile Cliffe's girl friend, whom I will call Anna, tagging along to monitor the experiment, was pleased with the results so far. She was cute, not as cute as some but cuter than others, and I immediately fell in love with her. It made me angry how Cliffe always criticized her for everything and I told her so.

We were sort of a threesome.

She was dying of a disease and told me so. Cliffe already knew. She only had a year to live. We both felt sorry for her, me sorrier, but it was Cliffe who died. This happened unexpectedly one afternoon.

It was time to make a new start so Anna and I moved to Park Slope, in Brooklyn. We pretended we were married and even got a baby carriage. We rolled up a towel in a blanket and pretended it was a baby and rolled it around the streets and sidewalks.

Then we discovered it really was a baby. I say "we" but Anna had known it all along. It was crying like crazy. Luckily by then we had a house. Now this had to happen!

Here I was, a big cockroach!

I tried to think of what to do. The bedroom door was shut but I knew that sooner or later Anna would come in and see me, flat on my back with six legs in the air. I had to figure out a way to communicate with her and let her know what was what, before she freaked out.

I was still figuring when the door opened and she came in and immediately started screaming. I could see she wasn't going to be much help, so I scurried under the bed as fast as lightning, cockroach style. Meanwhile she ran out of the room to get a broom, I figured, or something to kill me with.

I was on my own. That was when I remembered Cliffe's promise and wished he was still alive. But if wishes were pennies we'd all be rich. I scurried down through the walls and out of the house, making quick work of the front steps.

Here on the streets of Brooklyn I was less noticeable. Fast-moving, too. It was raining, and after lots of adventures which involved things like making a boat out of a leaf and riding on a roller skate like it was a bus, I made my way to the Gowanus Canal. I had a plan. I knew that with all the renovations in Brooklyn all the writers had ended up in one building, an old warehouse that wasn't hard to find. There were their names on the mailbox: Auster, Lethem, Whitehead, etc., plus a bunch of unknowns.

"This is not how you spell metaphor," they said, when I explained what had happened by walking through ink on scrap paper. I had spelled it with an F. I met with them all separately and together as well, but they were no help. Plus, the canal smelled good and I was beginning to face facts: the cockroach thing was for real.

I ate some paper. It was almost noon. I had to figure out a way to call in sick, at least. Then I might still have my job when things got straightened out.

I walked in a circle, thinking.

Then I met this old Jew. It was in the park. He almost stepped on me, then he picked me up and put me on the cuff of his shirt and started talking to me. It was in Hebrew but that was the least of my problems. His children had all died of this and that and he was fond of me. It turned out he was even older than he looked and knew lots of secrets, many of them Kabbalistic. He took out his pencil and outlined a Quest that would return me to normal.

I was off!

It took all day and involved more things like leaf boats and jumping onto the back of a pigeon and riding it like a dragon. I got to know the sewers too. I wished I had six little shoes.

But never mind, it worked, and by mid-afternoon I was normal, that is human, and full-sized. I was in the Bronx, but I made it home and knocked on the door at precisely five p.m.

To my surprise it was unlocked and swung open on its own. There was Anna with another lover, both of them nude.

"I thought you had turned into a cockroach," she said.

"It must have been your imagination," I said. I didn't want to get into it. Especially in front of this other dude who was pulling on his pants.

If you are thinking I was devastated, you're right. But at least I was no longer a cockroach. I looked in the mirror to make sure.

I'd had nothing to eat all day but paper, so I fixed a bowl of Cheerios while Anna got rid of her lover, who it turned out she hardly knew.

"Maybe we can make a new start," said Anna, pulling on her panties and replacing the barrettes in her hair. That was okay by me, I told her, and we were just about to watch TV when we heard the baby crying like crazy. We had forgotten all about it!

Well, it had turned into a cockroach too. There it was with six tiny legs, waving about, and I could see why Anna had screamed so on seeing me.

I looked at her. She looked at me. I knew what she was thinking. We had neither of us wanted this baby and now it was a cockroach.

She was just about to step on it when the phone rang. It was her father, the doctor.

"Your year is up," he said.

Was our happiness about to come to an end? She had agreed as part of a medical experiment to come into his office after a year and be chemically killed. It wasn't a disease at all.

"My father pressured me into it," she told me.

"I'll go with you," I said. I felt sorry for her. Plus I had a plan. I got a gun out of the box of them I had won in the Lottery and stuck it into my belt. My plan was to kill him before he killed her.

"What's with the gun?" she asked, and I told her.

"You'll need an alibi," she said, mysteriously. Her father's office was also near the Gowanus Canal, so I found myself retracing my steps, following her. It didn't smell so sweet this time. It turned out Anna had a plan as well. On the way, she showed me the items in her purse: a huge pair of scissors and a weird-looking thing.

"What's this thing?" I asked.

"It's a cockroach hat." She showed me how it worked. When she put it on, she looked exactly like a cockroach, six legs and all. I tried it on myself. We were passing a health food store and I saw myself reflected in the plate glass window. It worked!

She had made it herself out of stuff around the house. "You gave me the idea," she said. "I thought it might come in handy."

Indeed it did. "Before you kill me," she told her father, "I want you to try on this hat. I made it myself."

Like a fool, he did. I shot him and she cut him up with the scissors, careful to leave the hat on his "head." When the police came they were puzzled but we had an alibi.

"He looked to us like a big cockroach," said Anna.

"We believe you," said the police.

"I love you," she said (to me, Sam), but that came later.

First, they let us go and we walked home, hand in hand along the canal, holding our noses comically. It was a beautiful spring night in Brooklyn and I had learned a thing or two about love. It was time to make a new start.

We quickened our steps. We had forgotten to step on the baby.

J.P.K.

We have a difficult time imagining Kafka laughing; the myth instructs us that he was somber and doomed, unhappy in his work and at odds with the universe. This is a Kafka that his friends would not recognize. There are reports of him in stitches as he read the opening of the *The Trial* in public. Perhaps the misperception that Kafka did have not a sense of humor arises because he, like Bisson, is utterly deadpan as he writes about the ridiculous.

J.K.

The temptation to reference "The Metamorphosis" in the most obvious way, by serving up insects and entrapment, is hard to avoid for anyone who engages with Kafka's signature story. I love the way Bisson blithely skates past such difficulties with postmodern aplomb. This is likely the fiercest deconstruction of Kafka in the anthology. Enormities are passed off in single phrases.

MICHAEL BLUMLEIN:

Here are things I like about Franz Kafka:

He was dark.

He was funny.

He drank from the fountain of dreams.

He had a sense of the absurd.

He got a weird idea, he ran with it. He was a great riffer.

He wrote about sex.

He had a bug for a protagonist. That bug was a stroke of genius. Deep down we're all bugs. We have bug-like qualities, that is. There's a thread connecting us to them. You know that movie *Five Million Years to Earth*? It's the real deal. FK says check it out.

He wrote about the ridiculous.

He wrote about torment.

He had a protagonist with only the initial K for his last name. An anonymous hero. An everyman. A guy he could pour everything into, all his thoughts and feelings, all his humanity, and at the same time keep at arm's length. He could care about K, maybe even love the poor guy, without getting too attached.

He wrote about hunger.

He wrote about an ape lecturing men.

He crystallized a world view.

He gave us the word Kafkaesque.

He changed the way I thought about writing. From the moment I read him, I felt in the presence of a kindred spirit. The man's been dead nearly a hundred years, and that spirit is still alive today.

Hymenoptera

Michael Blumlein

THE WASP APPEARED in the salon that morning. It was early spring and unusually cold. The windows were laced with ice, and there was frost on the ground outside. Linderstadt shifted uneasily on the sofa, fighting both chill and dream. He had quarreled the night before, first with Madame Broussard, his head seamstress and lifelong friend, and then with Camille, his favorite model, accusing her of petty treacheries for which she was blameless. After they left, he drank himself into a stupor, stumbling from one workshop to another, knocking down mannequins, pulling dresses from their hangers, sweeping hats to the floor. The Spring Show, the most important of the year, was scarcely a week away, and the Spring Collection was complete. Normally, this was a time of excitement in the salon. Normally, the Linderstadt creations were worthy of excitement. Just the month before, Linderstadt had been dubbed, for the umpteenth time, the Earl of Elegance, the King of Couturier. He was a Genius. A Master. His attention to detail, to sleeve, waist and line were legendary. His transcendent gowns were slavishly copied and praised. He was at the peak of his powers, it was said, yet he felt, with this collection, just the opposite. It was bland, it was dull, it was uninspired. It reeked of old ideas and tired themes. It was the product of a man not at the height of his creativity but at the nadir and possibly the end. He had lost his way with this new line. He had lost his touch. He felt stagnant, bankrupt, pinched of vision, and insecure. Had he been cinched up in one of his own breath-defying corsets, he couldn't have felt more in need of fresh ideas and air.

Nothing had prepared him for this, and in his despair he came unglued, quarreling and drinking and cursing his empire of taffeta, satin, and silk. He raged against the poverty of his newest collection. He raged against himself and the poverty of his own spirit. It was a dark day in his life, and he drowned himself in the bottle, until, at last, he fell into a fitful sleep. There was a couch at one end of the room, where he lay in a disheveled, quasi-morbid state, half-draped in the train of a bridal gown he had appropriated from one of the ateliers for warmth. With dawn, sunlight appeared along the edges of the heavily curtained windows, penetrating the salon with a wan, peach-colored light.

The wasp was at the other end of the room, broadside to him and motionless. Its wings were folded back against its body, and its long belly was curled under itself like a comma. Its two antennae were curved delicately forward but otherwise as rigid as bamboo.

An hour passed and then another. When sleep became impossible, Linderstadt staggered off the couch to relieve himself. He returned to the salon with a pounding headache and a tall glass of water, at which point he noticed the wasp. From his father, who had been an amateur etymologist before dying of yellow fever, Linderstadt knew something of insects. This one he located somewhere in the family Sphecidae, which included wasps of primarily solitary habit. Most nested in burrows or natural cavities of hollow wood, and he was a little surprised to find the animal in his salon. Then again, he was surprised to have remembered anything at all about the creatures. He had scarcely thought of insects since his entry forty years before into the world of high fashion. He had scarcely thought of his father, preferring the memory of his mother Anna, his mother the caregiver, the seamstress, for whom he had named his first shop and his most famous dress. But his mother was not here, and the wasp most unmistakably was. Linderstadt downed his glass of water in a single gulp, wiped his lips, and pulled the bridal train over his shoulders like a shawl. Then he crossed the room to take a closer look.

The wasp stood chest high and about eight feet long. Linderstadt recognized the short hairs on its legs that used to remind him of the stubble on his father's chin, and he remembered, too, the forward palps by which the insect centered its jaws to tear off food. Its waist was pencil-thin, its wings translucent. Its exoskeleton, what Linderstadt thought of as its coat, was blacker than his blackest faille, blacker than coal. It seemed to absorb light, creating a small pocket of cold night right where it stood. Nigricans. He remembered the wasp's name. *Ammophila nigricans.* He was tempted to touch it, and instinctively, his eyes drifted down its belly to the pointed stinger that extruded like a rapier from its rear. He recalled that this was actually a hollow tube through which the female deposited eggs into her prey, where they would hatch into larvae and eat their way out. Males possessed the same tube but did not sting. As a boy he had always had trouble telling the sexes apart, and examining the creature now in the pale light, he wondered which it was. He felt a little feverish, which he attributed to the aftereffects of the alcohol. His mouth was parched, but he was reluctant to leave the salon for more water for fear the wasp would be gone when he returned. So he stayed, shivering and thirsty.

An hour passed. The temperature hovered near freezing. The wasp did not move. It was stiller than Martine, his stillest and most patient model. Stiller in the windless salon than the jewel-encrusted chandelier and the heavy damask curtains that hung like pillars and led to the dressing rooms. Linderstadt himself was the only moving thing in that cold, cold room. He paced to stay warm. He swallowed his own saliva to slake his thirst, but ultimately the need for water drove him out. He returned as quickly as possible, wearing shoes and sweater, carrying pencils, a pad of paper and a large pitcher of water. The wasp was exactly as he had left it, statuesque and immobile, as though carved in stone.

He began to draw, quickly, deftly, using broad, determined strokes. He worked from different angles, sketching the wasp's neck, its shoulders and waist. He imagined the creature in flight, its wings stiff and finely veined. He drew it feeding, resting, poised to sting. He clothed it in a variety of garments, experimenting with different designs, some stately and elegant, others pure whimsy. He found that he had already assumed the wasp was female. His subjects had never been anything but. He remembered Anouk, his very first model, the scoliotic girl his mother had brought home to test her adolescent son's fledgling talent. He felt as supple as he had then, his mind unlocked, as inventive and free-spirited as ever.

He worked all day and into the night, hardly daring to stop, resting only for a few brief hours in the early morning. He was woken at first light by the sound of church bells. It was Sunday, and near and far the call went out for prayer. In his youth he had been devout, and religious allusions were common in his early collections. But piety had given way to secularity. It had been years since he'd set foot in a church, and he felt both pleasure and guilt at the sound of the bells.

The morning brought no visitors, and he had the salon to himself. It was as cold as the day before, and the wasp remained inert. When the temperature hadn't climbed by noon, Linderstadt felt secure in leaving. His drawings were done, and his next task was to locate a suitable form on which to realize them. This was how gowns and dresses were made, and he owned hundreds of mannequins and torsos, of every conceivable shape, some bearing the name of a specific patron, others simply marked with an identifying number. He had other shapes as well, baskets, cylinders, mushrooms, triangles, all of which had found their way at one time or another into a collection. As long as an object had dimension, Linderstadt could imagine it on a woman. Or rather, he could imagine a woman in the object, in residence, giving it her own distinctive form and substance, imbuing each tangent and intersect with female spirit, joie de vivre and soul. He was wide-ranging and broad-minded in his tastes, and he expected to have no trouble in finding something suitable to the wasp, to serve as a model. Yet nothing caught his eye, not a single object or geometric form in his vast collection seemed remotely appropriate to the creature. It was odd but tantalizing. No simulation would do. He would have to work directly on the animal.

He returned to the salon and approached his subject. To a man accustomed to the divine plasticity of flesh, the armorlike hardness and inflexibility of the wasp's exoskeleton presented challenges. Each cut would have to be perfect, each seam precise. There was no bosom to softly fill a swale of fabric, no hip to give shape to a gentle waist. It would be like working with bone itself, like clothing a skeleton.

Intrigued, he stepped up and touched the wasp's body. It was cool and hard as metal. He ran a finger along one of its wings, half-expecting that his own nervous energy would bring it to life. Touch for him had always evoked the strongest emotions, which is why he used a pointing stick with his models. He might have done well to use the same stick with the wasp, for his skin tingled from the contact. For a moment he lost track of himself. His hand drifted, then touched one of the wasp's legs.

He felt a brief shock. It was not so different from a human leg. The hairs were soft like human hairs (hairs that his models assiduously bleached, waxed and shaved). The knee and ankle were jointed like their human counterparts, the claw as pointed and bony as a foot. His attention shifted to the animal's waist, in a human the pivot point between leg and torso. In the wasp it was lower and far narrower than anything human. It was as thin as a pipestem, a marvel of invention he was easily able to encircle in the tiny loop formed by his thumb and forefinger.

From a pocket he took out a tape and began to make his measurements: elbow to shoulder, shoulder to wing-tip, hip to claw, jotting each down in a notebook. From time to time he paused and stepped back to imagine a detail, a particular look…a melon sleeve, a fringed collar, a flounce. Sometimes he made a notation; occasionally, a quick sketch. He worked swiftly and confidently. All doubt and despair were gone.

When it came time to measure the chest, he had to lie on his back underneath the wasp. From that vantage he had a perfect view of its hairless and plated torso, as well as its stinger, which was poised like a pike and pointed directly between his legs. He felt a shiver of fear and excitement. After a moment's hesitation he took the stinger's measurement too. Idly, he wondered if this were one of those wasps that died after stinging, and if so, was there some way he could memorialize such a transformative event in a dress. Then he crawled out and looked at his numbers.

The wasp was symmetrical, almost perfectly so. Throughout his career Linderstadt had always sought to thwart symmetry, focusing instead on the subtle variations in the human body, the natural differences between left and right. There was always something to emphasize in a woman's body, something unique to draw the eye, a hip that was higher, a shoulder more prominent, a breast. Even an eye, whose iris might be flecked a slightly different shade of blue than its twin, could trigger a report, an echo, somewhere in the color of the dress below. Linderstadt had an uncanny ability to uncover such asymmetries. This talent flowed from his belief that no two people were alike. A human being was a singular creature. Each was unique. Each was special and deserved to be seen as special. Each of his models, his patrons, even the commonplace women who bought off the rack, deserved to stand out.

The wasp presented difficulties. There was nothing that distinguished left from right, one side from the other. In all likelihood it was identical to every other wasp of its kind. It seemed to mock the very idea of singularity. And yet it was beautiful, stunningly beautiful, and it occurred to Linderstadt that perhaps he'd been wrong. Perhaps beauty lay, not in the differences between people but in the similarities. That, in fact, people were more alike than different. That he himself was not so very different from the women he clothed.

It was revelation to him. Heart racing, he took his notebook to the main atelier and began work on his first dress.

He had decided to start with something simple, a velvet sheath with narrow apertures for wing and leg and a white flounce of tulle at the bottom to hide the stinger. With no time for a muslin fitting, he worked directly with the fabric itself. It was a job normally handled by his assistants, but the master had lost none of his skill with scissors and thread. The work went fast. Partway through the sewing, he remembered the name of the order to which this wasp belonged. Hymenoptera, after ptera, for wing, and hymeno, for the Greek god of marriage, referring to the union of the wasp's front and hind wings. He himself had never married, had never touched a woman outside his profession, certainly not intimately. It was possible he feared intimacy, or rejection, but more likely what he feared was a test of the purity of his vision. His women, he often thought, were extensions of himself. They were the best he had to offer, his most prized possessions. He clothed them to admire them and to have them admired. And to be admired himself. They were jewels, and they lived in the palace of his imagination and the stronghold of his dreams. He placed them on a pedestal, just as he himself wanted to be placed. The object of all eyes. Adored. Untouchable. Safe.

Yet now, inspired by the wasp, riding a wave of creativity, authenticity and passion unlike any he'd ever known, he knew it was not the time to be safe.

He finished the first dress and hurried to the salon. The wasp offered no resistance as he lifted its claws and pulled the dark sheath into place. The image of his father, gently unfolding a butterfly's wing and pinning it to his velvet display board, played across his mind. The Linderstadt men, it seemed, had a special gift with animals.

He straightened the bodice and zipped up the back of the gown, then stepped back for a look. The waist, as he expected, needed taking in, and one of the shoulders needed to be realigned. The choice of color and fabric, however, was excellent. Black on black, night against night. It was an auspicious start.

He did the alterations, then hung the gown in one of the dressing rooms and returned to his workshop. His next outfit was a broad cape of lemon guipure with a gold chain fastener, striking in its contrast to the wasp's jet-black body. He made a matching toque to which he attached a pair of lacquered sticks to echo the wasp's antennae. The atelier was as frigid as the salon, and he worked in overcoat, scarf and kid gloves whose fingertips he had snipped off with a scissors. His face was bare, and the bracing chill against his cheeks recalled the freezing winters of his child-hood when he was forced to stand stock-still for what seemed hours on end while his mother used him as a form for the clothes she was making. They had no money for heat, and Linderstadt had developed a stoical attitude toward the elements. The cold reminded him of the value of discipline and self-control. But more than that, it reminded him how he had come to love the feel of the outfits his mother had fitted and fastened against his skin. He loved it when she tightened a waist or took in a sleeve. The feeling of confinement warmed his blood. It was like a pair of hands holding and caressing him. He felt comforted, nurtured, restrained and paradoxically freed. What he remembered of the cold was not the numb-ness in his fingers, the misting of his breath, the goosebumps on his skin. It was his mother he remembered: her steady hand and hard work, her stubborn practicality and abiding love. He remembered the pleasure of wearing her creations. The flights of fantasy they stirred in him. The cold had become synonymous with these.

He worked through the night to finish the cape. When Monday morning arrived, he locked the doors of the salon, turning away the seamstresses, stockroom clerks, salesgirls and models who had come to work. He held the door against Camille and even Broussard, his confidante, who knew his moods as well as anyone. Half-hidden by the curtain that was strung across the broad glass entrance doors, he announced that the collection was complete, the final alterations to be done in private by himself. He assured them all was well. The House of Linderstadt had risen from the ashes. The House was intact. He invited each and every one of them to return in a week for the unveiling of the new collection. It would be a seminal event, and what better time than spring, the season of birth.

He withdrew to his workshop, where he started on his next creation, an off-the-shoulder blue moiré gown with a voluminous skirt festooned with bows. He sewed what he could by machine, but the bows had to be done by hand. He sewed like his mother, one knee crossed over the other, head bent, pinkie finger crooked out as though he were sipping a cup of tea. The skirt took a full day, during which he broke only once, to relieve himself. Food did not enter his mind, and in that he seemed in tune with the wasp. The creature showed neither hunger nor thirst. On occasion one of its antennae would twitch, but Linderstadt attributed this to subtle changes in the turgor of the insect's blood. He assumed the wasp remained immobilized by the cold, though he couldn't help but wonder if its preternatural stillness sprang from some deeper design. He thought of his father, so ordinary on the surface, so unfathomable beneath. Given the chance, the man would spend days with his insects, meticulously arranging his boards, printing the tiny specimen labels, revising and updating his collection. Often he seemed devoted to nothing else. Linderstadt was awed by his father's obsessiveness, frightened at times, envious at other times. There was something enticing, almost sacred, about it. His mother said the man was in hiding, but what did a child know about that?

The weather held, and on Wednesday he wheeled one of the sewing machines from the atelier to the salon so that he could work without leaving the wasp's side. Voices drifted in from the street, curiosity seekers, passersby trying in vain to get a glimpse inside the celebrated salon. The phone rang incessantly, message after message from concerned friends who hadn't heard from him, from clients, from the press. M. Jesais, his personal psychic, called daily with increasingly dire warnings. Linderstadt was unmoved. He heard but a single voice. He had, now, but a single vision.

All his life he'd worked with women. They were the world to him, sirens of impossible beauty and magic, divinities of mystery and might. Juliette in satin, Eve in furs, the Nameless Queen in stiff and imperious brocade. He had prized them and praised them. In private he had worshipped them. In public he had triumphed with them. But these triumphs, alas, were short-lived. Time and again he was left with an empty feeling inside. Something was missing in his life. Women were not the only beauties. They were not the only bodies begging to be wrapped in gossamer and adored.

He eyed the wasp and crossed his arms. Idly, he ran his fingers down his chest. He was tall, with narrow shoulders and hips. He'd been skinny as a boy and had scarcely thickened with age. His models, who slaved to stay thin, marveled at how he kept his figure. They joked that he could be a model himself. This was meant, of course, as praise, but there were times it felt like a curse. In his heart of hearts he would have preferred a different body, or two bodies: the one he bore, the other with more flesh and curves.

The wasp had no flesh. Chitin was the furthest thing from it. But it had curves aplenty. Head, torso, stinger, legs. Six of them, six shapely cylinders, each broken by multiple joints, a welter of angle, line and dimension. And wings with gently curving tips, wings as beautiful as those of the angel Gabriel himself, a painting of whom hung in the salon and had been the inspiration for Linderstadt's groundbreaking '04 collection. And eyes, rounded, compound eyes, able to see god-knew-what. And finely arching antennae, to sample and savor the world's delights.

He stitched a sleeve and then another. He imagined Camille as an insect, crawling down the runway, striking a pose. Camille on her hands and feet, like a beetle, Camille on her belly, inching along like a caterpillar, or a worm. Would she do it if he asked? Did he dare? It was a monstrous idea. He was a monstrous man. His adoration of women had made him blind to women. He saw what he wanted to see. Surfaces, gestures, poses, shapes. How little he understood of what lived underneath. How little he understood of himself.

He thought again of his father, closeted with his insect collection. Absorbed to the point of estrangement from his wife and son. In hiding, said his mother. Linderstadt, too, was in hiding. Hiding, it seemed, was a family trait.

He finished the last seam and held up the dress. The shimmering moiré reminded him of rippling water, the six-legged gown of a sea creature adrift beneath the waves. To a lesser talent the sleeves would have been a nightmare, but in the Master's able hands they flowed and were joined effortlessly into the bodice. Each one sported a ruffled cap and was zippered to aid in getting it on. Once the gown was in place, he stepped back to have a look. The fit was uncanny, as though some hidden hand had been guiding his own. It had been that way from the start. There were five gowns now. Five in five days. One more, he thought, one more to complete the collection.

He knew what that one was. The bridal gown, his signature piece. For forty years he had ended every show with such a gown. Brides signified life. They signified love and the power of creation. What better way, with this newest collection, to signal his own rebirth?

The dress took two days. The second was Sunday, and Linderstadt felt a little shiver of pleasure when the bells began to toll. He was working on the veil, a gorgeous bit of organza that looked like mist, sewing and thinking what a pity it would be to cover the wasp's extraordinary face. And so he had devised an ingenious interlocking paneled design that simultaneously hid the face and revealed it. After finishing the veil, he started on the train, using ten feet of egg-white chiffon that he gathered in gentle waves to resemble foam. Where it attached to the skirt, he cut a hole for the stinger and ringed it with white silk roses. The bodice of the dress was made of rich and creamy satin with an Imperial collar and long sleeves of lace. Queen, Mother, Bride—the holy trinity of women. The gown, to his mind, embodied all three and was triumphant.

He completed it Sunday night and hung it in the dressing room with the other gowns. Then he wrapped himself in his overcoat and

Kafkaesque

scarf and fell asleep on the couch. He planned to get up early Monday and make the final preparations for the show.

That night the cold spell broke. A warm front swept in from the south, brushing away the chill like a cobweb. In his sleep Linderstadt unbuttoned his coat and pulled off his scarf. He dreamed of summer, flying a kite with his mother at the beach. When he woke, it was almost noon. The room was thick with heat. A crowd had gathered outside the salon for the opening. The wasp was gone.

In a panic he searched the workshops, the stockroom, the dressing rooms and the offices. He looked in the basement and the boiler room. He climbed to the roof and swept his eyes across the sky. It was nowhere to be found.

In shock he returned to the salon.

Near where it had been he noticed a paper sphere the size of a pot-bellied stove. One side of it was open, and inside were multiple tiers of hexagonal cells, all composed of the same papery material as the outside of the sphere. Linderstadt had a glimmer of understanding, and when he discovered that his gowns had also vanished—every one of them—he realized his mistake. The wasp was not a Sphecida at all, but a Vespida, a paper wasp. Its diet consisted of wood, leaves and other natural fibers. It had eaten the collection.

Numbly, Linderstadt surveyed the remains of his work. The nest had a delicate beauty of its own, and briefly he considered showing it in lieu of the collection. Then he spied a bit of undigested material peeking out from behind the papery sphere. It was the bridal veil, and it stood on the floor like a fountain of steam frozen in air. No dress, no train, only this, the filmy, translucent veil. Meant to hide the bride until that moment it was lifted and she emerged, in all her newness, freshness and radiance.

Outside, the crowd clamored to be let in. Linderstadt hesitated for a minute, then drew back the heavy curtains and lifted the gossamer veil. The sun seemed to set it aflame. His heart quickened, and the tiny hairs on his neck and his arms stood on end as he placed it on his head. With everything gone there was nothing left to lose or conceal. A single thread would have sufficed. Raising his face, throwing his shoulders back, standing proud and erect, he opened the doors.

J.K.

Another giant insect story. But this story's resemblance to Kafka rests more, it seems to me, in the way the presence (or absence) of the giant insect reflects the psychological state of the viewpoint character.

JAMES PATRICK KESSEL:

A bug and questions of identity again, only this time in a doppelgänger story. The transformation, while equally fantastic, exists only in the protagonist's imagination.

JORGE LUIS BORGES:

[Kafka's] work could be defined as a parable or series of parables on the theme of the moral relationship of the individual with his God and with his God's incomprehensible universe. For all their contemporary setting, his stories are less close to what is conventionally called modern literature than they are to the Book of Job. They presuppose a religious conscience, specifically a Jewish conscience; formal imitation of Kafka in another context would be unintelligible. Kafka saw his work as an act of faith, and he did not want it to discourage other men. Because of this, he asked his friend to destroy it. However, I suspect further reasons. Kafka knew he could dream only nightmares and was aware that reality is a continuous sequence of melancholy nightmares. Added to which, he appreciated the dramatic potential of delays and postponements; this is apparent throughout his work. But both these themes, melancholy and delay, undoubtedly wearied him in the end. He might perhaps have preferred to be the author of a few happy pages—such as his honesty would not allow him to write.

—from his foreword to *Franz Kafka: Stories 1904–1924*, translated by J. A. Underwood)

The Lottery in Babylon

Jorge Luis Borges

Translated by Andrew Hurley

LIKE ALL THE men of Babylon, I have been proconsul; like all, I have been a slave. I have known omnipotence, ignominy, imprisonment. Look here—my right hand has no index finger. Look here—through this gash in my cape you can see on my stomach a crimson tattoo—it is the second letter, *Beth*. On nights when the moon is full, this symbol gives me power over men with the mark of Gimel, but it subjects me to those with the Aleph, who on nights when there is no moon owe obedience to those marked with the Gimel. In the half-light of dawn, in a cellar, standing before a black altar, I have slit the throats of sacred bulls. Once, for an entire lunar year, I was declared invisible—I would cry out and no one would heed my call, I would steal bread and not be beheaded. I have known that thing the Greeks knew not—uncertainty. In a chamber of brass, as I faced the strangler's silent scarf, hope did not abandon me; in the river of delights, panic has not failed me. Heraclides Ponticus reports, admiringly, that Pythagoras recalled having been Pyrrhus, and before that, Euphorbus, and before that, some other mortal; in order to recall similar vicissitudes, I have no need of death, nor even of imposture.

I owe that almost monstrous variety to an institution—the Lottery—which is unknown in other nations, or at work in them imperfectly or secretly. I have not delved into this institution's history. I know that sages cannot agree. About its mighty purposes I know as much as a man untutored in astrology might know about the moon. Mine is a dizzying country in which the Lottery is a major element of reality; until this day, I have thought as little about it as about the conduct of the indecipherable gods or of my heart. Now, far from Babylon and its beloved customs, I think with some bewilderment about the Lottery, and about the blasphemous conjectures that shrouded men whisper in the half-light of dawn or evening.

My father would tell how once, long ago—centuries? years?—the lottery in Babylon was a game played by commoners. He would tell (though whether this is true or not, I cannot say) how barbers would take a man's copper coins and give back rectangles made of bone or parchment and adorned with symbols. Then, in broad daylight, a drawing would be held; those smiled upon by fate would, with no further corroboration by chance, win coins minted of silver. The procedure, as you can see, was rudimentary.

Naturally, those so-called "lotteries" were a failure. They had no moral force whatsoever; they appealed not to all a man's faculties, but only to his hopefulness. Public indifference soon meant that the merchants who had founded these venal lotteries began to lose money. Someone tried something new: including among the list of lucky numbers a few *unlucky* draws. This innovation meant that those who bought those numbered rectangles now had a twofold chance: they might win a sum of money or they might be required to pay a fine—sometimes a considerable one. As one might expect, that small risk (for every thirty "good" numbers there was one ill-omened one) piqued the public's interest. Babylonians flocked to buy tickets. The man who bought none was considered a pusillanimous wretch, a man with no spirit of adventure. In time, this justified contempt found a second target: not just the man who didn't play, but also the man who lost and paid the fine. The Company (as it was now beginning to be known) had to protect the interest of the winners, who could not be paid their prizes unless the pot contained almost the entire amount of the fines.

A lawsuit was filed against the losers: the judge sentenced them to pay the original fine, plus court costs, or spend a number of days in jail. In order to thwart the Company, they all chose jail. From that gauntlet thrown down by a few men sprang the Company's omnipotence—its ecclesiastical, metaphysical force.

Some time after this, the announcements of the numbers drawn began to leave out the lists of fines and simply print the days of prison assigned to each losing number. That shorthand, as it were, which went virtually unnoticed at the time, was of utmost importance: *It was the first appearance of nonpecuniary elements in the lottery.* And it met with great success—indeed, the Company was forced by its players to increase the number of unlucky draws.

As everyone knows, the people of Babylon are great admirers of logic, and even of symmetry. It was inconsistent that lucky numbers should pay off in round silver coins while unlucky ones were measured in days and nights of jail. Certain moralists argued that the possession of coins did not always bring about happiness, and that other forms of happiness were perhaps more direct.

The lower-caste neighborhoods of the city voiced a different complaint. The members of the priestly class gambled heavily, and so enjoyed all the vicissitudes of terror and hope; the poor (with understandable, or inevitable, envy) saw themselves denied access to that famously delightful, even sensual, wheel. The fair and reasonable desire that all men and women, rich and poor, be able to take part equally in the Lottery inspired indignant demonstrations—the memory of which, time has failed to dim. Some stubborn souls could not (or pretended they could not) understand that this was a *novus ordo seclorum,* a necessary stage of history.... A slave stole a crimson ticket; the drawing determined that that ticket entitled the bearer to have his tongue burned out. The code of law provided the same sentence for stealing a lottery ticket. Some Babylonians argued that the slave deserved the burning iron for being a thief; others, more magnanimous, that the executioner should employ the iron because thus fate had decreed.... There were disturbances, there were regrettable instances of bloodshed, but the masses of Babylon at last, over the opposition of the well-to-do, imposed their will; they saw their generous objectives fully achieved. First, the Company was forced to assume all public power. (The unification was necessary because of the vastness and complexity of the new operations.) Second, the Lottery was made secret, free of charge, and open to all. The mercenary sale of lots was abolished; once initiated into the mysteries of Baal, every free citizen automatically took part in the sacred drawings, which were held in the labyrinths of the god every sixty nights and determined each citizen's destiny until the next drawing. The consequences were incalculable. A lucky draw might bring about a man's elevation to the council of the magi or the imprisonment of his enemy (secret, or known by all to be so), or might allow him to find, in the peaceful dimness of his room, the woman who would begin to disturb him, or whom he had never hoped to see again; an unlucky draw: mutilation, dishonor of many kinds, death itself. Sometimes a single event—the murder of C in a tavern, B's mysterious apotheosis—would be the inspired outcome of thirty or forty drawings. Combining bets was difficult, but we must recall that the individuals of the Company were (and still are) all-powerful, and clever. In many cases, the knowledge that certain happy turns were the simple result of chance would have lessened the force of those outcomes; to forestall that problem, agents of the Company employed suggestion, or even magic. The paths they followed, the intrigues they wove, were invariably secret. To penetrate the innermost hopes and innermost fears of every man, they called upon astrologers and spies. There were certain stone lions, a sacred latrine called Qaphqa, some cracks in a dusty aqueduct—these places, it was generally believed, *gave access to the Company,* and well- or ill-wishing persons would deposit confidential reports in them. An alphabetical file held those *dossiers* of varying veracity.

Incredibly, there was talk of favoritism, of corruption. With its customary discretion, the Company did not reply directly; instead, it scrawled its brief argument in the rubble of a mask factory. This *apologia* is now numbered among the sacred Scriptures. It pointed out, doctrinally, that the Lottery is an interpolation of chance into the order of the universe, and observed that to accept errors is to strengthen chance, not contravene it. It also noted that those lions, that sacred squatting-place, though not disavowed by the Company (which reserved the right to consult them), functioned with no official guarantee.

This statement quieted the public's concerns. But it also produced other effects perhaps unforeseen by its author. It profoundly altered both the spirit and the operations of the Company. I have but little time remaining; we are told that the ship is about to sail—but I will try to explain.

However unlikely it may seem, no one, until that time, had attempted to produce a general theory of gaming. Babylonians are not a speculative people; they obey the dictates of chance, surrender their lives, their hopes, their nameless terror to it, but it never occurs to them to delve into its labyrinthine laws or the revolving spheres that manifest its workings. Nonetheless, the semiofficial statement that I mentioned inspired numerous debates of a legal and mathematical nature. From one of them, there emerged the following conjecture: If the Lottery is an intensification of chance, a periodic infusion of chaos into the cosmos, then is it not appropriate that chance intervene in *every* aspect of the drawing, not just one? Is it not ludicrous that chance should dictate a person's death while the circumstances of that death—whether private or public, whether drawn out for an hour or a century—should *not* be subject to chance? Those perfectly reasonable objections finally prompted sweeping reform; the complexities of the new system (complicated further by its having been in practice for centuries) are understood by only a handful of specialists, though I will attempt to summarize them, even if only symbolically.

Let us imagine a first drawing, which condemns an individual to death. In pursuance of that decree, another drawing is held; out of that second drawing come, say, nine possible executors. Of those nine, four might initiate a third drawing to determine the name of the executioner, two might replace the unlucky draw with a lucky one (the discovery of a treasure, say), another might decide that the death should be exacerbated (death with dishonor, that is, or with the refinement of torture), others might simply refuse to carry out the sentence.... That is the scheme of the Lottery, put symbolically. *In reality, the number of drawings is infinite.* No decision is final; all branch into others. The ignorant assume that infinite drawings require infinite time; actually, all that is required is that time be infinitely subdivisible, as in the famous parable of the Race with the Tortoise. That infinitude coincides remarkably well with the sinuous numbers of Chance and with the Heavenly Archetype of the Lottery beloved of Platonists.... Some distorted echo of our custom seems to have reached the Tiber: In his *Life of Antoninus Heliogabalus,* Ælius Lampridius tells us that the emperor wrote out on seashells the fate that he intended for his guests at dinner—some would receive ten pounds of gold; others, ten houseflies, ten dormice, ten bears. It is fair to recall that Heliogabalus was raised in Asia Minor, among the priests of his eponymous god.

There are also *impersonal* drawings, whose purpose is unclear. One drawing decrees that a sapphire from Taprobana be thrown into the waters of the Euphrates; another, that a bird be released from the top of a certain tower; another, that every hundred years a grain of sand be added to (or taken from) the countless grains of sand on a certain beach. Sometimes, the consequences are terrible.

Under the Company's beneficent influence, our customs are now steeped in chance. The purchaser of a dozen amphoræ of Damascene wine will not be surprised if one contains a talisman, or a viper; the scribe who writes out a contract never fails to include some error; I myself, in this hurried statement, have misrepresented some splendor, some atrocity—perhaps, too, some mysterious monotony.... Our historians, the most perspicacious on the planet, have invented a method for correcting chance; it is well known that the outcomes of this method are (in general) trustworthy—although, of course, they are never divulged without a measure of deception. Besides, there is nothing so tainted with fiction as the history of the Company.... A paleographic document, unearthed at a certain temple, may come from yesterday's drawing or from a drawing that took place centuries ago. No book is published without some discrepancy between each of the edition's copies. Scribes take a secret oath to omit, interpolate, alter. *Indirect* falsehood is also practiced.

The Company, with godlike modesty, shuns all publicity. Its agents, of course, are secret; the orders it constantly (perhaps continually) imparts are no different from those spread wholesale by impostors. Besides— who will boast of being a mere impostor? The drunken man who blurts out an absurd command, the sleeping man who suddenly awakes and turns and chokes to death the woman sleeping at his side—are they not, perhaps, implementing one of the Company's secret decisions? That silent functioning, like God's, inspires all manner of conjectures. One scurrilously suggests that the Company ceased to exist hundreds of years ago, and that the sacred disorder of our lives is purely hereditary, traditional; another believes that the Company is eternal, and that it shall endure until the last night, when the last god shall annihilate the earth. Yet another declares that the Company is omnipotent, but affects only small things: the cry of a bird, the shades of rust and dust, the half dreams that come at dawn. Another, whispered by masked heresiarchs, says that *the Company has never existed, and never will.* Another, no less despicable, argues that it makes no difference whether one affirms or denies the reality of the shadowy corporation, because Babylon is nothing but an infinite game of chance.

Editors' notes

J.K.
Borges in this story and others (notably "The Library of Babel") uses the structure that Kafka uses in "The Metamorphosis" and others, where the story progresses not by a conventional Aristotelian plot—with protagonist, antagonist, a series of events comprising a rising action, climax, and denouement—but by assertion of a fact in contradiction to reality and elaboration/qualification/evolution from that assertion. Note the "sacred latrine called Qaphqa" where people petitioning the mysterious Company deposit confidential reports.

J.P.K.
The game of life, according to Borges, is subject to the laws of thermodynamics: You must play, you can't win, you can't break even, and you can't quit. Meanwhile, God may or may not be paying attention, if He even exists.

T. Coraghessan Boyle:

   Kafka, too. I forget Kafka. Kafka is one of the earliest influences before I even discovered Flannery O'Connor. Absolutely. Again, I don't even know how old I was— probably seventeen or so, when I first went to college. Kafka produced a different kind of story from what I had been familiar with. More akin to skewed folk tales than the realist stories of the fifties and sixties—the early sixties anyway. You know, Hemingway and Steinbeck and so on. His work was a revelation to me. To this day I reference "A Hunger Artist" all the time because it speaks so much to what we do in our work.

   —interview in *thepedestalmagazine.com*, Jun–Aug 2005

The Big Garage

T. Coraghessan Boyle

For K.

B. STANDS AT the side of the highway, helpless, hands behind his back, the droopy greatcoat like a relic of ancient wars. There is wind and rain—or is it sleet?—and the deadly somnolent rush of tires along the pavement. His own vehicle rests on the shoulder, stricken somewhere in its slippery metallic heart. He does not know where, exactly, or why— for B. is no mechanic. Far from it. In fact, he's never built or repaired a thing in his life, never felt the restive urge to tinker with machinery, never as a jittery adolescent dismantled watches, telephone receivers, pneumatic crushers. He is woefully unequal to the situation at hand. But wait, hold on now—shouldn't he raise the hood, as a distress signal? Isn't that the way it's done?

Suddenly he's in motion, glad to be doing something, confronting the catastrophe, meeting the challenge. He scuttles round to the front of the car, works his fingers under the lip of the hood and tugs, tugs to no effect, slips in the mud, stumbles, the knees of his trousers soaked through, and then rises to tug again, shades of Buster Keaton. After sixty or seventy seconds of this it occurs to him that the catch may be inside, under the dashboard, as it was in his late wife's Volvo. There are wires—bundles of them—levers, buttons, handles, cranks and knobs in the cavern beneath the steering wheel. He had no idea. He takes a bundle of wire in his hand—each strand a different color—and thinks with a certain satisfaction of the planning and coordination that went into this machine, of the multiple factories, each dominating its own little Bavarian or American or Japanese town, of all the shifts and lunch breaks, the dies cast and what do you call them, lathes—yes, lathes—turned. All this—but more, much more. Iron ore dug from rock, hissing white hot vats of it, molten recipes, chromium, tall rubber trees, vinyl plants, crystals from the earth ground into glass. Staggering.

"Hey pal—"

B. jolted from his reverie by the harsh plosive, spasms of amber light expanding and contracting the interior of the car like the pulse of some predatory beast. Looking up into a lean face, slick hair, stoned eyes. "I was ah trying to ah get the ah latch here—"

"You'll have to ride back in the truck with me."

"Yeah, sure," B. sitting up now, confused, gripping the handle and swinging the door out to a shriek of horns and a rush of air. He cracks something in his elbow heaving it shut.

"Better get out this side."

B. slides across the seat and steps out into the mud. Behind him, the tow truck, huge, its broad bumper lowering over the hood of his neat little German-made car. He mounts the single step up into the cab and watches the impassive face of the towman as he backs round, attaches the grappling hook and hoists the rear of the car, spider and fly. A moment later the man drops into the driver's seat, door slamming with a metallic thud, gears engaging. "That'll be forty-five bucks," he says.

A white fracture of sleet caught up in the headlights, the wipers clapping, light flashing, the night a mist and a darkness beyond the windows. They've turned off the highway, jerking right and left over a succession of secondary roads, strayed so far from B.'s compass that he's long since given up any attempt at locating himself. Perhaps he's dozed even. He turns to study the crease folded into the towman's cheek. "Much farther?" he asks.

The man jerks his chin and B. looks out at a blaze of light on the dark horizon, light dropped like a stone in a pool of oil. As they draw closer he's able to distinguish a neon sign, towering letters stamped in the sky above a complex of offices, outbuildings and hangars that melt off into the shadows. Eleven or twelve sets of gas pumps, each nestled under a black steel parasol, and cars, dark and driverless, stretching across the whitening blacktop like the reverie of a used-car salesman. The sign, in neon grid, traces and retraces its colossal characters until there's no end and no beginning: GARAGE. TEGELER'S. BIG. GARAGE. TEGELER'S BIG GARAGE.

The truck pulls up in front of a deep, brightly lit office. Through the steamed-over windows B. can make out several young women, sitting legs-crossed in orange plastic chairs. From here they look like drum majorettes: white calf boots, opalescent skirts, lace frogs. And—can it be?—Dale Evans hats! What is going on here?

The towman's voice is harsh. "End of the road for you, pal."

"What about my car?"

A cigarette hangs from his lower lip like a growth, smoke squints his eyes. "Nobody here to poke into it at this hour, what do you think? I'm taking it around to Diagnosis."

"And?"

"Pfft." The man fixes him with the sort of stare you'd give a leper at the Inaugural Ball. *"And* when they get to it, they get to it."

B. steps into the fluorescent blaze of the office, coattails aflap. There are nine girls seated along the wall, left calves swollen over right knees, hands occupied with nail files, hairbrushes, barrettes, magazines. They are dressed as drum majorettes. Nappy Dale Evans hats perch atop their layered cuts, short-and-sassies, blown curls. All nine look up and smile. Then a short redhead rises, and sweet as a mother superior welcoming a novice, asks if she can be of service.

B. is confused. "It…it's my car," he says.

"Ohhh," running her tongue round her lips. "You're the Audi."

"Right."

"Just wait a sec and I'll ring Diagnosis," she says, high-stepping across the room to an intercom panel set in the wall. At that moment a buzzer sounds in the office and a car pulls up to the farthest set of gas pumps. The redhead jerks to a halt, peers out the window, curses, shrugs into a fringed suede jacket and hurries out into the storm. B. locks fingers behind his back and waits. He rocks on his feet, whistles sotto voce, casts furtive glances at the knee-down of the eight majorettes. The droopy greatcoat, soaked through, feels like an American black bear (*Ursus americanus*) hanging round his neck.

Then the door heaves back on its hinges and the redhead reappears, stamping round the doormat, shaking out the jacket, knocking the Stetson against her thigh. "Brrrr," she says. In her hand, a clutch of bills. She marches over to the cash register and deposits them, then takes her seat at the far end of the line of majorettes. B. continues to rock on his feet. He clears his throat. Finally he ambles across the room and stops in front of her chair. "Ahh…"

She looks up. "Yes? Can I help you?"

"You were gong to call Diagnosis about my car?"

"Oh," grimacing. "No need to bother. Why, at this hour they're long closed up. You'll have to wait till morning."

"But a minute ago—"

"No, no sense at all. The Head Diagnostician leaves at five, and here it's nearly ten. And his staff gets off at five-thirty. The best we could hope for is a shop steward—and what would he know? Ha. If I rang up now I'd be lucky to get hold of a janitor." She settles back in her chair and leafs through a magazine. Then she looks up again. "Listen. If you want some advice, there's a pay phone in the anteroom. Better call somebody to come get you."

The girl has a point there. It's late already and arrangements will have to be made about getting to work in the morning. The dog needs walking, the cat feeding. And all these hassles have sapped him to the point where all he wants from life is sleep and forgetfulness. But there's no one to call, really. Except possibly Dora—Dora Ouzel, the gay divorcée he's been dating since his wife's accident.

One of the majorettes yawns. Another blows a puff of detritus from her nail file. "Ho hum," says the redhead.

B. steps into the anteroom, searches through his pockets for change, and forgets Dora's number. He paws through the phone book, but the names of the towns seem unfamiliar and he can't seem to find Dora's listing. He makes an effort of memory and dials.

"Hello?"

"Hello, Dora?—B. Listen, I hate to disturb you at this hour but—"

"Are you all right?"

"Yes, I'm fine."

"That's nice, I'm fine too. But no matter how you slice it my name ain't Dora."

"You're not Dora?"

"No, but you're B., aren't you?"

"Yes...but how did you know?"

"You told me. You said: 'Hello, Dora?—B.'...and then you tried to come on with some phony excuse for forgetting our date tonight or is it that you're out hooching it up and you want me—if I was Dora and I bless my stars I'm not—to come out in this hellish weather that isn't fit for a damn dog for christsake and risk my bones and bladder to drive you home because only one person inhabits your solipsistic universe—*You* with a capital Y—and *You* have drunk yourself into a blithering stupor. You know what I got to say to you, buster? Take a flyer. Ha, ha, ha."

There is a click at the other end of the line. In the movies heroes say "Hello, hello, hello," in situations like this, but B., dispirited, the greatcoat beginning to reek a bit in the confines of the antechamber, only reaches out to replace the receiver in its cradle.

Back in the office B. is confronted with eight empty chairs. The redhead occupies the ninth, legs crossed, hat in lap, curls flaring round the cover of her magazine like a solar phenomenon. Where five minutes earlier there were enough majorettes to front a battle of the bands, there is now only one. She glances up as the door slams behind him. "Any luck?"

B. is suddenly overwhelmed with exhaustion. He's just gone fifteen rounds, scaled Everest, staggered out of the Channel at Calais. "No," he whispers.

"Well that really is too bad. All the other girls go home at ten and I'm sure any one of them would have been happy to give you a lift.... You know it really is a pity the way some of you men handle your affairs. Why if I had as little common sense as you I wouldn't last ten minutes on this job."

B. heaves himself down on one of the plastic chairs. Somehow, somewhere along the line, his sense of proportion has begun to erode. He blows his nose lugubriously. Then hides behind his hands and massages his eyes.

"Come on now." The girl's voice is soft, conciliatory. She is standing over him, her hand stretched out to his. "I'll fix you up a place to sleep in the back of the shop."

The redhead (her name is Rita—B. thought to ask as a sort of quid pro quo for her offer of a place to sleep) leads him through a narrow passageway which gives on to an immense darkened hangar. B. hunches in the greatcoat, flips up his collar and follows her into the echo-haunted reaches. Their footsteps clap up to the rafters, blind birds beating at the roof, echoing and reechoing in the darkness. There is a chill as of open spaces, a stink of raw metal, oil, sludge. Rita is up ahead, her white boots ghostly in the dark. "Watch your step," she cautions, but B. has already encountered some impenetrable, rock-hard hazard, barked his shin and pitched forward into what seems to be an open grease pit.

"Hurt yourself?"

B. lies there silent—frustrated, childish, perverse.

"B.? Answer me—are you all right?"

He will lie here, dumb as a block, till the Andes are nubs and the moon melts from the sky. But then suddenly the cavern blooms with light (a brown crepuscular light, it's true, but light just the same) and the game's up.

"So there you are!" Arms akimbo, a grin on her face. "Now get yourself up out of there and stop your sulking. I can't play games all night, you know. There's eleven sets of pumps out there I'm responsible for."

B. finds himself sprawled all over an engine block, grease-slicked and massive, that must have come out of a Sherman tank. But it's the hangar, lit like the grainy daguerreotype of a Civil War battlefield, that really interests him. The sheer expanse of the place! And the cars, thousands of them, stretching all the way down to the dark V at the far end of the building. Bugattis, Morrises, LaSalles, Daimlers, the back end of a Pierce-Arrow, a Stutz Bearcat. The rounded humps of tops and fenders, tarnished bumpers, hoods thrown open like gaping mouths.

Kafkaesque

Engines swing on cables, blackened grilles and punctured cloth tops gather in the corners, a Duesenberg, its interior gutted, squats over a trench in the concrete.

"Pretty amazing, huh?" Rita says, reaching out a hand to help him up. "This is Geriatrics. Mainly foreign. You should see the Contemp wings."

"But what do you do with all these—?"

"Oh, we fix them. At least the technicians and mechanics do."

There is something wrong here, something amiss. B. can feel it nagging at the edges of his consciousness…but then he really is dog-tired. Rita has him by the hand. They amble past a couple hundred cars, dust-embossed, ribs and bones showing, windshields black as ground-out eyes. Now he has it: "But if you fix them, what are they doing here?"

Rita stops dead to look him in the eye, frowning, schoolmarmish. "These things take time, you know" She sighs. "What do you think: they do it overnight?"

The back room is the size of a storage closet. In fact, it is a storage closet, fitted out with cots. When Rita flicks the light switch B. is shocked to discover three other people occupying the makeshift dormitory: two men in rumpled suits and a middle-aged woman in a rumpled print dress. One of the men sits up and rubs his eyes. His tie is loose, shirt filthy, a patchy beard maculating his cheeks. He mumbles something—B. catches the words "drive shaft"—and then turns his face back to the cot, already sucking in breath for the first stertorous blast: *hkk-hkk-hkkkkkkgg*.

"What the hell is this?" B. is astonished, scandalized, cranky and tired. Tools and blackened rags lie scattered over the concrete floor, dulled jars of bolts and screws and wing nuts line the shelves. A number of unfolded cots, their fabric stained and grease-spotted, stand in the corner.

"This is where you sleep, silly."

"But—who?"

"It's obvious, isn't it? They're customers, like yourself, waiting for their cars. The man in brown is the Gremlin, the one with the beard is the Cougar—no, I'm sorry, the woman is the Cougar—he's the Citroën."

B. is appalled. "And I'm the Audi, is that it?"

Suddenly Rita is in his arms, the smooth satiny feel of her uniform, the sticky warmth of her breath. "You're more to me than a machine, B. Do you know that I like you? A lot." And then he finds himself nuzzling her ear, the downy ridge of her jawbone. She presses against him, he fumbles under the cheerleader's tutu for the slippery underthings. One of the sleepers groans, but B. is lost, oblivious, tugging and massaging like a horny teenager. Rita reaches behind to unzip her uniform, the long smooth arch of her back, shoulders and arms shedding the opalescent rayon like a holiday on ice when suddenly a buzzer sounds—loud and brash—end of the round, change classes, dive for shelter.

Rita freezes, then bursts into motion. "A customer!" she pants, and then she's gone. B. watches her callipygian form recede into the gloom of the Geriatrics Section, the sharp projection in his trousers receding with her, until she touches the light switch and vanishes in darkness. B. trundles back into the closet, selects a cot, and falls into an exploratory darkness of his own.

B.'s. breath is a puff of cotton as he wakes to the chill gloom of the storage closet and the sound of tools grating, whining and ratcheting somewhere off in the distance. At first he can't locate himself—What the? Where?—but the odors of gas and kerosene and motor oil bring him back. He is stranded at Tegeler's Big Garage, it is a workday, he has been sleeping with strangers, his car is nonfunctional. B. lurches up from the cot with a gasp—only to find that he's being watched. It is the man with the patchy beard and rancid shirt. He is sitting on the edge of a cot, stirring coffee in a cardboard container, his eyes fixed on B. My checkbook, my wallet, my wristwatch, thinks B.

"Mornin'," the man says. "My name's Rusty," holding out his hand. The others—the man in brown (or was it gray?) and the Cougar woman—are gone.

B. shakes the man's hand. "Name's B.," he says, somewhere between wary and paranoid. "How do I get out of here?"

"Your first day, huh?"

"What do you mean?" B. detects an edge of hysteria slicing through his voice, as if it belonged to someone else in some other situation. A pistol-whipped actress in a TV melodrama, for instance.

"No need to get excited," Rusty says. "I know how disquieting that first day can be. Why Cougar here—that woman in the print dress slept with us last night?—she sniveled and whimpered the whole time her first night here. Shit. It was like being in a bomb shelter or some frigging thing. Sure, I know how it is. You got a routine—job, wife at home, kids maybe, dog, cat, goldfish—and naturally you're anxious to get back to it. Well let me give you some advice. I been here six days already and I still haven't even got an appointment lined up with the Appointments Secretary so's I can get in to see the Assistant to the Head Diagnostician, Imports Division, and find out what's wrong with my car. So look: don't work up no ulcer over the thing. Just make your application and sit tight."

The man is an escapee, that's it, an escapee from an institution for the terminally, unconditionally and abysmally insane. B. hangs tough. "You expect me to believe that cock-and-bull story? If you're so desperate why don't you call a cab?"

"Taxis don't run this far out."

"Bus?"

"No buses in this district."

"Surely you've got friends to call—"

"Tried it, couldn't get through. Busy signals, recordings, wrong numbers. Finally got through to Theotis Stover two nights ago. Said he'd come out but his car's broke down."

"You could hitchhike."

"Spent six hours out there my first day. Twelve degrees F. Nobody even slowed down. Besides, even if I could get home, what then? Can't get to work, can't buy food. No sir. I'm staying right here till I get that car back."

B. cannot accept it. The whole thing is absurd. He's on him like F. Lee Bailey grilling a shaky witness. "What about the girls in the main office? They'll take you—one of them told me so."

"They take you?"

"No, but—"

"Look: they say that to be accommodating, don't you see? I mean, we *are* customers, after all. But they can't give you a lift—it's their job if they do."

"You mean—?"

"That's right. And wait'll you see the bill when you finally do get out of here. Word is that cot you're sitting on goes for twelve bucks a night."

The bastards. It could be weeks here. He'll lose his job, the animals'll tear up the rugs, piss in the bed and finally, starved, the dog will turn on the cat.... B. looks up, a new worry on his lips: "But what do you eat here?"

Rusty rises. "C'mon, I'll show you the ropes." B. follows him out into the half-lit and silent hangar, past the ranks of ruined automobiles, the mounds of tires and tools. "Breakfast is out of the machines. They got coffee, hot chocolate, candy bars, cross-ants and cigarettes. Lunch and late-afternoon snack you get down at the Mechanics' Cafeteria." Rusty's voice booms and echoes through the wide open spaces till B. begins to feel surrounded. Overhead, the morning cowers against the grimed sky-lights. "And eat your fill," Rusty adds, "—it all goes on the tab."

The office is bright as a cathedral with a miracle in progress. B. squints into the sunlight and recognizes the swaying ankles of a squad of majorettes. He asks for Rita, finds she's off till six at night. Outside, the sound of scraping, the putt-putt of snowplow jeeps. B. glances up. Oh, shit. There must be a foot and a half of snow on the ground.

The girls are chewing gum and sipping coffee from personalized mugs: Mary-Alice, Valerie, Beatrice, Lulu. B. hunches in the greatcoat, confused, until Rusty bums a dollar and hands him a cup of coffee. Slurping and blowing, B. stands at the window and watches an old man stoop over an aluminum snow shovel. Jets of fog stream from the old man's nostrils, ice cakes his mustache.

"Criminal, ain't it?" says Rusty.

"What?"

"The old man out there. That's Tegeler's father, seventy-some-odd years old. Tegeler makes him earn his keep, sweeping up, clearing snow, polishing the pumps."

"No!" B. is stupefied.

"Yeah, he's some hardnose, Tegeler. And I'll tell you something else too—he's set up better than Onassis and Rockefeller put together. See that lot across the street?"

B. looks. TEGELER'S BIG LOT. How'd he miss that?

"They sell new Tegelers there."

"Tegelers?"

"Yeah—he's got his own company: the Tegeler Motor Works. Real lemons from what I hear... But will you look what time it is!" Rusty slaps his forehead. "We got to get down to Appointments or we'll both grow old in this place."

The Appointments Office, like the reward chamber in a rat maze, is located at the far end of a complicated network of passageways, crossways and counterways. It is a large carpeted room with desks, potted plants and tellers' windows, not at all unlike a branch bank. The Cougar woman and the man in the brown suit are there, waiting along with a number of others, all of them looking bedraggled and harassed. Rusty enters deferentially and takes a seat beside Brown Suit, but B. strides across the room to where a hopelessly walleyed woman sits at a desk, riffling through a bundle of papers. "Excuse me," he says.

The woman looks up, her left iris drowning in white.

"I'm here—" B. breaks off, confused as to which eye to address: alternately one and then the other seems to be scrutinizing him. Finally he zeroes in on her nose and continues: "—about my car. I—"

"Do you have an appointment?"

"No, I don't. But you see I'm a busy man, and I depend entirely on the car for transportation and—"

"Don't we all?"

"—and I've already missed a day of work." B. gives her a doleful look, a look charged with chagrin for so thwarting the work ethic and weakening the national fiber. "I've got to have it seen to as soon as possible. If not sooner." Ending with a broad grin, the bon mot just the thing to break the ice.

"Yes," she says, heaving a great wet sigh. "I understand your anxiety and I sympathize with you, I really do. But," the left pupil working round to glare at him now, "I can't say I think much of the way you conduct yourself—barging in here and exalting your own selfish concerns above those of the others here. Do you think that there's no one else in the world but you? No other ailing auto but yours? Does Tegeler's Big Garage operate for fifty-nine years, employing hundreds of people, constantly expanding, improving, streamlining its operations, only to prepare itself for the eventuality of your breakdown? Tsssss! I'm afraid, my friend, that your arrogant egotism knows no bounds."

B. hangs his head, shuffles his feet, the greatcoat impossibly warm.

"Now. You'll have to fill out the application for an appointment and wait your turn with the others. Though you really haven't shown anything to deserve it, I think you may have a bit of luck today after all. The Secretary left word that he'd be in at three this afternoon."

B. takes a seat beside the Cougar woman and stares down at the form in his hand as if it were a loaded .44. He is dazed, still tingling from the vehemence of the secretary's attack. The form is seven pages long. There are questions about employment, annual income, collateral, next of kin. Page 4 is devoted to physical inquiries: Ever had measles? leprosy? irregularity? The next delves deeper: Do you feel that people are out to get you? Why do you hate your father? The form ends up with two pages of IQ stuff: if a farmer has 200 acres and devotes $\frac{1}{16}$ of his land to soybeans, $\frac{5}{8}$ to corn and $\frac{1}{3}$ to sugar beets, how much does he have left for a drive-in movie? B. glances over at the Cougar woman. Her lower lip is thrust forward, a blackened stub of pencil twists in her fingers, an appointment form, scrawled over in pencil with circled red corrections, lies in her lap. Suddenly B. is on his feet and stalking out the door, fragments of paper sifting down in his wake like confetti. Behind him, the sound of collective gasping.

Out in the corridor B. collars a man in spattered blue coveralls and asks him where the Imports Division is. The man, squat, swarthy, mustachioed, looks at him blank as a cow. "No entiendo," he says.

"The. Imports. Division."

"No hablo inglés—y no me gustan las preguntas de cabrones tontos." The man shrugs his shoulder out from under B.'s palm and struts off down the hall like a ruffled rooster. But B. is encouraged: Imports must be close at hand. He hurried off in the direction from which the man came (was he Italian or only a Puerto Rican?), following the corridor around to the left, past connecting hallways clogged with mechanics and white-smocked technicians, following it right on up to a steel fire door with the words NO ADMITTANCE stamped across it in admonitory red. There is a moment of hesitation…then he twists the knob and steps in.

"Was ist das?" A workman looks up at him, screwdriver in hand, expression modulating from surprise to menace. B. finds himself in another hangar, gloomy and expansive as the first, electric tools screeching like an army of mechanical crickets. But what's this?: he's surrounded by late-model cars—German cars—Beetles, Foxes, Rabbits, sleek Mercedes sedans! Not only has he stumbled across the Imports Division, but luck or instinct or good looks has guided him right to German Specialties. Well, ha-cha! He's squinting down the rows of cars, hoping to catch sight of his own, when he feels a pressure on his arm. It is the workman with the screwdriver. "Vot you vant?" he demands.

"Uh—have you got an Audi in here? Powder blue with a black vinyl top?"

The workman is in his early twenties. He is tall and obscenely corpulent. Skin pale as the moon, jowls reddening as if with a rash, white hair cropped across his ears and pinched beneath a preposterously undersized engineer's cap. He tightens his grip on B.'s arm and calls out into the gloom—"Holger! Friedrich!"—his voice reverberating through the vault like the battle cry of some Mesozoic monster.

Two men, flaxen-haired, in work clothes and caps, step from the shadows. Each grips a crescent wrench big as the jawbone of an ass. "Was gibt es, Klaus?"

"Mein Herr vants to know haff we got und Aw-dee."

"How do you say it?" The two newcomers are standing over him now, the one in the wire-rimmed spectacles leering into his eyes.

"Audi," B. says. "A German-made car?"

"Aw-dee? No, never heard of such a car," the man says. "A cowboy maybe—family name of Murphy?"

Klaus laughs, "Har-har-har," booming at the ceiling. The other fellow, short, scar on his cheek, joins in with a psychopathic snicker. Wire-rims grins.

Uh-oh.

"Listen," B. says, a whining edge to his voice, "I know I'm not supposed to be in here but I saw no other way of—"

"Cutting trew der bullshit," says Wire-rims.

"Yes, and finding out what's wrong—"

"On a grassroot level," interjects the snickerer.

"—right, at the grassroot level, by coming directly to you. I'm getting desperate. Really. That car is my life's breath itself. And I don't mean to get dramatic or anything, but I just can't survive without it."

"Ja," says Wire-rims, "you haff come to der right men. We haff your car, wery serious. Ja. Der bratwurst assembly broke down and we haff sent out immediately for a brötchen und mustard." This time all three break into laughter, Klaus booming, the snickerer snickering, Wire-rims pinching his lips and emitting a high-pitched hoo-hoo-hoo.

"No, *seriously*," says B.

"You vant to get serious? Okay, we get serious. On your car we do a compression check, we put new solenoids in der U joints und we push der push rods," says Wire-rims.

"Ja. Und we see you need a new vertical stabilizer, head gasket and PCV valve," rasps the snickerer.

"Your sump leaks."

"Bearings knock."

"Plugs misfire."

B. has had enough. "Wiseguys!" he shouts. "I'll report you to your superiors!" But far from daunting them, his outburst has the opposite effect. Viz., Klaus grabs him by the collar and breathes beer and sauerbraten in his face. "We are Chermans," he hisses, "—we haff no superiors."

"Und dammit punktum!" bellows the snickerer. "Enough of dis twaddle. We haff no car of yours und furdermore we suspect you of telling to us fibs in order maybe to misappropriate the vehicle of some otter person."

"For shame," says Wire-rims.

"Vat shall we do mit him?" the snickerer hisses.

"I'm tinking he maybe needs a little lubrication," says Wire-rims. "No sense of humor, wery dry." He produces a grease gun from behind his back.

And then, for the first time in his life, B. is decorated—down his collar, up his sleeve, crosshatched over his lapels—in ropy, cake-frosting strings of grease, while Klaus howls like a terminally tickled child and the snickerer's eyes flash. A moment later he finds himself lofted into the air, strange hands at his armpits and thighs, swinging to and fro before the gaping black mouth of a laundry chute—"Zum ersten! zum andern! zum dritten!"—and then he's airborne, and things get very dark indeed.

B. is lying facedown in an avalanche of cloth: grimy rags, stiffened chamois, socks and undershorts yellowed with age and sweat and worse, handkerchiefs congealed with sputum, coveralls wet with oil. He is stung with humiliation and outrage. He's been cozened, humbugged, duped, gulled, spurned, insulted, ignored and now finally assaulted. There'll be lawsuits, damn them, letters to Congressmen—but for now, if he's to salvage a scrap of self-respect, he's got to get out of here. He sits up, peels a sock from his face, and discovers the interior of a tiny room, a room no bigger than a laundry closet. It is warm, hot even.

Two doors open onto the closet. The one to the left is wreathed in steam, pale shoots and tendrils of it curling through the keyhole, under the jamb. B. throws back the door and is enveloped in fog. He is confused. The Minotaur's labyrinth? Ship at sea? House afire? He can see nothing, the sound of machinery straining at his ears, moisture beading along eyebrows, nostril hairs, cowlick. Then it occurs to him: the carwash! Of course. And the carwash must give onto the parking lot, which in turn gives onto the highway. He'll simply duck through it and then hitchhike—or, if worse comes to worst, walk—until he either makes it home or perishes in the attempt.

B. steps through the door and is instantly flattened by a mammoth, water-spewing pom-pom. He tries to get to his feet, but the sleeve of his coat seems to be caught in some sort of runner or track—and now the whole apparatus is jerking forward, gears whirring and clicking somewhere off in the mist. B., struggling to free the coat, finds himself jerking along with it. The mechanism heaves forward, dragging B. through an extended puddle of mud, suds and road salt. A jet of water flushes the right side of his face, a second pom-pom lumbers out of the haze and pins his chest to the floor, something tears the shoe from his right foot. Soap in his ears, down his neck, sudsing and sudsing: and now a giant cylinder, a mill wheel covered with sponges, descends and rakes the length of his body. B. shouts for help, but the machinery grinds on, squeaking and ratcheting, war of the worlds. Look out!: cold rinse. He holds his breath, glacial runoff coursing over his body, a bitter pill. Then there's a liberal blasting with hot wax, the clouds part, and the machine turns him loose with a jolt in the rear that tumbles him out the bay door and onto the slick permafrost of the parking lot.

He staggers to his feet. There's a savage pain in his lower back and his right shoulder has got to be dislocated. No matter: he forges on. Round the outbuildings, past the front office and on out to the highway.

It has begun to get dark. B., hair frozen to his scalp, shoeless, the greatcoat stiff as a dried fish, limps along the highway no more than a mile from the garage. All around him, as far as he can see, is wasteland: crop-stubble swallowed in drifts, the stripped branches of the deciduous trees, rusty barbed wire. Not even a farmhouse on the horizon. Nothing. He'd feel like Peary running for the Pole but for the twin beacons of Garage and Lot at his back.

Suddenly a fitful light wavers out over the road—a car coming toward him! (He's been out here for hours, holding out his thumb, hobbling along. The first ride took him south of Tegeler's about two miles—a farmer, turning off into nowhere. The second—he didn't care which direction he went in, just wanted to get out of the cold—took him back north about three miles.)

B. crosses the road and holds out his thumb. He is dancing with cold, clonic, shoulder, arm, wrist and extended thumb jerking like the checkered flag at the finish of the Grand Prix. Stop, he whispers, teeth clicking like dice, stop, please God stop. Light floods his face for an instant, and then it's gone. But wait—they're stopping! Snot crusted to his lip, shoe in hand, B. double-times up to the waiting car, throws back the door and leaps in.

"B.! What's happened?"

It is Rita. Thank God.

"R-r-r-ita?" he stammers, body racked with tremors, the seatsprings chattering under him. "The ma-ma-machine."

"Machine? What are you talking about?"

"I-I need a r-r-r-ride. Wh-where you going?" B. manages, falling into a sneezing jag.

Rita puts the car in gear, the tires grab hold of the pavement. "Why—to work, of course."

The others smack their lips, sigh, snore, toss on their cots. Rusty, Brown Suit, the Cougar woman. B. lies there listening to them, staring into the darkness. His own breathing comes hard (TB, pleurisy, pneumonia—bronchitis at the very least). Rita—good old Rita—has filled him full of hot coffee and schnapps, given him a brace of cold pills and put him to bed. He is thoroughly miserable of course—the car riding his mind like a bogey, health shot, job lost, pets starved—but the snugness of the blanket and dry mechanic's uniform Rita has found for him, combined with the country-sunset glow of the schnapps, is seducing him off to sleep. It is very still. The smell of turpentine hangs in the air. He pulls the blanket up to his nose.

Suddenly the light flicks on. It is Rita, all thighs and calves in her majorette's outfit. But what's this? There's a man with her, a stranger. "Is this it?" the man says.

"Well, of course it is, silly."

"But who are these chibonies?"

"It's obvious, isn't it? They're customers, like yourself, waiting for their cars. The man in brown is the Gremlin, the one with the beard is the Citroën, the woman is the Cougar and the old guy on the end is the Audi."

"And I'm the Jaguar, is that it?"

"You're more to me than a machine, Jeff. Do you know that I like you? A lot."

B. is mortally wounded. Enemy flak, they've hit him in the guts. He squeezes his eyes shut, stops his ears, but he can hear them just the same:

heavy breathing, a moan soft as fur, the rush of zippers. But then the buzzer sounds and Rita gasps. "A customer!" she squeals, struggling back into her clothes and then hurrying off through the Geriatrics hangar, her footsteps like pinpricks along the spine. "Hey!" the new guy bellows. But she's gone.

The new guy sighs, then selects a cot and beds down beside B. B. can hear him removing his things, gargling from a bottle, whispering prayers to himself—"Bless Mama, Uncle Ernie, Bear Bryant…"—then the room dashes into darkness and B. can open his eyes.

He fights back a cough. His heart is hammering. He thinks how pleasant it would be to die…but then thinks how pleasant it would be to step through the door of his apartment again, take a hot shower and crawl into bed. It is then that the vision comes to him—a waking dream—shot through with color and movement and depth. He sees Tegeler's Big Lot, the ranks of cars, new Tegelers, lines of variegated color like beads on a string, windshields glinting in the sun, antennae jabbing at the sky, stiff and erect, like the swords of a conquering army....

In the dark, beneath the blanket, he reaches for his checkbook.

J.K.

The Trial as slapstick surrealism. Of course it's a German garage. I love the three mechanics, with their vaudeville German accents and aura of menace. Sexy Rita provides the counterpart to Kafka's Leni, the seductive nurse who works for K's lawyer, with cowboy boots instead of a webbed hand. Instead of K's fellow defendant Block we have the three bedraggled car owners living in the garage as they await repairs that may never come.

Paul Di Filippo:

I first encountered the work of Franz K. in my tender, teenage, high school years, when "The Metamorphosis" cropped up on a reading list. We often lament the sorry state of public education in the USA, but I have to say that teaching "The Metamorphosis" to teens is one of the genius moves of education professionals, and should be highly applauded. What better fable to console and validate adolescent angst than this! "Screw school today, Ma—I feel just like a giant bug with a rotting apple stuck in my back, and I'm just gonna lie under the bed until I die!" But much as I appreciated this first peek into the Kafkaverse, I neglected to follow up on my own by tracking down more of his fiction. Too busy reading Aldiss, Dick, Ballard, and Moorcock to make a lateral foray into literary territory. So several years passed until I met Franz again, in college, in the form of "In the Penal Colony" and "A Hunger Artist." Now I was solidly hooked, and began reading all I could. But it was only when I got belatedly to *Amerika* a few years ago that I was inspired to write an homage. That novel, I realized with a jolt, is an utter cartoon version of reality, a comic strip take on a land Kafka had never seen, one part *Katzenjammer Kids*, one part *Flash Gordon*, one part *Dick Tracy*, one part *Gasoline Alley*. Having undergone this epiphany, I had no recourse except to turn Franz himself into the Caped Crusader, all neurosis and guilt and vengeance. And thus did my decades-long fascination with a man who died thirty years before my birth, but who has lived in my brain and many others forever after, reach its unnatural climax.

The Jackdaw's Last Case

Paul Di Filippo

"Whatever advantage the future has in size, the past compensates for in weight...."
—The Diaries of F. K.

PALE LIGHT THE color of old straw trodden by uneasy cattle pooled from a lone streetlamp onto the greasy wet cobbles of the empty street. Feelers of fog like the live questing creepers of a hyperactive Amazonian vine twined around standards and down storm drains. The aged, petulant buildings lining the dismal thoroughfare wore the blank brick countenances of industrial castles. Some distance away, the bell of a final trolley sounded. A minute later, as if in delayed querulous counterpoint, a tower clock tolled midnight. A rat dashed in mad claw-clicking flight across the street.

Shortly after the tolling of the clock, a rivet-studded steel door opened in one of the factories, and a trickle of weary workers flowed out in spurts and ebbs, the graveyard shift going home. Without many words, and those few consisting of stale ritual phrases, the laborers apathetically trudged down the hard urban trail toward their shabby homes.

The path of many of the workers took them past the mouth of a dark alley separating two of the factories like a wedge in a log. None of the tired men and women took notice of two ominous figures crouched deep back in the alley's shadows like beasts of prey in the mouth of their burrow.

When it seemed the last worker had definitely passed, one of the gloom-cloistered lurkers whispered to the other. "Are you sure she's still coming?"

"Yeah, yeah, don't sweat it. She's always late for some reason. Maybe tossing the boss a quickie or something."

"You'd better be right, or our goose is cooked. We promised Madame Wu we'd bag her one last dame. And the boat for Shanghai leaves on the dot of two. And we still gotta get the baggage down to the dock."

"Don't get ants in your pants, fer chrissakes! Jesus, you'd think you'd never kidnapped a broad before! Ain't the white slavery racket a lot better'n second-story work?"

"I guess so. But I just got this creepy feeling tonight—"

"Well, keep it to yourself! You got the chloroform ready?"

"Sure, sure, I'm not gonna screw up. But there's something—"

"Quiet! I hear footsteps!"

Closer the lonely click-clack of a woman walking in heels sounded. A bare white arm and a skirted leg swung into the frame of the alley-mouth. Then the assailants were upon the unsuspecting woman, pinioning her arms, slapping an ether-drenched cloth to her face.

"OK, she's out! You get her legs, I'll take her arms. Once we're in the jalopy, we're good as there—"

Suddenly the night was split by an odd cry, half avian, half human, a spine-tingling ululation ripe with sardonic, caustic derision.

The kidnappers dropped their unconscious burden to the pavement and began to tremble.

"Oh, shit, no! Not him!"

"Where the hell is he! Quick!"

"There! I see him! Up on the roof!"

Standing in silhouette on a high parapet loomed the enigmatic and fearsome bane of evildoers everywhere, a heart-stopping icon of justice and fair play.

The Jackdaw.

The figure was tall and cadaverous. On his head perched a wide-brimmed, split-crown felted hat. An ebony feathered cape, fastened around his neck, hung from his outstretched arms like wings. A cruel beaked raptor's mask hid the upper half of his face. From his uncovered mouth now burst again his piercing trademark cry, part caw, part madman's exultant defiance.

"Don't just stand there! Blast him!"

The frightened yeggs drew their pistols, took aim, and snapped off several shots.

But the Jackdaw was no longer there.

Facing outward, the forgotten woman behind their backs, and swiveling nervously about like malfunctioning automata on a Gothic town-square barometer, the kidnappers strained their ears for the slightest sound of movement. Only the drip, drip, drip of condensing fog broke the eerie stillness.

"We did it! We scared off the Jackdaw! He ain't such hot shit after all!"

"OK, quit bragging! We still gotta get this broad to the docks—"

"I think not, gentlemen."

The kidnappers swung violently around, teeth chattering. Bestriding the unconscious woman, the Jackdaw had twin pistols clutched in his yellow-gloved hands and trained on the quaking assailants. Before the thugs could react, the Jackdaw fired, his strange guns emitting not the flash and boom of gunpowder, but only a subtle *phut, phut.*

The kidnappers had time only to slap at the darts embedded in their necks before crumpling to the ground.

Within a trice, the Jackdaw had the men hogtied with stout cord unwrapped from around his waist. Picking up the girl and hoisting her in a fireman's carry over one shoulder, one gloved hand resting not unfamiliarly on her buttocks, the Jackdaw said, "A hospital bed will suit you better than a brothel's doss, *liebchen.* And I should still have time to meet that Shanghai-bound freighter. Altogether, this promises to be a most profitable night."

With this observation the Jackdaw plucked a signature feather from his cape and dropped it between the recumbent men. Then, with a repetition of his fierce cry, he was gone like the phantasm of a fevered brain.

When Mister Frank Kafka reached the office of his employer at 1926 Broadway on the morning of July 3, 1925, he found the entire staff transformed from their normally staid and placid selves into a milling, chattering mass resembling a covey of agitated rooks, or perhaps the inhabitants of an invaded, ax-split termite colony.

Hanging his dapper Homburg on the wooden coatrack that stood outside the door to his private office, Kafka winced at the loud voices before reluctantly approaching the noisy knot formed by his coworkers. The center of their interest and discussion appeared to be that morning's edition of the *Graphic,* a New York tabloid that was the newest addition to the stable of publications owned by the very individual for whom they too labored—that is, under normal conditions. All labor seemed suspended now.

The clot of humanity appeared an odd multilimbed organism composed of elements of male and female accoutrements: starched detachable collars, arm garters, ruffled blouses, high-buttoned shoes. Employing his above-average height to peer over the shoulders of the congregation, Kafka attempted to read the large headlines dominating the front page of the newspaper. Failing to discern their import, he turned to address an inquiry to a woman who resolved herself as an individual on the fringes of the group.

"Millie, good morning. What's this uproar about?"

Millie Jensen turned to fix her interlocutor with sparkling, mischievous eyes. A young woman in her early twenties with wavy dark hair parted down the middle, she exhibited a full face creased with deep laugh lines. Today she was clad in a black rayon blouse speckled with white dots and cuffed at the elbows, as well as a long black skirt belted with a wide leather cincture.

"Why, Frank, I swear you live in another world! Haven't you heard yet? The streets are just buzzing with the news! It's that mysterious vigilante, the Jackdaw—he struck again last night!"

Kafka yawned ostentatiously. "Oh, is that all? I'm afraid I can't be bothered keeping current with the doings of every Hans, Ernst, and Adolf who wants to take the law into his own hands. What did he accomplish this time? Perhaps he managed to foil the theft of an apple from a fruit-vendor's cart?"

"Oh, Frank!" Millie pouted prettily. "You're such a cynic! Why can't you show a little idealism now and then? If you really want to know, the Jackdaw broke up a white-slavery ring! Imagine—they were abducting helpless working girls just like me and shipping them to the Orient, where they would addict them to opium and force them into lewd, unnatural acts!"

Kafka smiled in a world-weary manner. "It all seems rather a short-sighted and unnecessary waste of time and effort on the part of these outlaw international entrepreneurs. Surely there are many women in town who would have volunteered for such a position. I counted a dozen on Broadway alone last night as I walked home."

Millie became serious. "You strike this pose all the time, Frank, but I know it's not the real you."

"Indeed, then, Millie, you know more about me than I do myself."

Kafka yawned again, and Millie studied him closely. "Didn't get much sleep last night, did you?"

"I fear not. I was working on my novel."

"*Bohemia,* isn't that the title? How's it going?"

"I draw the words as if out of the empty air. If I manage to capture one, then I have just this one alone and all the toil must begin anew for the next."

"Tough sledding, huh? Well, you can do it, Frank, I know it. Anybody who can write that lonely hearts column the way you do—well, you're just the bee's knees with words, if you get my drift." Millie laid a hand on the sleeve of Kafka's grey suitcoat. "Step aside, a minute, won't you, Frank? I—I've got a little something for you."

"As you wish. Although I can't imagine what it could be."

The pair walked across the large open room to Millie's desk. There, she opened a drawer and took out a small gaily wrapped package.

"Here, Frank. Happy birthday."

Kafka seemed truly touched, his self-composure disturbed for a moment. "Why, Millie, this is very generous. How did you know?"

"Oh, I happened to be rooting around in the personnel files the other day and a certain date and name just caught my eye. It's your forty-first, right?"

"Correct. Although I never imagined myself ever attaining this advanced age."

Millie smiled coyly. "You sure don't look that old, Frank."

"Even into my late twenties, I was still being mistaken for a teenager."

"Was that back in Prague?"

Kafka cocked his head alertly. "No. I left my native city in 1902, when I was only nineteen. That was the year my Uncle Lowy in Madrid took me under his wing and secured me a job with his employer, the Spanish railways."

"And that's what led to all those years of traveling the globe as a civil engineer, building railways?"

"Yes." Kafka fixed Millie with a piercing gaze. "Why this sudden inquisition, Miss Jensen? It seems purposeless and unwarranted."

"Oh, I don't know. I like you, I guess. I want to know more about you. Is that so strange? And you're so close-mouthed, it's a challenge. Even after two years of working almost side by side, I feel we hardly know each other. No, don't protest, it's true. Oh, I admit you contribute to the general office conversation, but never anything personal. Getting anything vital out of you is like pulling teeth."

Kafka seemed about to reply with some habitual rebuff, then hesitated as if summoning fresh words. "There is some veracity to your perceptions, Millie. But you must rest assured that the fault lies with me, and not yourself. Due to my early warped upbringing, I have been generally unfitted for regular societal intercourse. Oh, I put up a good facade, but most of the time I feel clad in steel, as if my arm muscles, say, were an infinite distance away from myself. It is only when—well, at certain times I feel truly human. Then, I have a feeling of true happiness inside me. It is really something effervescent that fills me completely with a light, pleasant quiver and that persuades me of the existence of abilities of whose nonexistence I can convince myself with complete certainty at any moment, even now."

Millie stood with jaw agape before saying, "Jiminy, Frank—that's deep! And see, it didn't hurt too much to share that with me, did it?"

Kafka sighed. "I suppose not, for whatever it accomplished. You must acknowledge that if I am not always agreeable, I strive at least to be bearable."

Millie threw her arms around Kafka, who stood rigid as a garden beanpole. "Don't worry, Frank! Everybody feels a little like a caged animal now and then!"

"Not as I do. Inside me is an alien being as distinctly and invisibly hidden as the face formed from elements of the landscape in a child's picture puzzle."

Releasing Kafka, Millie stepped back. "Gee, that is a weird way to feel, Frank. Well, anyhow, aren't you going to open your present?"

"Certainly."

Discarding the colored paper and bow, Kafka delicately opened the box revealed. From within a nest of excelsior, he withdrew a small carving.

"Very nice, Millie. A figurine for my desk, I presume."

"Do you recognize it?"

Kafka twirled the object, showing no emotion. "A bird of some sort, obviously. A crow?"

"A *jackdaw,* actually. How do you say that in Czech?"

"Why, something tells me you already know, Millie. Back home we say, '*kavka.*'"

Smiling as if she had just been awarded a trophy, Millie repeated, "'*Kavka.*'" Then, rather alarmingly, she flapped her arms, crowed softly, and winked.

Closing his office door gently behind him so as not to make a loud report that would disturb his acutely sensitive hearing, Kafka bestowed a long appraisal on his desk, where a Corona Model T typing machine reigned in midblotter like a machine-age deity. Wearily, he shook his head. Nothing good could be done on such a desk. There was so much lying about, it formed a disorder without proportion and without that compatibility of disordered things which otherwise made every disorder bearable.

Kafka set about cleaning up the mess. Soon he had a stack of unopened mail, one of interoffice memos, and another of miscellaneous documents. Finally he could truly work.

However, just as soon as he had positioned himself behind the writing machine, ivory-handled letter opener in one hand and faintly perfumed envelope in another, a male shadow cast itself on the frosted glass of his door, followed by a tentative knock.

Sighing, Kafka urged entrance in a mild voice.

Carl Ross, the office boy, was a freckled youth whose perpetually ink-smeared face bore a constant smile of impish goodwill. "Boss wants you, Mr. Frank."

"Very well. Did he say why?"

"Nope. He seemed a tad steamed though."

"Undoubtedly at me. Well, the fault is probably all mine. I shall not reproach myself, for shouted into this empty day it would have a disgusting echo. And after all, the office has a right to make the most definite and justified demands on me."

"Cripes, Mr. Frank, why do you want to go and beat up on yourself like that for, before you even get called on the carpet? Let the Boss do it if he's going to. Otherwise, you're just going to suffer twice!"

Kafka stood and advanced to lay a hand on Carl's tousled head. "Good advice, Carl. Perhaps we should trade jobs. Well, there's no point putting this off. Let's go."

At the end of a long, blank corridor was a door whose gilt lettering spelled out the name of Kafka's employer: *Bernarr Macfadden*. Kafka knocked and was admitted with a gruff "Come in!"

Bernarr Macfadden—that prolific author, self-promoter, notorious nudist and muscleman, publishing magnate, stager of beauty contests, inventor of Physical Culture and the Macfadden Dietary System—was upside down. His head was firmly ensconced on a thick scarlet pillow with gold-braid trim placed against one wall of his large office, against which vertical surface his inverted body was braced. In his expensive suit and polished shoes, his vibrant handsome mustachioed face suffused with blood, Macfadden reminded Kafka of some modern representation of the Hanged Man Tarot card, an evil omen one would not willingly encounter.

As if to reinforce Kafka's dire whimsy, Macfadden now bellowed, "Have a seat and hang in there, Frank! I'll be done in a couple of seconds!"

Kafka did as ordered. True to his words, in only a moment or two Macfadden broke his swami's pose, coiling forward in a deft somersault that brought him to his feet, breathing noisily.

"There! Now I can think clearly again! Sure wish I could get you to join in with me once in a while, Frank!"

"I appreciate your interest, sir. However, I have a nightly course of exercises of my own devising which keep me fit."

"Well, can't argue with success!" Macfadden snatched up a stoppered vacuum bottle from his desktop and gestured with it at Kafka. "Care for a glass of Cocomalt?"

"No, thank you, sir."

"No matter, I'll have one." Macfadden poured himself a glass of the chilled food-tonic. "Anyhow, I must confess you're looking mighty fit. You're following my diet rules though, aren't you?"

"Indeed."

"Good, good. You were on the road to goddamn ruin when you first applied for a job here. I can't believe you ever fell for Fletcherism! Chew every mouthful a dozen times! Hogwash! As long as you lay off the tobacco and booze, you'll be A-OK! Why, look at me!" Abruptly, Macfadden stripped off his coat, rolled back one sleeve, and flexed the biceps thus exposed. "I'm fifty-seven years young, and at the peak of health! A little grey at the temples, but that's just frost on the roof. The fire inside is still burning bright! You can expect the same, if you just stay the course!"

Kafka coughed in a diversionary manner. "As you say, sir. Uh, I believe you needed to speak to me about a work-related matter…?"

Macfadden grew solemn. He propped one lean buttock on the corner of his expansive desk. "That's right, son. It's about your column."

"So then. I assume that 'Ask Josephine' is losing popularity with the readers of *True Story*. Or perhaps you've had a specific complaint…?"

"No, no, no, nothing like that. Your copy's as popular as ever, and no one's complained. It's just that your advice to the readers is so—so eccentric! Always has been, but I just read the latest issue and, son— you're moving into some strange territory!"

"I'm afraid I don't see—"

"Don't see! Why, how do you justify this? 'Anxious in Akron' asks for your advice on whether she should have more than one child. Here's your reply in its entirety: 'The convulsive starting up of a lizard under our feet on a footpath in Italy delights us greatly, again and again we are moved to bow down, but if we see them at a dealer's by hundreds crawling over one another in confusion in the large bottles in which otherwise pickles are packed, then we don't know what to do.'"

"Very clear, I thought."

"Clear? It's positively lurid!"

Kafka smiled with his typical demure sardonicism. "A charge you yourself have frequently had leveled at your own writings, sir."

"Harumph! Well, yes, true. But hardly the same thing! What about this one? 'Pining in Pittsburgh' wants to know how she can get her reluctant beau to pop the question. Your counsel? 'The messenger is already on his way. A powerful, indefatigable man, now pushing with his right arm, now with his left, he cleaves a way for himself through the throng. If he encounters resistance he points to his breast, where the symbol of the sun glitters. The way is made easier for him than it would be for any other man. But the multitudes between him and you are so vast; their numbers have no end. If he could reach the open fields how fast he would fly, and soon doubtless you would hear the welcome hammering of his fists on your door. But he is still only making his way through the inner courts of a palace infinite in extent. If at last he should burst through the outermost gate—but never, never can that happen—the whole imperial capital would lie before him, the center of the world, crammed to bursting with its own sediment. Nobody could fight his way through there. But you sit at your window when evening falls and dream it to yourself.'"

For a space of time Kafka was silent. Then he said, "It's best, I think, not to raise false hopes...."

Macfadden slammed down the magazine from which he had been reading. "False hopes! My god, boy, that's hardly the issue here! With such mumbo jumbo, who can even tell if you're talking about this planet or another one! I know the motto of our magazine is 'Truth is stranger than fiction,' but this kind of malarkey really beats the band!"

Kafka seemed stung. "The readers appear to take adequate solace from my parables."

"I'll grant you that if someone's heartsick enough they can find comfort in any old gibberish. But that's not what we're about at Macfadden enterprises. The plain truth plainly told! No flinching from hard facts, no mincing or obfuscation. If you can only keep that in mind, Frank!"

Rising to his feet, Kafka said, "I will do my best, sir. Although my nature is not that of other men."

Macfadden got up also, and put an arm around Kafka's shoulders.

"That brings me to another point, son. You know I like to keep a fatherly eye on my employees and their home lives. And it has risen to my attention that you're becoming something of a reclusive loner, a regular hermit bachelor type. Now, take this advice of mine to heart, both as a stylistic example and on a personal level. You cannot work for yourself alone, and rest content. You need a satisfying love life, and the home and children with which it is sanctified. It is the stimulus of love that makes service divine. To work for yourself alone is cold, selfish, and meaningless. You need a loved one with whom you can double your joys and divide your sorrows."

During this speech Macfadden had been escorting his subordinate to the exit. Now, opening the door, he slapped Kafka with hearty bonhomie on the back, sending the slighter man staggering forward a step or two.

"Have a yeast pill, son, and get back in the harness!"

Silently, Kafka accepted the offered tablet and departed.

Back in his office, Kafka deposited the yeast pill in a drawer containing scores of others. Then he picked up the envelope the slitting of which had been interrupted by his boss's summons and extracted its contents.

"Dear Josephine," the letter began. "I hardly know where to start! My sick, elderly parents are about to be evicted from our farm because they had a number of bad years and can't pay their loans, and my own job—our last hope of survival—could be in danger itself. It's my boss, you see. He has made improper advances toward me, advances I've modestly refused. Still, I get the impression that he won't respect my virtuous stand much longer, and I'll have to either bend to his will or be fired! I've made myself sick with worry about this, can't sleep, can't eat, etc., until I almost don't care about anything anymore, just wish I could escape from it all somehow. Does this make me a bad daughter? Please help!"

Kafka rolled a sheet of paper into his typing machine. Attempting to keep Macfadden's advice in mind, he moved his fingers delicately over the keys.

"Don't despair, not even over the fact that you don't despair. Just when everything seems over with, new forces come marching up, and precisely that means that you are alive." Kafka paused, then added a codicil. "And if they don't, then everything is over with here, once and for all."

Seated in the study of his Fifth Avenue apartment at a desk that was the tidy twin to its office mate, with the dusk of another evening mantling his shoulders like a moleskin cape, Kafka composed with pen in their native German his weekly letter to his youngest and favorite sister, Ottla, now resident with her husband Joseph David in Berlin.

Dearest Ottla,

I am gratified to hear that you are finally feeling at ease in your new home and environs. The claws of our "little mother" Prague are indeed difficult to disengage from one's skin. Sometimes I envision all of Prague's more sensitive citizens as being metaphorically suspended from the city's towers and steeples on lines and flesh-piercing hooks, like Red Indians engaged in ritual excruciations. Although I myself have been a wandering expatriate for some two decades now, I still recall my initial disorientation, when Uncle Alfred took me under his wing and forcibly launched me on my globe-circling career. I think that my strong memories of Bohemia and my intense feelings for our natal city were what prevented me from settling down until recently. Although, truth be told, I soon came to enjoy my peripatetic mode of existence. The lack of close and enduring ties with other people was not unappealing, neither were the frequent stimulating changes of scenery.

Of course, all that changed after "The Encounter," which I have expatiated about to you in, I fear, far too copious and boring detail. That meeting in the rarefied reaches of the Himalayas with the Master—hidden like a pearl of great worth in his alpine hermitage—and my subsequent revelatory year's tutelage under him has finally resulted in my settling down to pursue a definitive course of action, one calculated to make the best use of my talents. My adopted country, I feel confident in saying, is now Amerika, practically the last country unvisited by me in an official engineering capacity, yet one of which I have often dreamed—right down to spurious details such as a sword-wielding Statue of Liberty! It is here, at the dynamic new center of the century, that I have finally planted sustainable roots.

As for your new role as wife and mother, you must accept my sincerest congratulations. You know that I esteem parenthood most highly—despite having many reasons well known to you for the likely development of exactly the opposite opinion. Once I actually dared dream of such a role for myself. But such a happy circumstance was not to be. For although there have been many women in my life, none seemed equal to my idiosyncratic needs. (Any regrets I may have once had regarding my eternal bachelorhood are long extinguished, of course.) Curiously enough, my employer, Herr Macfadden, saw fit to accost me on this very topic today. Perhaps I shall take his blunt advice to heart and resume courting the fair sex, if only for temporary amusement. Although the rigors of my curious manner of existence have grown, if anything, even more demanding than before....

Fleshing out his letter with another page or two of trivial anecdotes and polite domestic and familial inquiries, Kafka paused at the closing endearment. After some thought, he finally inscribed it: "Give my regards to Mother—and Mother alone." Weighing the sealed letter with a small balance, he affixed the precisely requisite postage to it, then took the elevator down to the lobby of his building, where he left the missive with the concierge.

But then, instead of returning to his apartment or exiting onto the busy Manhattan street, Kafka moved to an innocuous door in a forlorn corner of the lobby. Looking about to ascertain whether anyone was observing him, he quickly insinuated himself through the portal.

A wanly lit flight of stairs led downward. Soon Kafka was in the basement. Crossing that nighted realm, Kafka reached another set of stairs. Within seconds, he was in a subcellar.

This underground kingdom seemed even darker than the level above, save for a distant flickering glow. Kafka moved toward this partially shielded light source.

Heat mounted. On the far side of a gap-slatted wooden partition, Kafka came face to face with an enormous, Moloch-like furnace. Its door was open, and from an enormous pile of coal a half-naked man shoveled scoop after scoop of black lumps.

For some time Kafka watched the brawny sweating man work. He knew neither the man's name nor his history. Kafka assumed he lived here, within reach of his fiery charge, for no matter when Kafka visited he found the stoker busy tending his demanding master.

The congruence with his own situation did not go unregarded by Kafka.

On the floor stood a pail of cinder-flecked water with a dipper in it. Kafka took up the dipper and raised it to the stoker's lips. Without stopping his shoveling, the laborer greedily drank the warm sooty liquid. After several repetitions of this beneficence, the man signaled by a grunt his satisfaction.

Feeling free now to tend to his own business, Kafka stepped around the bulk of the furnace. Behind this asbestos-clad monster was another door, seemingly placed without sense. Through this door Kafka stepped.

And into the Jackdaw's sanctum.

Strange machines and devices bulked in the shadows not entirely dispelled by several low-wattage bulbs. An exit leading who-knows-where could be vaguely discerned. Near the entrance door on a peg hung the famous feathered cape; on a table sat mask, hat and canary-colored gloves. In a glass case was a gun belt and sundry other portable gadgetry.

With lingering, almost fetishistic pleasure, Kafka donned his disguise. A transformative surge passed through him, rendering him somehow larger than life.

Emitting a mild *sotto voce* version of his shrill cry, the Jackdaw stepped to a ticker-tape device. Picking up the trailing paper, he began to scan its contents.

"Hmmm… The Mousehole Gang suspected in daring daylight bank robbery, but police on the case… Dogface Barton in prison break, but likely hideout believed known… The dirigible *Shenandoah* to make maiden flight… Ku Klux Klan to stage Washington rally… Yes, yes, but nothing here for me—Wait, what's this? 'The Federal Bureau of Investigation under its new director Mr. Hoover is pursuing reports of an extortion attempt upon oil and steel magnate John D. Rockefeller by a hitherto unknown Zionist agent provocateur using the pseudonym of "The Black Beetle...."' Ah, this has the Jackdaw's name writ large upon it!"

The door to Kafka's office opened and Millie Jensen entered, carrying a sheaf of papers. She stood quietly for a moment, regarding the affecting sight before her, which evoked a tender sigh from her sympathetic nature.

Kafka's face rested insensibly on a surface definitely not intended for such a purpose: the uncomfortable keys and platen of his Corona typing machine. Gentle snores issued from the sleeping columnist.

Millie tried awakening him by tapping her foot. When this method produced no effect, she began to cough, at first femininely, then with increasing violence, until her ultimate efforts resembled the paroxysms of a tuberculosis victim.

Her ploy worked at last, for Kafka jolted awake with a start, almost like a caged dangerous beast, taking in his situation with a single wild-eyed glance before his usual mask of calm fell into place.

"Ah, Miss Jensen, please excuse my inattention. I was inspecting the mechanism. Its performance was unsatisfactory—"

"Oh, you don't need to make excuses with me, Frank," said Millie, not unkindly. "I know you're exerting yourself night and day to accomplish—certain things."

"Yes, quite correct. My, um, novel is presenting me with certain intractable difficulties. Important lines of the plot refuse to resolve themselves—"

"Yeah, gotcha, kiddo." Millie regarded Kafka slyly and with a humorous glint in her green eyes. "Say, did you ever think that by relaxing a little, you might find an answer to your problems unconsciously?"

Kafka smiled. "Why, Millie, you sound positively like a disciple of Herr Freud."

"Oh, a girl likes to keep abreast of the latest fads. But I'm serious. You like the movies, don't you?"

"I believe that the cinema represents a valid new sensory experience akin to the exteriorization of one's dreams."

"And their popcorn generally ain't so bad either. Well, it's a Friday, and the new Chaplin is playing downtown. *The Gold Rush.* Wanna catch it with me tonight?"

Kafka deliberated momentarily before brightening and giving a surprisingly hearty and colloquial assent. "Millie, I'm your man!"

Turning to leave—or so that she could regard Kafka coquettishly over one shoulder—Millie replied, "That remains to be seen!"

Streaming out from the doors of the Nature Theater of Oklahoma—a popular begemmed movie palace owned by the most famous and successful son of that prairie state, the comedian Will Rogers—the happy moviegoers soon dispersed into the evening bustle of Manhattan. Left behind were a single man and woman; the pair seemed hesitant or unsure of their next destination, like moths deprived of their phototropism.

After a protracted silence, Millie chirpily asked Kafka, "So, Frank, whadda'd you think? What a riot, huh?"

Millie's date seemed lost in thought, his dark features enrapt in a fugue of consternation. "That scene where Chaplin is starving and forced to eat his own shoe made me feel so strange.... It corresponded exactly to an enervating emotion I myself have had on numerous occasions."

"Really? Gosh, I feel plenty bad for you, Frank. Look at you—you're wound up so tight you're ready to burst to pieces! What you need is a feminine presence in your life, someone to take care of you and nurture you. Don't you think that would be nice?"

"If you speak of marriage, Miss Jensen, I fear that such a normal mortal luxury is forever denied me. A formal union with a woman would result not only in the dissolution of the nothingness that I am, but doom also my poor wife."

"Holy cats, Frank, you've been reading the fake sob stories in our rag too much! Or maybe you've even been dipping into *Weird Tales*! Life just isn't as complex or melodramatic as you or those three-hankie writers make it out to be!" Millie linked her arm through Kafka's and leaned her head on his shoulder. "A man and a woman together—what could be simpler?"

Kafka did not disengage, but instead, seeming to take some small encouragement from the simple human contact, managed to pull himself together with a visible effort.

"I'm sorry to be such a wet blanket, Millie, when all you sought was a gay night out. Truthfully, I have not felt so melancholy for nearly twenty years. This black humor was something I thought I had left behind in the dank and dismal streets of Prague. The cosmopolitan, globe-trotting engineer known as Frank Kafka was a mature, vibrant, self-assured fellow. But it appears now that he was only a paper cutout that quickly withers in the flames of frustration."

Since Kafka was at least communicating again, Millie's natural exuberance reasserted itself. "Oh, bosh and piffle, Frank! Everyone gets a dose of the blues now and then. It'll pass, you'll see! All we have to do is spend an hour or two doing something pleasant. What do you really, really like to do? How about grabbing a coffee and some pastry? The Hotel Occidental has a great coffee shop. I bet their jelly donuts will make you think of Vienna!"

"That sounds fine, Millie. But if you'd really like to know what I enjoy—"

"Yes, yes, Frank—tell me!"

"I like to contemplate the Brooklyn Bridge. Mr. Roebling's masterpiece reminds me of some of the humbler constructions I myself was once responsible for. Sometimes those noble buttresses alone seem endurable and without shame to me, amidst all the city's charade. But I don't suppose—"

"Frank, I'd love bridge-watching with you! Let's go!"

With Millie forcefully tugging on her coworker's arm, the mismatched couple began to move up Broadway. Soon, they were within sight of City Hall and not far from the majestic span across the East River.

As they crossed the small park in front of City Hall, the shrill scream of a hysterical woman brought them to an abrupt halt. This initial call of alarm was quickly followed by a swelling chorus of indignation, fear, confusion, and outrage.

Kafka raced toward the source of the noise, Millie trailing behind.

A growing, growling, agitated crowd lifted its gaze skyward. Atop the very roof of City Hall stood an ominous figure. Diminutive yet powerful, with the warped back and hypertrophied cranium of a Quasimodo, he was clad in a form-fitting black union suit that merged into face-concealing, antennae-topped headgear. From his back sprouted small, wire-stiffened cellophane wings; from his torso, parallel rows of artificial abdominal feelers. The creature could be none other than—

"The Black Beetle!" shouted an onlooker.

"Where're the cops?" yelled someone else.

"Where's the Jackdaw?" yelled another.

Kafka stood quivering beside Millie like a dog on a leash faced with an impudent raccoon or squirrel.

The Black Beetle began to harangue his audience in a slightly accented English, showering them with incomprehensible slogans and demands.

"Down with all anti-Semites! Up with Zionism! Palestine for the Jews! The Mufti of Jerusalem must die! America must support the Zionist cause! If she does not do so willingly, with guns and money, we shall compel her to! Take this as a sign of our seriousness!"

There was nothing equivocal or esoteric about the round bomb which the Black Beetle now produced from somewhere on his person. The sight of its sizzling fuse raised a loud inchoate cry from the crowd, and people began to scatter in all directions.

"Long live the Stern Gang!" shouted the Black Beetle as he hurled his explosive device.

Kafka knocked Millie to the ground and covered her body with his lanky form.

The bomb went off, filling their world with noise and the reek of gunpowder, hurtling shrapnel, flying cement chips, and clumps of sod.

Immediately after the detonation, Kafka leaped to his feet and surveyed the situation. By a miracle of Providence, it appeared that no person had been caught in the blast, the destruction confined to turf, sidewalk, and park benches.

As for the Black Beetle—in the confusion, he had made good his escape.

Kafka slumped in despair, muttering, "Useless, useless, all ambition. And yet what joy, imagining again the pleasure of a knife twisted in my heart...."

Millie had regained her feet and was brushing her clothes clean. "Frank—are you OK?"

Kafka straightened. "Millie, our night together is over. I trust you can find your own way home? I have—I must be going."

"Why, sure, Frank. See you in the office."

Kafka hurriedly departed. Millie hung back until he turned a corner. Then she slipped after him, always keeping a shield of pedestrians between them.

She followed her quarry as far as Times Square. There, in a squalid doorway apart from the more wholesome foot-traffic, as Millie watched from concealment behind a shuttered kiosk, Kafka approached two gaudy women of obvious ill repute, leaving, after a slight dickering, with both of the overpainted floozies, plainly headed toward the entrance of a nearby fleabag hotel.

"Oh, Frank! Why?" Millie exclaimed, and began to weep.

Dearest Ottla,

I write to you today hoping to clarify my own thoughts on one particular matter, that being our shared ancestry and heritage. A disturbing incident of late has unleashed a savage pack of old feelings and recriminations I thought long tamed. I have always admired at a suitable distance your passionate embrace of an ultra-modern synthesis of our old family religion—perhaps strictly for its certitude—although I could never myself feel comfortable in its suffocating clutches. Perhaps your perspective will aid me in seeing my own status afresh.

We are Jews, of course. Jews by birth, an inescapable heritage of the blood. You have affirmed this ancient taint wholeheartedly, passionately enlisting in such causes as the rescue of the *Ostjuden* and the formation of a Jewish homeland in the Palestine protectorate. I, on the other hand, have violently abandoned any such affiliations and attitudes, a decision enforced not solely by my rational intellect and the study of comparative cultures enabled by my extensive travels, but equally by my gut.

How you ever maintained any religious feeling, raised in our household as you were, I cannot imagine. Dragged by *him*, we went to synagogue a bare four times a year, and it was a farce, a joke. No, not even a joke. I've never been so bored in my life, I believe, except later on at dance lessons. I did enjoy the small distractions, such as the opening of the Ark, which always reminded me of a shooting gallery where, when you hit a bull's-eye, a door flips open the same way, except that at the gallery something interesting popped out, while here it was always the same old dolls without heads.

Later, I saw things in a slightly less harsh light and realized what could lead you to believe. You had actually managed to salvage some scraps of Judaism from that small, ghettolike congregation. For me, it was not to be, and I firmly affixed a Solomonic seal to the whole stinking corpse of my incipient, puerile Judaism and buried it deep.

But now, this old specter has arisen again, lashed into an unnatural afterlife by the chance meeting with a Zionist demagogue.

What I humbly request from you, dearest sister, are two things. First, a well-marshalled explanation and defense of your own faith. Second, and perhaps more vitally, some information regarding the chief figures of the European Zionist scene, specifically any particulars concerning a certain crook-backed firebrand...

The door to Kafka's office was thrust open so violently that it swung through a full half-circle of arc to bang against the wall in which it was hung, making the inset glass pane quiver like a shaken quilt.

Kafka clapped his hands to his ears and winced. "Millie, was that strictly necessary?"

Millie snorted, then stomped across the room. "That's 'Miss Jensen' to you, *Mr.* Kafka!" She flung an armful of papers down on Kafka's desk and pivoted to leave.

Kafka stood and moved to her side. "Millie—or if you insist, Miss Jensen. I realize that our date did not end in a particularly satisfying fashion, and that perhaps your nerves are still abuzz from our shared brush with death. And yet, I fancied that until that unforeseen, inaesthetic climax we were enjoying ourselves much like any other couple."

Millie's jade eyes flared with anger. "Oh, sure, right till we nearly got blown up things were hunky-dory. But what came *after* was the real shocker!"

"After? I don't understand—No, surely you couldn't have—"

"But I did, Mr. Barn Veeve-ant, Filly-der-joy Kafka! And let me just tell you this, buster! Any guy who'd pass up some heavy petting with me in favor of two clapped-out, gussied-up old trollops is not someone who's ever going to learn if I wear my stockings rolled!"

And with that obscure assertion, Millie departed as noisily as she had come.

Kafka sat down at his desk and cradled his head in his hands. There came a polite knock, followed by the entrance of officeboy Carl.

Kafka looked up. "The Boss?"

Carl simply nodded, his expression and demeanor conveying the utmost solemn sympathy.

Once more Kafka stood before the forbidding door to Bernarr Macfadden's office. Dispiritedly he knocked, wearily entered when bidden.

Macfadden was employing an apparatus of steel springs and Bakelite grips in exercises intended to strengthen his upper body. Seated behind his massive desk, he stretched and released the resistant springs like a demented candymaker fighting recalcitrant taffy. Sweat dripped from his aggressive mustache as, grunting, he nodded Kafka to a seat.

Watching in horrified fascination, Kafka sought within him for some last untapped resource of strength. A phrase of the Master's came back to him unbidden: "The axe that cleaves the frozen sea within us..." Why could he no longer lay his grip upon that once familiar haft?

Finally Kafka's superior finished his exertions. Dropping the device, he wiped his brow and then poured himself some brown sludge from his flask. That Kafka was not offered any of the drink, the advice columnist considered a bad omen.

Macfadden began to lecture, on a topic of seemingly small relevance.

"I'm not one of your hypocritical, church-going, priest-worshipping, narrow-minded Babbits, Frank. Far from it! Open-minded toleration and clear-sighted experimentation has always been my game plan. I'll endorse any mode of living that honors the body and the mind and the soul. But I draw the line at one thing. Do you know what that is?"

"No, sir. What?"

"Blasphemy!" thundered Macfadden. "Blasphemy of the sort contained in these galleys of yours, which I took the precaution of securing a look at before they reached print! And thank the Lord I did! I can't imagine the magnitude of the hue and cry that would have followed the publication of this corker!"

"Sir, to what are you referring...?"

"This answer of yours to 'Doubting in Denver.' 'If we were possessed by only a single devil, one who had a calm, untroubled view of our whole nature, and freedom to dispose of us at any moment, then that devil would also have enough power to hold us for the length of a human life high above the spirit of God in us, and even swing us to and fro so that we should never get to see a glimmer of it and therefore should not be troubled from that quarter.'"

Weakly, Kafka replied, "You misconstrue my meaning—"

Macfadden crumpled the galleys savagely. "Misconstrue, hell! It's the most blatant decadent Satanism I've ever seen! That poor girl! I hate to imagine how her life could have been ruined by these aberrant Nietzschean gutter-sweepings of yours! No, Frank, you've had your chance. You had a good job, but you threw it away. I want you to clean out your desk right now, collect your last wages, and be off."

Kafka said nothing in his own defense. He knew that all he could say would appear quite incomprehensible to Macfadden, and that whether a good or bad construction was to be put on his actions had all along depended solely on Macfadden's judgmental spirit. And besides, the summed weight of all the misunderstandings he was the center of now sat upon his shoulders like a sack of coal on a stevedore's back, robbing him of speech. A flickering, cool little flame had taken up residence in the left side of his head, and a tension over his left eye had settled down and made itself at home. Coming to his feet, Kafka turned to go.

Now that he had vented his spleen, Macfadden softened somewhat toward his ex-employee, to the point of offering advice. "Maybe you should try something that doesn't involve contact with the public so much, Frank. Go back to the railroads. Or you could always try the insurance industry. Lots of call for analysts and writers there."

Kafka left without a word.

On his way from the building, he was forced to thread an unwelcome, albeit generally friendly gauntlet of his ex-coworkers. Most of them uttered sympathetic farewells and useful advice, all of which pelted Kafka like hailstones.

The ultimate face in the series belonged to Millie. Seemingly genuine tears of sorrow had snailed her cheeks.

"Oh, Frank, I had no idea—"

Kafka came alert, straightening his back. "Millie, I regret anything I have done to cause you distress. For a time, I acted like a lost sheep in the night and in the mountains. Or rather, like a sheep which is running after this sheep. But now my course is clear."

"What's that, Frank?" sniffled Millie.

"To let my own devil fully possess me."

And with that, Kafka walked with what he hoped was a passably erect carriage through the door.

A wrinkled, disintegrating newspaper, half soaking in the wet gutter, half draped over the granite curb, bore large headlines just legible under the wan buttercup-colored glow of a streetlamp:

JACKDAW TERRORIZES UNDERWORLD!
POLICE HARD PUT TO JAIL ALL MALEFACTORS
DELIVERED TO THEIR DOOR!
COURTS CLOGGED!
"WHAT IS HE AFTER?" ASKS PUBLIC
COMMISSIONER O'HALLORAN SPECULATES:
"IT SEEMS HE HAS A GRUDGE AGAINST THE BLACK
BEETLE"

A booted foot ground down upon the discarded tabloid, pulping its substance. The foot moved on, followed by its mate, carrying their owner with determined stealth across the sidewalk and up to the very wall of a derelict building. There the boots halted.

The Jackdaw studied the structure before him. His keen eyes caught sight of a line of ornamental carvings above the second-story windows. Deftly the masked avenger uncoiled a grapple and cord from around his waist. In mere seconds he was standing on a ledge some dozen feet above the ground. From there he progressed rapidly up the side of the seemingly abandoned building until he crouched before the lighted panes of a sixth-floor window.

Inside, men clustered around a table on which bomb-making materials were scattered. Consulting a plan and arguing among themselves, they were oblivious to their watcher.

Chuckling softly to himself, the Jackdaw stood. Tugging the rope secured above him to test its stability, he next leaned backward into sheer space at an angle to the wall, supported by his yellow-gloved grip on the rope. With a kick, he propelled himself away from the wall. At the end of his short arc into darkness, he was aimed feet first for the glass and moving at some speed.

As he hit, glass and wood exploding inward, the Jackdaw emitted his nerve-shattering cry.

It was enough. The bombmakers fell cowering to the floor, failing even to reach for their weapons.

"We give up! Don't kill us! Please!"

The Jackdaw picked up one of the spineless hirelings of the Black Beetle with maniacal force. "Where is he! The Black Beetle! Talk!"

"Lower East Side! In the basement of Schnitzler's Market on Delancey Street! That's his headquarters! Honest!"

"Very well! Now, you gentlemen look as if you could use a little nap before your ride in the Black Maria—"

The pick in the lock of the rear door to Schnitzler's Market tickled the tumblers as delicately as a virgin toying with the strap of her camisole in some Weimar brothel. Within seconds, the Jackdaw had gained entrance. Tiptoeing across the shadowy storage room thus revealed the Jackdaw spied what was patently the basement door.

As he twisted its handle, there came a noise from above of rattling chains.

With a tremendous crash a large cage fell, trapping the Jackdaw!

Gas hissed out from hidden nozzles.

Consciousness departed from the Jackdaw like an offended customer offered inferior goods huffily exiting a carriage-trade establishment.

When he awoke, the Jackdaw found himself lying belly down on some kind of padded platform, secured at wrists, waist, and ankles, and stripped of his mask and cape. His chin was cupped in a kind of trough, and a leather strap went around his brow, forcing him to bend his neck at a strained angle. The sole sight before his eyes was a brick wall with flaking grey paint and blooming excrescences of niter.

Into the Jackdaw's view now walked a man.

The Black Beetle, bent of back, bulging of skull.

"So, we meet again after so long, Franz Kafka!"

Even in extremis, his careful deliberation of speech had not deserted Kafka. Far from blurting out a plea for mercy or a useless threat, Kafka now uttered a simple, "Again?"

An ooze of false sincerity and hollow bonhomie dripped from the Black Beetle's voice. "Ah, but of course! I am still masked. How discourteous! Allow me...." The Black Beetle doffed his headgear, so that the attached piece of his suit with its antennae hung down his back like an improperly molted skin. Kafka saw the gnomish face of a stranger his own age, in no way familiar.

"I see you are still puzzled by my identity," continued the Black Beetle. "Naturally, there is no reason for you to remember such a nonentity as Max Brod!"

"Max Brod? Weren't you at the Altstadter Gymnasium with me as a youth? But that was over two decades ago, and we hardly ever spoke a single word to each other even then!"

"Of course we never spoke! Who would bother to seek out conversation with a crippled, graceless overachiever such as I was then? Not the haughty, handsome Franz Kafka, by any means! Oh, no, he never had time to see the pitiful, adoring youngster who idolized him, who hung on the fringes of his precious little circle—Pollack, Pribam, Baum, that whole bunch!—desperately hoping for some little crumb of attention! And then, when you left me behind in Prague, the agonies of severed affection I suffered! The sleepless nights in a sweat-soaked bed, writhing under the lash of your image! The long hikes and swims intended to burn away your memory, but which only succeeded in somewhat alleviating my childhood bodily afflictions. Even your absence became a kind of presence, for the glorious figure of Engineer Kafka and his faraway glorious deeds were forever thrust before my eyes by all and sundry in the small world of Jewish Prague society."

The strain on Kafka's neck was beginning to nauseate him. "And—and have you tracked me down then only to sate your unnatural obsessions and take revenge?"

Brod laughed sourly. "Even now you cast all events with yourself at the center! Far from it, Mr. Vaunted Jackdaw! This victory is merely a sweet lagniappe. You see, the only way I was able to forget about you and recover my wits and energies was to plunge myself into a cause larger than myself. Zionism was the flame that reignited me!

"At first, I allied myself with one of your old buddies, Weltsch, and his journal *Selbstwehr*. But he proved too meek and mild for my tastes, and I soon found more radical companions. Willingly, to spite all those who see the Jew as the cockroach of civilization, I adopted this disguise. Now I and my comrades wage a worldwide campaign of terror and coercion with the aim of establishing a Jewish state in Palestine. You in your foolish crimefighting role stood in the way of my goals here in America, so I simply chose to stomp on you. The wonderful irony of our early connection was merely a token that Yahweh continues to smile on me."

"And now what will you do with me?"

From somewhere on his person, Brod produced a crisp crimson apple. After polishing it on his sleeve, he began to crunch it, chewing avidly, as if to mock his captive. "I shall enlist you in a scientific experiment. You are secured, you see, to the bed of a unique apparatus intended to convince the enemies of Zionism of their folly. Above you is an adjustable clockwork mechanism which can be set to reproduce certain movements in what we call 'the Harrow,' to which it is connected by various subtle motors.

"The Harrow features two kinds of needles arranged in multiple patterns. Each long needle has a short one beside it. The long needle does a kind of inkless tattoo writing directly into your flesh, and the shorter needle sprays a jet of water to wash away the blood and keep the inscription clear. Blood and water are then conducted here through small runnels into this main runnel and down a waste pipe."

"I see. And what text have you chosen to inscribe on my flesh?"

"A portion of the Talmud dealing with traitors to the Jewish race!"

Discarding the core of his apple, Brod moved out of Kafka's view. In the next second, Kafka felt his garments being slit open to expose his back.

"I am sorry you will not survive your reeducation, my dear Franz. But the process, to be effective, must be repeated hundreds of times over many hours!"

Kafka waited tensely for the start of the physical torture. But what came next was the last thing he expected.

"By the way," said Brod with fiendish glee, "your beloved *father* sends his usual sentiments!"

Kafka swooned straight away.

When he regained consciousness, the reeducation machine was already in action.

What felt like a bed of nails now touched Kafka's back, and he was instantly reminded of enduring a similar sensation under the Master's tutelage. Yet even those lessons in self-mastery were bound to disintegrate under repetitive assaults of the Harrow, especially when his psyche was weakened by the Black Beetle's psychological thrust.

Kafka strained against his bonds, to no avail.

"Perhaps you'd care to vent that ridiculous cry of yours once more? No, I thought not. Very well, prepare yourself—"

Suddenly a loud crash sounded from above them, followed by the clamor of urgent gruff voices.

"Damnation! Well, I see I must leave my fun. But not before witnessing the first prick!"

Dozens of dancing needles pierced Kafka as if he were Saint Sebastian, and he swore his skin could interpret the agonizing shapes of the Hebrew letters. It took all his Oriental training not to scream.

Footsteps galloped down a flight of wooden stairs. The needles continued their cruel and arcane tarantella. Shots rang out. Kafka lost his senses.

He swam up out of blackness apparently only moments later, and felt that his bleeding form was freed from the Harrow and cradled in a soft embrace. The tearful face of Millie Jensen regarded him from above.

"Oh, Frank! Tell me you're going to make it!"

Kafka groaned. "The palimpsest of my hide still has room for a few more passages…"

Millie bent to kiss him. "Thank God! I was sure we'd be too late! I've been haunting the police since the day you were fired, trying to convince them I knew who the Jackdaw was, trying to stop you for your own good! When those bombmakers finally came around and the police beat some information out of them, I tagged along! Everything's fine now, Frank!"

A certain lifelong tension inherent in his very sinews and musculature seemed to have been drained from Kafka along with his blood. Momentarily, he thought to ask whether the Black Beetle had escaped, then realized he didn't care. Max Brod's fanaticism would lead to his own undoing sooner or later, much as Kafka's had nearly led to his.

"Millie?"

"Yes, Frank?"

"Have you ever considered what marriage to me might entail?"

Millie kissed him again. "Well, you're nothing to crow about—"

Kafka winced. "Millie, please, my writer's sensibilities have not been extinguished—"

"But you'd be a feather in any girl's cap!"

J.K.

"Kafka" is "kavka" in Czech, meaning "crow" or "jackdaw." Di Filippo's story, which might on the face of it seem to take unacceptable liberties with Kafka's biography, is powered by it: "Millie" for instance, is based on Milena Jesenská, journalist and first translator of Kafka's stories into Czech, with whom Kafka carried on a correspondence and brief affair. He is also the iconic Kafka, the man torn between unbridgeable solitude and desire to engage with the world, unable to engage with the everyday life that others lead ("that step which it is impossible for him to climb even by exerting all this strength, that step which he cannot get up on and which he naturally can't get past either"[1]) and yet the man who did engage, and attempt to, though his friends, his sister Ottla, his fiancé Felice Bauer, Milena, and Dora Dymant. Writer as sacrificial ascetic. Rather like Batman.

J.P.K.

With over-the-top noir prose, quotes from Kafka's work, insider jokes about the actual biography, and a four-color comic book plot, this romp manages to be hilarious and oddly reverent at the same time.

1 "Letter to his Father"

Carol Emshwiller:

Kafka is my favorite writer. I've used his stories over and over as a model for my own. Whenever I wondered what to write next, I went and read some Kafka. Not so much recently, though, and not with my early stories, but through my whole middle period of writing. So this isn't the only story influenced by him.

What I like about Kafka is that his stories seem to symbolize so much and yet you can't quite put your finger on exactly what they're about. That's what I wanted to do in my work.

I'm so happy to be included in this book!

Report to the Men's Club

Carol Emshwiller

> There was nothing else for me to do, provided always that freedom
> was not to be my choice.
> —Franz Kafka

RESPECTED MEMBERS OF the Men's Club, you have conferred upon
me the highest honor that you are capable of conferring, though it is
certainly not, in your eyes, your highest honor. It is, in fact, something
that you yourselves take for granted, even though I am sure you are
always, on some deep level, aware of the magnificence of it, so that
you walk with a surer step, see with clearer eyes, and always have a
little half-smile hovering about your lips. Needless to say, it's something
that I never hoped to achieve…could not possibly have hoped for, and,
therefore, could not have striven for directly even though, on the other
hand, I can say that some part of me has been striving for it all my life,
from the very moment I began to understand which of us were the girls
and which were the boys.

Yours is a unique group. In any other similar organization, I might
not be fully accepted as one of you (though it's true, often those like
me have been accepted at an entirely different level as lesser members of
some such group), but here in this group, after the reception you have
been kind enough to give to me as well as to my researches, I am sure
that I am, at long last, to be numbered as one of you.

It was not after the formal initiation, where you allowed me to partake in the solemn ceremony—very moving, I may add, and of great beauty—of the drinking from the golden cup, the wearing of the crimson hood, the slow marching to that unique beat that is yours alone… it was not after that that I felt most particularly one of you, but it was in your allowing me to take part in the informal initiation. I mean no disrespect by this comment, but it should not be hard for you to see that that particular ceremony should be the most meaningful to me.

And I realize, Gentlemen, how hard it must have been for you to go through with that ceremony and to paint the blue stripe just there. How you must have yearned to avert your eyes, turn away, in fact, from the whole business. You must have felt, deep inside, that you had made a terrible mistake, but you went on with it. You persevered. And I, I would have lain as still as possible in order to help you, but I knew that it was customary to fight, and so I fought with all the strength I had, and I'm proud to say that I, and you, too, were as covered with blue after my fight as you were from the fight of the man the week before. By now the blue has worn off, but not the memory of it, nor my gratitude for those hilarious moments of brotherhood.

We are the sons of hunters, not of lovers. (I trust that now I may use the word "we" and include myself with all of you.) If all the lovers of the world were laid end to end, they would not be able to make one tiny dent in some great concept of the universe, and so we are not lovers. We put aside the body and pay little attention to its messy functions. Particularly messy, I must admit it, Gentlemen, particularly messy are the functions of the body of a woman. Birth itself a messy business and more than most men can stomach. (I speak from experience.) We are best left out of it altogether. And I, in spite of having once been enmeshed in such things, am, by your ceremonies, by your blue paint, if only figuratively speaking, now am cleansed.

All my life I have been a student of mankind. *Man*kind. I have watched men. I learned their ways, the thoughtful stroking of the chin, the walk with elbows out, the long, wide stride. I repeated what I saw. I sat with legs apart, and, if not an "I can lick you" look in my eyes (for, after all,

I couldn't), then certainly my gaze was level, never coquettish or cute. In fact, "cute" was what I never was, I'm proud to say. I made sure of that from before the age of three. I refused, above all else, to be cute even if I was forced to chop off my own hair to accomplish it. Mother was frantic. She wanted bows in my hair. (I can honestly say that I have never worn a bow for longer than a few seconds.)

Mother was not a woman to be reckoned with, but rather to be swept aside as one hurried towards the important things in life. A sad fact, but a true one. I saw this as a small girl when we went to the beach. Mother sat under a big umbrella with the baby while Father, along with all the other fathers and older children, frolicked in the water. "In the swim," as it were. I ranked myself, then and there, among the fathers and vowed that when I grew up I would never sit on the bank with a baby (though I must confess that I have done it, and more than once).

I have been thought to be amenable to training by many of the men I have encountered, not to mention my father, to whom I will be forever grateful for giving me a name (Leslie) that could be of either sex. (Lucky for me I had no brother, though too bad for Father.) It was from him that I learned never to be without a graphing calculator in my back pocket (though it was hard to have a back pocket most of the time). Perhaps my father saw something in me from the start—something of the enigma I wanted to be. I was frantic to be noticed by him and put on the most outlandish performances, sometimes climbing trees and screaming from the topmost branches (though I was terrified of heights) in hopes of attracting his attention.

But men are, as you know, Gentlemen, preoccupied with more important things than one small girl could ever hope to be, even one at the top of a tree. I did attract his attention, though not in ways I hoped. Often it was simply in the matter of climbing down. Mother could not help me in that regard (another sign of her inferiority).

Father always said a girl should know how to give one swift punch to the Adam's apple or one swift kick to the you-know-where. I practiced these. Perhaps I sensed, even then, what the future held.

*

Of course there soon came the problem of having breasts. What were these things doing on, of all bodies, *my* body? I had thought that, simply by the strength of will, I could at the very least stay neutral—not take sides so completely in this matter. So then I thought, at least I'll not be a woman like any others. I'll keep the faith with men. See their side of every question. And I'm happy to say I've done so to this day.

Also I'm happy to say that my mind is uncluttered by the imagination, that I stick to the facts, have not veered off into emotionalities. (Even when I had children of my own, I made a point of avoiding any talk of them in favor of more important subjects.) And I often make snap judgments worthy, if I may say so myself, of a military man.

But do not think I have lived without ecstasy. Though it is exactly that ecstasy—that falling gently into the damp, erotic, messy needs of the body—that misled me for a while. I became confused. My sources of pleasure were, after all, the very same as my sources of disdain and shame. I suffered in my ecstasy. I suffered, hardly knowing that I did, and yet, looking back on it, I know I did. I had come down from my trees, my rooftops, my high dives…down from all my dreams. In short, Gentlemen, I fell in love with one of you. Every day I asked him how he was coming along in the world I had left behind, and he answered me cheerfully enough for a while, but he soon grew tired of my endless probing, though even after he no longer answered me except in grunts and clearings of the throat, my goal still was: How to improve the quality of life for the opposite sex. For myself, I hoped only to *inspire* excellence in him and in my children. I did not hope to find any excellence in myself.

Only a lunatic, you will be saying to yourselves, would have put up with this for a minute. I can only agree with you, but that's where ecstasy can lead those of my sex.

But you are wondering, when was it that I began my preparations for being one of you in earnest? When I was not quite in my fourteenth year, I began a series of tests. Even I could not guess the meaning of them: Ice-cold showers, hands held over candles, a knife wound in my cheek, and so forth. I bear the scars to this day, as you can see. (As to the life I subsequently led masquerading as a boy, strange to say, I have few scars—though, since the initiation of last week, I've used a cane and have this sling.)

Was I self-destructive? Obviously I was, no matter that I would protest it and no matter how many reasons for it may have been in the forefront of my mind at the time. Or, and more important, was I mainly yearning for my freedom? Ah, there, gentlemen, well you might have thought so, but that would have been your biggest mistake, for freedom has never been my wish. I can assure you of that. I wanted to take my place among the powerful. Note that I don't say I wanted power. I simply wanted to be numbered among those that make the history and the money. I wanted to be among the people that the word "mankind" refers to.

But I soon saw that I might well destroy myself altogether if I continued to show myself no mercy. There was nothing for it but to attempt a daring escape across rooftops, fording streams, and off into the bogs of the arboretum....

As can well be imagined, guards to keep me prisoner in my life, as it should be lived, were everywhere, for it was in everyone's best interests that I stay. Children were on the stairs (their skates, their jump ropes to trip me, hoses in the garden, rakes left, tines up), Grandmother in the kitchen, Mother in the backyard, Father, though he had seemed to be in sympathy with my earlier efforts to better myself, was now aligned with all the others and stationed himself at the front door. (By then, my husband was long gone.) At night, too, someone was always awake and watching, if not a child with the pretext of a bad dream, then a grownup with insomnia. But I managed to bide my time until my oldest son was just my size, and, dressed in his clothes, my hair cut short, I walked past all my jailers quite easily one beautiful spring afternoon.

I brought nothing from that place except that one suit of clothes. After all, I had not earned a penny for all the work I did each day. I felt that nothing there really belonged to me, not even the apple that I put in my pocket. I left with all my longings newly kindled, but even then I could not put a name to what I wanted. It is you, Gentlemen, who have made it all come true at last—that for which I longed most.

What, after all is said and done, distinguishes us...us men from the women. What but the fact that we are *not* enmeshed in the body and that we do *not* fluctuate at the mercy of our glands—that the moon does *not* affect us. Isn't it, then, by all these *nots,* as well as by all our male values and virtues, that we are set apart from simply "being"? It is, in fact, exactly these questions, as you all well know, that I have made the essence of my investigations, and which I have recorded in what you have, most kindly, called: "Extraordinary detail," and that I have published under the title *Man*...simply *Man,* for that one word is enough—has always been enough. You have found this work worthy of some small notice, and for this I thank you.

But I have spoken too long already, and so, since I have presented my most important points, I'll not bore you with any more of my personal history: How I joined, for a time, a gang of runaway boys; nor will I mention the kindly intellectual who found me half-starved in the gutter and who took me in and brought me up as his own son. (I had, by then, reached a fairly early menopause, possibly due to my hardships, so more children were, happily, out of the question.) Without the help of this man, I would certainly not be here among you. I wish to give a special thanks to him.

So, as I step—or, rather, hobble; I've still not quite recovered from that wondrous initiation—down from this podium, I'll not be stepping down at all, but up. One giant step up into *Man*kind. Too bad Father isn't here to see me now, though Mother would probably say (not even knowing she was quoting Kafka) that it was hardly worth the trouble.

J.K.

Emshwiller borrows the form of her story from Kafka's "A Report to an Academy," producing multiple ironies as her female speaker takes the place of Kafka's ape, describing her experience trying to be recognized as a human being. Emshwiller understands Kafka's ability to be both serious and funny more than most.

J.P.K.

Of course, in Kafka's "A Report to an Academy" the narrator was addressing an all-male audience as well. Interesting that Kafka's ape announces "Let no one say that it was not worth the bother."

Jeffrey Ford:

When my novel, *The Physiognomy*, was first published by Avon, it got some great reviews, some good ones, and its share of lumps. The one thing that was fairly unanimous by the reviewers was the mention of Kafka in their reviews. When the book was issued in mass market paperback, between the front and back covers and the blurb pages in front, there were seven or eight mentions of Kafka. I showed the book to my neighbor, a retired NYC transit cop, and he told me, "You got to get rid of this Kafka shit. That's not doing you any favors. Get them to mention Tom Clancy, and then you'll sell some books."

As it turned out, my neighbor wasn't too far off. At first, I thought the proliferation of Kafka on my book was funny, but then I started to consider how old Franz, himself, might feel about having his masterful oeuvre compared to my Science Fiction/Fantasy/Horror/Mystery and realized he'd more than likely not be happy. After that I waited through long nights for him to eventually appear and kick my ass.

One night I dreamt he was standing at the bottom of my bed. The usually mild mannered insurance salesman, I could tell, was pissed. I could hear his teeth grinding like the mechanical workings of that contraption in "In the Penal Colony." When I woke, I decided I'd better do something to placate his bad will from beyond the grave, so I wrote "Bright Morning." In that story, I manufactured a means of escape for myself—you'll see.

When all is said and done, Kafka is one of the greatest fiction writers of all time, for his clarity, his ability to conjure the fantastic from the everyday, his ability to craft remarkable fabulations with characters that never quite succumb to the allegorical. If one needs be cursed by a great writer, I'll take Kafka any day.

Bright Morning

Jeffrey Ford

If THERE IS one thing that distinguishes my books from others it is the fact that in the review blurbs that fill the back cover and the page that precedes the title page inside, the name of "Kafka" appears no less than eight times. *Kafka, Kafkaesque, Kafka-like, in the tradition of Kafka.* Certainly more Kafka than one man deserves—a veritable embarrassment of Kafka riches. My novels are fantasy/adventure stories with a modicum of metaphysical whim-wham that some find to be insightful and others have termed "overcooked navel gazing." Granted, there are no elves or dragons or knights or wizards in these books, but they are still fantasies, none the less. I mean, if you have a flying head, a town with a panopticon that floats in the clouds, a monster that sucks the essence out of hapless victims through their ears, what the hell else can you call it? At first glance, it would seem that any writer would be proud to have their work compared to that of one of the twentieth century's greatest writers, but upon closer inspection it becomes evident that in today's publishing world, when a novel does not fit a prescribed format, it immediately becomes labeled as Kafkaesque. The hope is, of course, that this will be interpreted as meaning *exotic*, when, in fact, it translates to the book-buying public as *obscure*. Kafka has become a place, a condition, a boundary to which it is perceived only the pretentious are drawn and only total lunatics will cross.

As my neighbor, a retired New York City transit cop, told me while holding up one of my novels and pointing to the cover, "Ya know, this Kafka shit isn't doing you any favors. All I know is he wrote a book about a guy who turned into a bug. What the fuck?"

"He's a great writer," I said in defense of my blurbs.

"Tom Clancy's a great writer, Kafka's a putz."

What could I say? We had another beer and talked about the snow.

Don't get me wrong, I like what I've read of Kafka's work. The fact that Gregor Samsa wakes from a night of troubling dreams to find that he has been transformed into a giant cockroach is, to my mind, certain proof of existential genius firing with all six pistons. Likewise, a guy whose profession is sitting in a cage and starving himself while crowds throng around and stare, is classic everyman discourse. But my characters run a lot. There's not a lot of running in Kafka. His writing is unfettered by parenthetical phrases, introductory clauses, and adjectival exuberance. My sentences sometimes have the quality of Arabic penmanship, looping and knotting, like some kind of Sufi script meant to describe one of the names given to God in order to avoid using his real name. In my plots, I'm usually milking some nostalgic sentiment resulting from unrequited love or working toward a punch line of revelation like an old Borscht Belt comic with a warmed-over variation of the one about the traveling salesman, whereas Kafka seems like he's trying to curtly elicit that ambiguous perplexity that makes every man an island, every woman an isthmus, every child a continental divide.

My friend, Quigley, once described the book *The Autobiography of a Yogi* as "a miracle a page," and that's the kind of effect I'm striving for, building up marvels until it just becomes a big, hallucinogenic shitstorm of wonder. Admittedly, sometimes the forecast runs into a low-pressure system and all I get is a brown drizzle; such are the vicissitudes of the fiction writer. On the other hand, Kafka typically employed only one really weird element in each story (a giant mole, a machine that inscribes a person's crime upon their back) that he treats as if it were as mundane as putting your shoes on. Then he inspects it six ways to Sunday, turning the microscope on it, playing out the string, until it eventually curls up into a question mark at the end. There are exceptions, "A Country Doctor," for instance, that swing from start to finish. I don't claim to be anywhere near as accomplished a writer as Kafka. If I was on a stage with Senator Lloyd Bentsen and he said to me, "I knew Kafka, and you, sir, are no Franz Kafka," I'd be the first to agree with him. I'd shake his damn hand.

I often wondered what Kafka would make of it, his name bandied about, a secret metaphor for *fringe* and *destination remainder bin*. For a while it really concerned me, and I would have dreams where I'd wake in the middle of the night to find Kafka standing at the foot of my bed, looking particularly grim, half in, half out of the shaft of light coming in from the hallway. He'd appear dressed in a funeral suit with a thin tie. His hair would be slicked back and his narrow head would taper inevitably to the sharp point of his chin. Ninety pounds soaking wet, but there would be this kind of almost visible tension surrounding him.

"Hey, Franz," I'd say, and get out of bed to shake his hand, "I swear it wasn't my idea."

Then he'd get a look on his face like he was trying to pass the Great Wall of China and haul off and kick me right in the nuts. From his stories, you might get the idea that he was some quiet little dormouse, a weary, put upon pencil pusher in an insurance office, but, I'm telling you, in those nightmares of mine, he really ripped it up.

Do you think Kafka would be the type of restless spirit to reach out from beyond the pale? On the one hand, he was so unassuming that he asked Max Brod to burn all of his remaining manuscripts when he died, while on the other hand, he wrote an awful lot about judgment. He might not have as much to do with my writing as some people say, but me and Franz, we go way back, and I'm here to warn you: the less you have to do with him the better. His pen still works.

It was 1972 and I was a junior at West Islip High School on Long Island. I was a quiet kid and didn't have a lot of friends. I liked to smoke pot and I liked to read, so sometimes I'd combine those two pleasures. I'd blow a joint in the woods behind the public library and then go inside and sit and read or just wander through the stacks, looking through different books. In those days, I was a big science fiction fan, and I remember reading *Martians, Go Home, Adam Link, Space Paw, Time Out of Joint*, etc. In our library, the science fiction books had a rocket ship on the plastic cover down at the bottom of the spine. There were three shelves of these books and I read just about all of them.

One afternoon at the library, I ran into Bettleman, a guy in my class. Bettleman was dwarfish short with a dismorphic body—long chimp arms, a sort of hunchback, and a pouch of loose skin under his chin. He was also a certified math genius and had the glasses to prove it—big mothers with lenses thick as ice cubes. I came around a corner of the stacks and there he was: long, beautiful woman fingers paging through a book he held only inches from his face. He looked up, took a moment to focus, and said hello. I said hi and asked him what he was reading.

"Karl Marx," he said.

I was impressed. I knew Marx was the father of Communism, an ideology that was still viewed as tantamount to Satanism in those days when the chill of the cold war could make you dive under a desk at the sound of the noon fire siren.

"Cool," I said.

"What have you got there?" he asked me.

I showed him what I was carrying. I think it was *Dandelion Wine* by Bradbury. He pushed those weighty glasses up on his nose and studied it. Then he closed his eyes for a moment, as if remembering, and when he opened them proceeded to rattle off the entire plot.

"Sounds like it would have been a good one," I said.

"Yeah," he told me, "it's alright—fantasy with a dash of horror meets the child of Kerouac and Norman Rockwell."

"Cool," I said, not knowing what he was talking about, but recalling him correcting the math teacher on more than one occasion.

"Hey, you want to read something really wild?" he asked.

"Sure," I said uncertainly, thinking about the first time I was dared into smoking weed.

He closed the book in his hand and walked to the end of the aisle. I followed. Three rows down, he turned left and went to the middle of one of the stacks. Moving his face up close to the titles, he scanned along the shelf as if sniffing out the volume he was searching for. Finally, he stepped back, reached out a hand and grabbed a thick, violet-covered book from the shelf. When he turned to me he was wearing a wide smile that allowed me to see through his strange exterior for a split second and genuinely like him.

"There's a story in here called 'The Metamorphosis,'" he said. "Just check it out." Then he laughed loudly and that pouch of flesh that caused the other kids to call him *The Sultan of Chin* jiggled like the math teacher's flabby ass when she ran out of the room, embarrassed at her own ignorance in the face of Bettleman's genius.

He handed it over to me and I said, "Thanks." I turned the book over to see the title and the author and when I looked up again, he was gone. So I spent that sunny winter afternoon in the West Islip public library reading Kafka for the first time. That story was profound in a way I couldn't put my finger on. I knew it was heavy, but its burden was invisible like that of gravity. There was also sadness in it that surfaced as an unfounded self-pity, and underneath it all, somehow, a sense of humor that elicited in me that feeling of trying not to laugh in church. I checked the book out, took it home, and read every word of every tale and parable between its covers.

It took me a long time to read them all, because after ingesting one, I'd chew on it, so to speak, for a week or two, attempting to identify the flavor of its absurdity, what spices were used to give it just that special tang of nightmare. Occasionally, I'd see Bettleman at school and run a title by him. He'd usually push his glasses up with the middle finger of his left hand, give me a one-line review of the story in question, and before scuttling hastily off to square the circle, he'd let loose one of his Sultanic laughs.

"Hey, Bettleman, 'The Imperial Message,'" I'd say.

"Waiting for a sign from God that validates the industrious drudgery of existence while God waits for a sign to validate his own industrious drudgery."

"Yo, Bettleman, what do you say to 'The Hunter Gracchus'?"

"Siamese twins, altogether stuck. One judgment, one guilt, both unable to see their likeness in the other which would allow them to transcend."

"Yeah, whatever."

Then in the first days of spring, I came across a story in the Kafka collection that I will admit did have a true influence on me. Wedged in between "The Bucket Rider" and "Josephine the Singer, or the Mouse Folk," I discovered an unusual piece that was longer than the parables but not quite the length of a full-fledged story. Its title was "Bright Morning," and for all intents and purposes it seemed to me to be a vampire story. I read it at least a half dozen times one weekend and afterward couldn't get its imagery out of my mind.

I went to school Wednesday, hoping to find Bettleman and get his cryptic lowdown on it. Bettleman, it seems, had his own plans for that day. He sailed into the parking lot in the rust Palomino, three-door Buick Special, he'd inherited from his old man and didn't stop to park, but drove right up on the curb in front of the entrance to the school. When he got out of the car, he was wearing a Richard Nixon Halloween mask and lugging a huge basket of rotten apples. He climbed up on top of the hood of his car and then, laughing like a maniac behind the frozen leer of Tricky Dick, started beaning students and teachers with the apples.

Although Bettleman's genetic mishap of a body prevented him from being taken seriously by the sports coaches at school, those primate arms of his were famous for having the ability to hurl a baseball at Nolan Ryan speeds. He broke a few windows, nailed Romona Vacavage in the right breast, splattered a soft brown one against the back of Jake Harwood's head, and pelted the principal, No Foolin' Doolin', so badly he slipped and fell on the sauce that had dripped off his suit, dislocating his back. Everyone ran. Even the tough kids with the leather jackets and straight-pin-and-India-ink tattoos of the word SHIT on their ankles were afraid of his weirdness. Finally the cops came and took Bettleman away. He didn't come back to school. In the years that followed, I never heard anything more about him but half expected to discover his name on the Nobel lists when I'd run across them in the newspaper.

The Kafka collection didn't get returned to the library until the end of the summer. I'd run up a twenty-dollar late fee on it. In those days, twenty dollars was a lot of money, and my old man was pissed when he got the letter from the librarian. He paid for my book truancy, but

I had to work off the debt by raking and burning leaves in the fall. Under those cold, violet-gray skies of autumn, the same color as the cover of the book, I gathered and incinerated the detritus of August and considered Kafka and the plight of Bettleman. I realized the last thing that poor bastard needed was Kafka, and so when my labor was completed I put the two of them out of my mind by picking up a book by Richard Brautigan, *In Watermelon Sugar*. The light confection of that work gave me a rush that set me off on another course of reading, like "The Hunter Gracchus," in frustrated search of transcendence.

The hunt lasted throughout most of my senior year of high school, taking me through the wilds of Burroughs and Kerouac and Miller, but near the end, when I was about to graduate, I found myself one day in the stacks of the public library, returning to the absurd son of Prague for a hit of real reality before I went forth into the world. To my disbelief and utter annoyance, I discovered the book had been removed as soon as I had returned it at the end of the summer and never brought back. In its place was a brand new edition of *The Collected Stories of Franz Kafka*. I paged through the crisp, clean book, but could not find the story "Bright Morning." The incompleteness of this new volume put me off and I just said, "The hell with it!"—much to the dismay of the librarian who was within easy earshot of my epithet.

I went to college and dropped out after one semester, bought a boat and became a clammer on the Great South Bay for two years. All this time, I continued to read, and occasionally Kafka would rear his thin head in a mention by another author. These were usually allusions to "The Metamorphosis," which seemed the only work of his anyone ever mentioned.

One night on Grass Island out in the middle of the bay, a place where clammers congregated on Saturday nights to party, I ran into a guy I knew from having spoken to him previously, when I'd be out of the boat, with a tube and basket, scratch raking in the flats. If we were both working the same area, he'd take a break around three o'clock when the south wind would invariably pick up, and wander over to talk with me for a while. He was also a big reader, but usually his tastes ran to massive tomes like the Gulag books, Mann's *The Magic Mountain*, Proust.

That night on Grass Island, in the gaze of Orion, with a warm breeze from off the mainland carrying the sounds of Lela Ritz getting laid by Shab Wellow down in the lean-to, we were sitting atop the highest dune, passing a joint back and forth, when the conversation turned to Kafka. This guy from the bay, I don't remember his name, said to me, "I really like that story, 'Bright Morning.'"

"You know it?" I said.

"Sure." Then he proceeded to tell the entire thing just as I remembered it.

"Do you have a copy of it?" I asked.

"Sure," he said. "I'll bring it out with me someday for you."

The discussion ended then because we spotted Lela in the moonlight, naked, down by the water's edge. Lela Ritz had the kind of body that made Kafka seem like a bad joke.

In the days that followed, I'd see that guy from time to time who owned the book, and he'd always promise to remember to bring it out with him. But at the end of summer, I'd heard that he'd raked up the beringed left hand of a woman who, in June, had been knocked out of a boat, caught in the propeller, and supposedly never found. The buyer at the dock told me the guy gave up clamming because of it. That fall I returned to college and never saw him again.

I went to school for my undergraduate and masters degrees at SUNY, Binghamton, in upstate New York, where I studied literature and writing. It was there that I met and worked with novelist John Gardner, who did what he could to help me become a fiction writer. His knowledge of literature, short stories, and novels was encyclopedic, and when I was feeling mischievous, I would try to stump him by giving him merely a snippet of the plot of, what I considered to be, some obscure piece I had recently discovered: Bunin's "The Elaghin Affair," Blackwood's "The Willows," Collier's *His Monkey Wife*. He never failed to get them, and could discuss their merits as if he had read them but an hour earlier. Twice in conversation I brought up the story by Kafka, and on the first occasion he said he knew it. He even posited some interpretation of it, which I can't now remember. The second time I brought it up, in relation to having just read his own story, "Julius Caesar and the Werewolf," he shook his head and said that there

Kafkaesque

was no such piece by Kafka, but if there was, with that title, it would have to be a horror story.

What was even more interesting concerning the story during my college years, and really the last time I would hear anything about it for a very long time, was an incident that transpired at the motel where I lived with my future wife, Lynn. The Colony Motor Inn on Vestal Parkway had a string of single rooms that sat up on a hill, separated from the main complex of the establishment. These rooms were reserved for students, long-time borders, and the illegal Chinese immigrants who worked at the motel restaurant, The House of Yu. It was a dreary setting in which to live on a daily basis—a heaping helping of Susquehanna gothic. The maintenance guy had one arm and an eye patch, and two of the maids were mother and daughter *and* sisters, whose *other* job was slaughtering livestock.

Lynn was in nursing school and I was doing my literary thing, spending a lot of time writing crappy stories with pencil in composition books. The room we had was really small, and the bathroom doubled as a kitchen. We had a toaster oven in there on the counter, and we cooked our own food to save money. In the mornings I'd shave onto ketchup-puddled plates in the sink. The toilet was also the garbage disposal, and it wasn't unusual for me to try to hit the floating macaroni when I'd take a piss. That bathroom had no door, just a sliding curtain. Right next to the entrance, we kept an old Victrola, and if one of us was going in to do our thing, for a little privacy, we'd spin the "Blue Danube Waltz" at top volume.

When the weather was good and the temperature was still warm, we'd walk, in the mornings, down to the motel pool at the bottom of the hill. Lynn would swim laps, and I would sit at one of the tables and write. If we went early enough, we usually had the spot to ourselves.

On one typical day, while Lynn was swimming and I was hunched over my notebook, smoking a butt, trying to end a story without having the protagonist commit suicide or kill someone, I heard the little gate in the chain-link fence surrounding the pool open and close. I looked up and there stood this skinny guy dressed in a sailor's uniform, white gob hat tilted at an angle on his shaved head, holding a Polaroid camera. He said hello to me and I nodded, hoping he wasn't going to strike up a conversation. I watched his Adam's apple bob and his eyes shift back and forth and immediately knew I was in for it.

He came over and sat at my table and asked to bum a smoke. I gave him one and he lifted my matches and lit it.

"That your girl?" he asked, nodding toward Lynn as she passed by in the water.

"Yeah," I said.

"Nice hair," he said and grinned.

"You on leave?" I asked.

"Yeah," he said. "Got a big bunch of money and a week or so off. Bought this new camera."

"Where you staying?"

"Up on the hill," he said.

"They usually don't rent the places up on the hill unless you're staying for a long time," I said.

"I made it worth their while," he told me, flicking his ashes. "I wanted to be able to see everything."

I was going to tell him I had to get back to work, but just then Lynn got out of the pool and came over to the table.

"Ma'am," he said, and got up to let her sit down.

"Well, have a nice day," I told him, but he just stood there looking at us.

I was going to tell him to shove off, but finally he spoke. "Would you two like me to take your portrait?" he asked.

I shook my head no, and Lynn said yes. She made me get up and drew me over to stand against the chain-link fence with the Vestal Parkway in the background.

The sailor brought the Polaroid up to his eye and focused on us. "Let's have a kiss, now," he said, that Adam's apple bobbing like mad.

I put my arm around Lynn and kissed her for a long time. In the middle of it, I heard the pool gate open and close and saw the sailor running away across the parking lot toward the hill.

"Creep," said Lynn.

Then I read her my new story and she dozed off while sitting straight up.

That night, as we lay in bed on the verge of sleep, I heard a loud bang come from somewhere down the row of rooms. I knew immediately that it was a gunshot, so I grabbed Lynn and rolled onto the floor. We lay there breathing heavily from fear and she said to me, "What the hell was that?"

"Maybe Mrs. West's hair finally exploded," I said, and we laughed. Mrs. West was the maids' supervisor. She had a seven-story beehive hairdo she was constantly jabbing a sharpened pencil into to scratch her scalp.

About ten minutes later, I heard the police car pull up and saw the flashing red light through the split in the curtains. I hastily put my shorts and sneakers on and went outside. In the parking lot, I met Chester, our next-door neighbor.

"What's up?" I asked him.

He was shaking his head, and in that Horse Heads, New York, upstate drawl, said, "Man, that's gonna ruin my night."

"What happened?" I said.

"Admiral asshole blew his brains out down there in 268."

"The sailor?" I asked.

"Yeah, I heard the shot and went down to his room. The door was open part way. Jeez, there was a piece of jaw bone stuck in the wall and blood everywhere."

Two more cop cars pulled up and when the officers got out they told us to go back inside.

After I told Lynn what had happened, she didn't get much sleep, and I tossed and turned all night, falling in and out of dreams about that goofy sailor. I just remember one dream that showed him in a small boat in shark-infested waters, while in the background a volcano erupted. I awoke in the morning to the sound of someone knocking on the door; Lynn had already left for her shift at the hospital. I got out of bed and dressed quickly.

It was Mrs. West. She wanted to know if I wanted the room cleaned. I said no, and quickly shut the door. A second later, she knocked again. I opened up and she stood there, holding something out toward me. It was then that I noticed that her hands and arms were red.

"They had me here early this morning, cleaning the death," she said. "I found this amidst the fragments." She handed me what I took to be a square of paper. Only when I touched it did I realize it was a photograph—the picture of Lynn and me kissing, while all around us splattered flecks of red filled the sky like a blood rain.

That afternoon, I had the photo setting on the table next to where I was writing a story about a sailor who goes to a motel to commit suicide and falls in love with the maid. Every time I'd look up, there would be that picture. It gave me the willies, so eventually I turned it over. I hadn't noticed before, but written on the back in very light pencil were these words: *He stepped out into the bright morning and quietly evaporated...* I recognized it immediately as part of the last line of Kafka's elusive story. That photograph is still in my possession, at the bottom of a cardboard box, out in the garage or in the basement, I think.

Just when the synchronistic influence of that text seemed to be reaching a crescendo of revelation, it suddenly turned its back on me, and I heard nothing, saw nothing about it for years and years, until I could easily ignore my awareness of it. The avalanche of books and stories I read in the interim helped to bury it. Occasionally, when I was in a bookstore and would see some new edition of Kafka's stories, I would pick it up and scan the table of contents, hoping not to see the piece listed. I was never disappointed. So many other writers came to call, and their personalities and plots and words became ever so much more important to me than his.

Slowly, and I mean slowly, the stories I wrote became less and less crappy and I actually had a few published by small-press magazines. The amount of time it took me to become a professional writer is reminiscent of the adage of a hundred apes in a room with a hundred typewriters, at work for a hundred years, eventually producing Hamlet's soliloquy. From there, it was only a matter of more time, and then one day I sold a novel to a major publisher. I could less believe it than the fact that the sailor had known "Bright Morning" well enough to quote it. When my novel was published, the blurb the publisher had written for it mentioned Kafka twice. At the time, I wasn't thinking about all the incidents that had been related to the Kafka story; they seemed light-years away. All I thought was, "Hey, Kafka, it's better than Harold Robbins." Or was it? The book didn't sell all too well, but it got great reviews. Nearly every critic who wrote about it mentioned Kafka at least once, so that when the paperback edition came out, it carried all of the critical blurbs and the back cover was lousy with Kafka.

In four years, I'd published three fantasy novels, a dozen short stories also in the genre, and a couple of essays. The first novel won a World Fantasy Award, the first two were *New York Times* Notable Books of the Year; one of the stories was nominated for a Nebula Award, another appeared in *The Year's Best Fantasy and Horror*; there were starred reviews in *Publishers Weekly, Kirkus Review,* the *Library Journal*; three stories in one year made *Locus* magazine's recommended reading list. I tell you all of this not by way of bragging, because there are others who have written more and garnered more accolades, there are others who *are* better writers, but for me it was a goad. I thought that to stop for a moment would mean to let all I had worked for slip away. At the same time, I was teaching five classes, over a hundred writing students a semester, at a community college an hour and a half from my house, and I had two young sons with whom I needed to spend a considerable amount of time. So I slept no more than four hours a night, smoked like mad when writing, and lived on coffee and fast food. It was an insane period and it made me into a bloated zombie. Finally I hit an impasse and needed a break. I couldn't think of one more damn fantasy story I could write. And as it turned out, what stood between me and a vacation from it all was just one more story.

Like a good soldier, I had finished off all the pieces I had promised to editors, and then all that remained was a final story for a collection of short fiction I really wanted to see published. When the project had first presented itself I had, with reckless largesse, promised to write a piece for it that would appear nowhere else. My imagination, though, was emptier than the dark, abandoned railway station I visited every night in my dreams. In four years, I'd done just about everything *I* could possibly do in fantasy. I told you already about the flying head, the cloud city with attendant panopticon, but there was much more—demons, werewolves, men turned to blue stone, evil geniuses, postmodern fairy-tale kingdoms, giant moths, zombies, parodies of fantasy heroes, an interview with Jules Verne, big bug-aliens enamored of old movies, Lovecraft rip-offs, experimental hoodoo, and that's just for starters. The only fantasy I could now conceive of was sneaking in a nap on Saturday afternoon after the kids' basketball games and before the obligatory family trip to the mall. I was burnt crisper than a fucking cinder on the whole genre.

The deadline for the story collection was fast approaching, and all I had was a computer file full of aborted beginnings, all of which stunk. I was determined not to fail, so when the college I taught at closed for spring break and I had a week to write, I said to myself, "Okay, get a grip." Driving home the last night before the vacation, I had a brainstorm. Why reinvent the wheel? I decided I'd just take one of the old fantasy tropes and work it over a little—a ready-made theme. Upon arriving home, I went to my office and scanned the bookshelves for an idea, and that's when I came upon a book I had bought at a yard sale back when Lynn and I were still in college. I'd almost forgotten I'd owned the thing—an anthology of vampire stories. That night and the next day, I read almost all of the pieces in it. There was one great one, "Viy," by Gogol, that reinvigorated my imagination somewhat. As I sat down to compose, though, a memory of Kafka's "Bright Morning" came floating up from where it had been buried, and breached the surface of my consciousness like the hand of that corpse at the end of the movie *Deliverance*. I thought to myself, "If I could just read that story one more time, that would be all I'd need to get something good going."

Sitting back in my office chair, I lit a cigarette and tried to remember what I could about the piece. Bettleman and his apples; Gregor Samsa lying in bed on his back, six legs kicking; the sailor's hat; the worm-filled wound of the kid in "The Country Doctor"—all passed through my mind as I called forth the intricacies of the plot. Then I imagined I was back in the West Islip public library on a winter's afternoon, reading from the violet book. Ironically enough, it dawned on me that "Bright Morning" centered around a frustrated writer, F.—a young dilettante of literary aspirations, who feels he has all of the aesthetic acumen and an overabundance of style, but, for the life of him, cannot conceive of a story worth telling. It is intimated that the reason for this is that he has spent all of his days with his nose in a book and is devoid of life experience. There is more to it than that, but that's how the story begins. Somewhere along the way he hooks up with this haggard, bent, old man, a Mr. Krouch, whose face is "a mask of wrinkles." I think they meet at night on the bridge leading into the small town that is the story's setting. The old man offers his life story to the young writer in exchange for half the proceeds if the book is ever published. The writer is reticent, but then the old man tells him just one short tale about when he was a sailor, shipwrecked on a volcanic island in the Indian Ocean, south of Sumatra, and encountered a species of ferocious blue lizards as big as horses.

The young man is soon convinced he will become famous writing the old man's biography. Each night, after their initial meeting, the old man comes to F.'s house. On the first night, as a gift to the writer, the old man gives him, from his tattered traveling bag, a beautiful silver pen and a bottle of ink. The pen feels to the young man as if it has been specifically designed for his grip; the ink flows so smoothly it is as if the words are writing themselves. Then the old man begins to recount his long, long life, a chapter a night. In that wonderfully compressed style Kafka utilizes in his parables, he gives selections from the annals of Krouch. Years tending the tombs of monarchs in some distant eastern land, a career as a silhouette puppeteer in Venice, a love affair with a young woman half his age—these are a few I remember, but there were more and they were packed into the space of two or three modestly sized paragraphs.

At the end of each session, Krouch leaves just before dawn, and F. falls asleep to the sounds of bird song that accompanies the coming of the sun. The work has an exhausting effect upon him and he sleeps all day, until nightfall, when he wakes only an hour before the old man returns. The gist of the story is that, as the auto/biography grows, F. slowly wastes away while Krouch gets younger and more robust. It becomes evident as to how the old man has managed to fit so many adventures into one lifetime, and the reader begins to suspect that there have been other unsuspecting writers before F. By the time the young man places the last period at the end of the last sentence—a sentence about him placing the last period at the end of the last sentence—he is no longer young but has become shriveled and wrinkled and bent.

"Now off to the publisher with it," Krouch commands and gives a hearty laugh. F. can barely stand. He struggles to lift the pile of pages and then, knees creaking, altogether out of breath, he shuffles toward the door. "Allow me," says Krouch, and he leaps from his chair and moves to open the door.

It takes much of his remaining energy, but F. manages to whisper, "Thank you."

He steps out into the bright morning and quietly evaporates, the pages scattering on the wind like frightened ghosts.

It is one thing to vaguely remember a story by Kafka and quite another to actually have the book before you. There is that wonderfully idiosyncratic style: the meek authorial voice, the infrequent but strategically placed metaphor, a businesslike approach to plot, and those deceptive devices of craft, nearly as invisible as chameleons that make all the difference to the beauty of the imagery and the impact of the tale. I knew I needed that story in my hands, before my eyes, and that I would obsess over it, unable to write a word of my own, until I had it.

I enlisted the help of my older son, and together we scoured the Internet, made phone calls to antiquarian and used book shops as far away as Delaware; the western wilds of Pennsylvania; Watertown, New York, up by the Canadian border. Nothing. Most had never heard of the story. One or two said they had a very vague recollection of the violet edition but couldn't swear to it. The used book sites on the Web were crammed with copies of the more recent Schocken edition and some even had expensive originals from Europe, but none of the abstracts described the book I was searching for. I drove around one day to all the used bookstores I knew of and, in one, found the violet-covered book. I was so frantic to have my hands on it, I could hardly control my shaking as I forked over the $23.50 to the clerk. When I got out to my car and opened it, I discovered that it was really a copy of *Mansfield Park* by Jane Austen. I was livid, and on my way home as I drove across an overpass, I opened the window and tossed the damned thing out into the traffic below.

My week off was nearing its end and I was no closer to Kafka's story, no closer to my own. The frustration of the search, my fear of impending failure, finally peaked and then dropped me into a sullen depression. On Saturday afternoon, between basketball and the mall, I received a phone call. Lynn answered it and handed me the receiver.

"Hello?" I said.

"I understand you are looking for the violet Kafka," said the voice.

I was rendered speechless for a moment. Then I blurted out, "Who is this?"

"Am I correct?" asked the voice.

"Yes," I said. "The one with the story..."

"'Bright Morning,'" he said. "I know the story. Very rare."

"Supposedly it doesn't exist," I said.

"That's interesting," he said, "because I have a copy of the volume before me as we speak. I'm selling it."

"How much?" I inquired, too eagerly.

"That depends. I have another client also interested in it. I thought perhaps you and he would like to bid for it. The bidding starts at eighty dollars."

"That seems rather low," I said.

"Come tonight," he said, and gave me a set of directions to his place. The location was not too far from me, directly south, in the Pine Barrens. "Eight o'clock, and if you should decide to participate, I will explain more than the price."

"What is your name?" I asked.

He hung up on me.

I was altogether elated that this voice had validated the existence of the story, but at the same time I found the enigmatic nature of the call somewhat disturbing. The starting price was suspiciously low, and the fact that the caller would not give a name didn't bode well. I envisioned myself going to some darkened address and being murdered for my wallet. This alternated with a vision of discovering an abandoned railway station in the woods where the angry Kafka of my dreams would be waiting to bite my neck. At seven o'clock, though, I drove down to the money machine in town, withdrew five hundred dollars (more than I could afford), and then headed south on route 206.

My fears were allayed when, at precisely 7:45, I pulled up in front of a beautifully well-kept Victorian of near-mansion dimensions on a well-lit street in the small town of Pendricksburg. I parked in the long driveway and went to the front door. After knocking twice, a young woman answered and let me in.

"Mr. Deryn will see you. Come this way," she said.

I followed. The place was stunning, the woodwork and floors so highly polished, it was like walking through a hall of mirrors. There were chandeliers and Persian carpets and fresh flowers, like something from one of my wife's magazines. Classical music drifted through the house at low volume, and I felt as though I was touring a museum. We came to a door at the back of the house; she opened it and invited me to step inside.

The first thing I noticed were the bookcases lining the walls, and then I gave a start because sitting behind the desk was what I at first took to be a human frog, smoking a cigar. When I concentrated on the form it resolved its goggle eyes, hunch, and pouch into nothing more than an oddly put together person. But what was even more incredible, it was Bettleman. He was older, with a few days' growth of beard, but it was most definitely him. Not rising, he waved his hand to indicate one of the chairs facing his desk.

"Have a seat," he said.

I walked slowly forward and sat down, experiencing a twinge of déjà vu.

"Bettleman," I said.

He looked quizzically at me, and said, "I'm sorry, you must be mistaken. My name is John Deryn." Then he laughed and the pouch undulated, convincing me even more completely it was him.

"You're not Christian Bettleman?" I asked.

He shook his head and smiled.

I quickly decided that if he wanted to play-act it was fine by me; I was there for the book. "The violet Kafka," I said, "can I see it?"

He reached into a drawer in front of him and pulled out a thick volume. There it was, in seemingly pristine condition. Paging through it with his long graceful fingers, he stopped somewhere in the middle and then turned it around and laid it on the desk facing me. "Bright Morning," he said.

"My God," I said. "I was beginning to think it had merely been a delusion."

"Yes, I know exactly what you mean," he said. "I've spent a good portion of my life tracing the history of that story."

"Is it a forgery?" I asked.

"Nothing of the sort, though, in its style it is slightly unusual for Kafka, somewhat reminiscent of Hoffmann."

"What can you tell me about it?" I asked.

"I will try to keep this brief," he said, drawing on his cigar. His exposition came forth wrapped in a cloud. "In the words of Kafka's Czech translator and one-time girl friend, Milena Jesenska, Kafka 'saw the world as full of invisible demons, who tear apart and destroy defenseless people.' She was not speaking metaphorically. From the now expurgated portions of his diaries, we know that he had a recurring dream of one of these demons, who appeared to him as an old man named Krouch. Of course, knowing Kafka's problems with his father, the idea of it being an 'old man' admittedly has its psychological explanations.

"In 1921, when Franz was in the advanced stages of tuberculosis, he attests to his friend Max Brod, as evidenced in Brod's own journal, that this demon, Krouch, is responsible for his inability to write. He feels that every day that goes by that he does not write a new story, the disease becomes stronger. Being the mystic that he is, Kafka devises a plan to exorcise the demon. What he does is utterly brilliant. He writes a story about the vampiric Krouch, ensnaring him in the words. At the end of the tale, F., the figure who represents Kafka, disappears from the story back to the freedom of this reality. One believes upon reading it that the young writer is, himself, trapped, but not so, or at least not in Kafka's mind. This is all documented in a letter to the writer, Franz Werfel. Hence the non-indicative but promising title of the story, 'Bright Morning.'

"It becomes clear to Kafka soon after that, although he has effectively imprisoned the demon in the words of the story, Krouch still has a limited effect on him when the text is in close proximity. So what does he do? In 1922, at his last meeting with Milena, in a small town known as Gmünd, on the Czech-Austrian border, he gives her all of his diaries. Along with those notebooks and papers is 'Bright Morning.' How effective Kafka's plan was is open to question. He only lived until 1924, but consider the further life of poor Milena, now the owner of the possessed text: she nearly dies in childbirth; has an accident which causes a fracture of her right knee, leaving her partially crippled for the rest of her life; becomes addicted to morphine; is arrested in Prague for her pro-Jewish writing, and is sent, in 1940, to Ravensbrück concentration camp in Germany where she suffers poor health. A kidney is removed when it gets infected, and not too long afterward the other fails and she dies.

"Here, 'Bright Morning' seems to quietly evaporate for some time until 1959 when the Pearfield Publishing Company of Commack, Long Island, New York, publishes an edition of Kafka containing the story. At the time, the building that houses the small publisher catches fire, burns to the ground, and of the few boxes of books salvaged, one contains twelve copies of the violet edition. Six of them went to local libraries, six to the local USO."

"And so, it carries a curse," I said.

"That is for you to decide," he said. "I acquired this copy years ago from a shellfish harvester who worked the waters of the Great South Bay. He might have said something about a curse, but then people who make a living on the water are usually somewhat superstitious. Another might laugh at the idea. I will admit that I have had my own brushes with fate."

"You cannot deny that you are Bettleman," I said.

He stared at me and a moment later the young woman was at the door. "Mr. Deryn," she said, "the other gentleman is here. Shall I show him in?"

"Please do," he told her. When she left to carry out his wish, he turned back to me. "I have chosen to only tell you the story behind the story," said Deryn. "For old time's sake." Then he smiled and with his middle finger pushed his glasses up the bridge of his nose. By now, the cigar was a smoldering stub, and he laid it in the ashtray to extinguish itself.

I was, of course, about to make some inane exclamation, like "I knew it!" or "Did you think I could be so easily fooled?" but the other bidder entered the room and saved Bettleman and myself from the embarrassment.

Not only had I recognized Bettleman, but with one glance, I also knew my competition in the auction. I should have been more startled by the synchronicity of it all, but the events that preceded this fresh twist allowed me to take it in stride. He was another writer, working also in my genre, a big, oafish lout by the name of Jeffrey Ford. You might have heard of him, perhaps not. A few years ago he wrote a book called *The Physiognomy* which, by some bizarre fluke, perhaps the judges were drugged, won a World Fantasy Award. I'd met and spoken to him before on more than one occasion at various conferences. What the critics and editors saw in his work, I'll never know. Our brief careers, so far, had been very similar, but there was no question I was the better writer. He leaned over the desk and shook Bettleman's hand, and then he turned to me and, before sitting, nodded but said nothing.

Bettleman, in his affable Mr. Deryn guise, allowed Ford to inspect the book. Once that was finished, the bidding was to begin. Ford wanted to know why it was to start as low as eighty dollars, and Deryn told him only, "I have my reasons."

I had been slightly put off the book by what I had been told, but once Ford started making offers, I couldn't resist. I felt like if he were to win, he would be walking out of there with my best plot ever. We two cheapskate writers upped the ante at ten dollars an increment, but even at this laggardly pace, we were soon in the three-hundred-dollar range. Bettleman was smiling like Toad of Toad Hall, and when he stopped for a moment to light another cigar, my gaze moved around the room. Off in the corner, behind his desk, wedged into a row of books, I saw a large bell jar, and floating in it, a delicate, beringed hand. For some reason the sight of this horrid curio jogged my memory, and I recalled, perhaps for the first time something that I had wanted to suppress, that the woman who had fallen off the boat back in the bay and was lost those many years ago, was not a woman at all but a young girl, Lela Ritz. For a brief moment, I saw her naked in the moonlight. Then Bettleman croaked and the bidding resumed.

As we pushed onward, nickel-and-diming our way toward my magic number, five hundred dollars, I could not dismiss all of the tragedy left in the wake of "Bright Morning." I thought about Lynn and the kids and how I might be jeopardizing their safety or maybe their lives by this foolish desire. Still my mouth worked, and I let the prices roll off my tongue. By the time I took control of myself and fully awoke to the auction, my counterpart had just proposed four hundred and fifty.

He added, "And I mean it. It is my absolute final offer."

Ford now turned to look at me, and I knew I had him. By a good fifty dollars, I had him.

"Your apple," said Bettleman, looking at me from behind his thick lenses. Now he was no longer smiling, but I saw a look of sadness on his face.

That long second of my decision was like a year scratch raking for hands in the pool of the Colony Inn. The truth was, I didn't know what I wanted. I felt the margins of the story closing in, the sentences wrapping around my wrists and ankles, the dots of i's swimming in schools across my field of vision. Experiencing now the full weight of my weariness, I finally said, "I pass."

"Very well," said Bettleman.

I rose and shook his hand, nodded to Ford, who was already reaching into the pocket of his two-sizes-too-small jeans to retrieve a crumpled wad of money, and left.

Call me a superstitious fool if you like, I might very well deserve the appellation. As it turned out, I never finished the promised story, and the publisher of the collection, Golden Gryphon Press, retracted their offer to do the book. Of all the ironies, they filled my spot on their list with a collection by Ford. He even wrote, especially for it, a story entitled "Bright Morning," making no attempt to disguise his swiping of Kafka's material. One of the early, prepublication critics of the book wrote in a scathing review, "Ford is Kafka's monkey." Nothing could have interested me less. I returned to my teaching job. I spent time with my family. I slept at night with no frightening visits from old or thin demons. In the mornings I woke to the beauty of the sun.

A year later, after retiring from my brief career as a fantasy writer, I read that Ford, two weeks prior to the publication of his collection, had given a reading from his manuscript of "Bright Morning" at one of the conventions (I believe in Massachusetts). According to the article, which appeared in a reputable newspaper, after receiving a modest round of applause from the six or seven people in attendance, he stepped out into the bright morning and quietly evaporated, the pages scattering on the wind like frightened ghosts.

J.P.K.

The conceit of the vanishing story is pure Kafka but the metafictional moves that Ford makes are his own. If the fictional Ford, who has become "Kafka's monkey" steps into the bright morning and evaporates, then perhaps the real Ford has exorcised Kafka's ghost at long last. Or do we ever get over Kafka?

Theodora Goss:

I first read Kafka in high school. I suppose high school is the perfect place to read Kafka for the first time. There are certainly places that make you feel more Kafkaesque, more as though you are caught up in circumstances over which you have no control, than the average American high school. But for most of us, high school is rather like being in one of Kafka's novels. In my high school, we were tracked based on our supposed academic ability, which meant that I spent my day with the same group of students in honors classes, all of us bound for college, none of us with any standing in the school's social hierarchy. We understood "The Metamorphosis." One morning, you wake up as an insect. That made sense.

I'm sure we read more than *Hamlet*, "The Metamorphosis," and *Rosencrantz and Guildenstern Are Dead* in honors English that year, but those are the texts I remember, I suppose because each of them taught me something about the possibilities of literature. When I later read Kafka's short stories, they confirmed what I had taken from him as a teenager: a lesson about the fundamental strangeness of life and the ability of literature, particularly fantastical literature, to express it. Kafka was my first introduction to the notion that there was a literary version of the mass market fantasies that I read for fun, on my own time. A literary version that said something different about life: that sometimes there was no hero, sometimes the world could not be saved. That sometimes the world was scarcely comprehensible.

The summer before my senior year, I went back to Hungary, where I had been born, to visit my grandparents. This was during the communist era, and when I think back to high school, those are the experiences I remember: honors English and my visit. I still remember the men with machine guns at the airport. Which was more Kafkaesque, high school or communist Hungary? I honestly don't know. But I do know that Kafka influenced how I thought about both. That is the mark of a great writer: we begin to see the world through that writer's eyes, that writer's stories. Kafka is one of the writers who taught me how to see. If one morning I wake up as an insect, I won't be surprised.

The Rapid Advance of Sorrow

Theodora Goss

I SIT IN one of the cafés in Szent Endre, writing this letter to you, István, not knowing if I will be alive tomorrow, not knowing if this café will be here, with its circular green chairs and cups of espresso. By the Danube, children are playing, their knees bare below school uniforms. Widows are knitting shapeless sweaters. A cat sleeps beside a geranium in the café window.

If you see her, will you tell me? I still remember how she appeared at the University, just off the train from Debrecen, a country girl with badly cut hair and clothes sewn by her mother. That year, I was smoking French cigarettes and reading forbidden literature. "Have you read D. H. Lawrence?" I asked her. "He is the only modern writer who convincingly expresses the desires of the human body." She blushed and turned away. She probably still had her Young Pioneers badge, hidden among her underwear.

"Ilona is a beautiful name," I said. "It is the most beautiful name in our language." I saw her smile, although she was trying to avoid me. Her face was plump from country sausage and egg bread, and dimples formed at the corners of her mouth, two on each side.

She had dimples on her buttocks, as I found out later. I remember them, like craters on two moons, above the tops of her stockings.

Sorrow: A feeling of grief or melancholy. A mythical city generally located in northern Siberia, said to have been visited by Marco Polo. From Sorrow, he took back to Italy the secret of making ice.

That autumn, intellectual apathy was in fashion. I berated her for reading her textbooks, preparing for her examinations. "Don't you know the grades are predetermined?" I said. "The peasants receive ones, the bourgeoisie receive twos, the aristocrats, if they have been admitted under a special dispensation, always receive threes."

She persisted, telling me that she had discovered art, that she wanted to become cultured.

"You are a peasant," I said, slapping her rump. She looked at me with tears in her eyes.

The principal export of Sorrow is the fur of the arctic fox, which is manufactured into cloaks, hats, the cuffs on gloves and boots. These foxes, which live on the tundra in family groups, are hunted with falcons. The falcons of Sorrow, relatives of the kestrel, are trained to obey a series of commands blown on whistles carved of human bone.

She began going to museums. She spent hours at the Vármuzeum, in the galleries of art. Afterward, she would go to cafés, drink espressos, smoke cigarettes. Her weight dropped, and she became as lean as a wolfhound. She developed a look of perpetual hunger.

When winter came and ice floated on the Danube, I started to worry. Snow had been falling for days, and Budapest was trapped in a white silence. The air was cleaner than it had been for months, because the Trabants could not make it through the snow. It was very cold.

She entered the apartment carrying her textbooks. She was wearing a hat of white fur that I had never seen before. She threw it on the sofa.

"Communism is irrelevant," she said, lighting a cigarette.

"Where have you been?" I asked. "I made a paprikás. I stood in line for two hours to buy the chicken."

"There is to be a new manifesto." Ash dropped on the carpet. "It will not resemble the old manifesto. We are no longer interested in political and economic movements. All movements from now on will be purely aesthetic. Our actions will be beautiful and irrelevant."

"The paprikás has congealed," I said.

She looked at me for the first time since she had entered the apartment and shrugged. "You are not a poet."

The poetry of Sorrow may confuse anyone not accustomed to its intricacies. In Sorrow, poems are constructed on the principle of the maze. Once the reader enters the poem, he must find his way out by observing a series of clues. Readers failing to solve a poem have been known to go mad. Those who can appreciate its beauties say that the poetry of Sorrow is impersonal and ecstatic, and that it invariably speaks of death.

She began bringing home white flowers: crocuses, hyacinths, narcissi. I did not know where she found them, in the city, in winter. I eventually realized they were the emblems of her organization, worn at what passed for rallies, silent meetings where communication occurred with the touch of a hand, a glance from the corner of an eye. Such meetings took place in secret all over the city. Students would sit in the pews of the Mátyás Church, saying nothing, planning insurrection.

At this time we no longer made love. Her skin had grown cold, and when I touched it for too long, my fingers began to ache.

We seldom spoke. Her language had become impossibly complex, referential. I could no longer understand her subtle intricacies.

She painted the word ENTROPY on the wall of the apartment. The wall was white, the paint was white. I saw it only because soot had stained the wall to a dull gray, against which the word appeared like a ghost.

One morning I saw that her hair on the pillow had turned white. I called her name, desperate with panic. She looked at me and I saw that her eyes were the color of milk, like the eyes of the blind.

It is insufficient to point out that the inhabitants of Sorrow are pale. Their skin has a particular translucence, like a layer of nacre. Their nails and hair are iridescent, as though unable to capture and hold light. Their eyes are, at best, disconcerting. Travelers who have stared at them too long have reported hallucinations, like mountaineers who have stared at fields of ice.

I expected tanks. Tanks are required for all sensible invasions. But spring came, and the insurrection did nothing discernible.

Then flowers appeared in the public gardens: crocuses, hyacinths, narcissi, all white. The black branches of the trees began to sprout leaves of a delicate pallor. White pigeons strutted in the public squares, and soon they outnumbered the ordinary gray ones. Shops began to close: first the stores selling Russian electronics, then clothing stores with sweaters from Bulgaria, then pharmacies. Only stores selling food remained open, although the potatoes looked waxen and the pork acquired a peculiar transparency.

I had stopped going to classes. It was depressing, watching a classroom full of students, with their white hair and milky eyes, saying nothing. Many professors joined the insurrection, and they would stand at the front of the lecture hall, the word ENTROPY written on the board behind them, communicating in silent gestures.

She rarely came to the apartment, but once she brought me poppy seed strudel in a paper bag. She said, "Péter, you should eat." She rested her fingertips on the back of my hand. They were like ice. "You have not joined us," she said. "Those who have not joined us will be eliminated."

I caught her by the wrist. "Why?" I asked.

She said, "Beauty demands symmetry, uniformity."

My fingers began to ache with cold. I released her wrist. I could see her veins flowing through them, like strands of aquamarine.

Sorrow is ruled by the absolute will of its Empress, who is chosen for her position at the age of three and reigns until the age of thirteen. The Empress is chosen by the Brotherhood of the Cowl, a quasi-religious sect whose members hide their faces under hoods of white wool to maintain their anonymity. By tradition, the Empress never speaks in public. She delivers her commands in private audiences with the Brotherhood. The consistency of these commands, from one Empress to another, has been taken to prove the sanctity of the Imperial line. After their reigns, all Empresses retire to the Abbey of St. Alba, where they live in seclusion for the remainder of their lives, studying astronomy, mathematics, and the seven-stringed zither. During the history of Sorrow, remarkable observations, theorems, and musical arrangements have emerged from this Abbey.

No tanks came, but one day, when the sun shone with a vague luminescence through the clouds that perpetually covered the city, the Empress of Sorrow rode along Váci Street on a white elephant. She was surrounded by courtiers, some in cloaks of white fox, some in jesters' uniforms sewn from white patches, some, principally unmarried women, in transparent gauze through which one could see their hairless flesh. The eyes of the elephant were outlined with henna, its feet were stained with henna. In its trunk it carried a silver bell, whose ringing was the only sound as the procession made its way to the Danube and across Erzsébet Bridge.

Crowds of people had come to greet the Empress: students waving white crocuses and hyacinths and narcissi, mothers holding the hands of children who failed to clap when the elephant strode by, nuns in ashen gray. Cowled figures moved among the crowd. I watched one standing ahead of me and recognized the set of her shoulders, narrower than they had been, still slightly crooked.

I sidled up to her and whispered, "Ilona."

She turned. The cowl was drawn down and I could not see her face, but her mouth was visible, too thin now for dimples.

"Péter," she said, in a voice like snow falling. "We have done what is necessary."

She touched my cheek with her fingers. A shudder went through me, as though I had been touched by something electric.

Travellers have attempted to characterize the city of Sorrow. Some have said it is a place of confusion, with impossible pinnacles rising to stars that cannot be seen from any observatory. Some have called it a place of beauty, where the winds, playing through the high buildings, produce a celestial music. Some have called it a place of death, and have said that the city, examined from above, exhibits the contours of a skull.

Some have said that the city of Sorrow does not exist. Some have insisted that it exists everywhere: that we are perpetually surrounded by its streets, which are covered by a thin layer of ice; by its gardens, in which albino peacocks wander; by its inhabitants, who pass us without attention or interest.

I believe neither of these theories. I believe that Sorrow is an insurrection waged by a small cabal, with its signs and secrets; that it is run on purely aesthetic principles; that its goal is entropy, a perpetual stillness of the soul. But I could be mistaken. My conclusions could be tainted by the confusion that spreads with the rapid advance of Sorrow.

So I have left Budapest, carrying only the mark of three fingertips on my left cheek. I sit here every morning, in a café in Szent Endre, not knowing how long I have to live, not knowing how long I can remain here, on a circular green chair drinking espresso.

Soon, the knees of the children will become as smooth and fragile as glass. The widows' knitting needles will click like bone, and geranium leaves will fall beside the blanched cat. The coffee will fade to the color of milk. I do not know what will happen to the chair. I do not know if I will be eliminated, or given another chance to join the faction of silence. But I am sending you this letter, István, so you can remember me when the snows come.

J.P.K.

The nature of Sorrow is unclear and its powers mysterious, yet the narrator attests to its power to change reality. In a Kafka story, the rapid advance of Sorrow would have overtaken and overwhelmed the narrator in the end; here he has fled but his escape would seem to be temporary.

Eileen Gunn:

I didn't set out to write a story that referenced "The Metamorphosis." I had been reading David Attenborough's *Life on Earth: A Natural History*, and I was very taken with the evocative, if excessively anthropomorphic, language of the book. There was a passage about insect exoskeletons that particularly spoke to me:

> Many limbs carry special tools moulded from the chitin—pouches for holding pollen, combs for cleaning a compound eye, spikes to act as grappling irons, and notches with which to fiddle a song.

This is a pretty artful sentence from a scientist, even if you dismiss the religious implication of "moulded." It almost pleads with the reader to toss science aside and to think about insects as one might see them in a children's book, in little hobbit-houses, taking a pinch from the pollen pouch, combing their compound eyelashes, and then jigging about to "Turkey in the Straw."

The first scene derived from that: I imagined waking up in the morning with a chitinous comb in my hand, and the rest of the scene followed rather naturally. I tossed my red-and-white quilt into the story, and my partner John. And then, having written the first part, I had no idea what should come next. This happens frequently, so I asked myself, as I often do, what the story was about.

My subconscious answered immediately: "It's about working at Microsoft." Since I had only recently left my job at that company—in order to have time to write—it was natural enough that I'd address the issues I have with corporate hierarchies and conformity, not to mention carved vegetables, and express my love for earrings shaped like little blue airplanes.

When I finished the story, I was dissatisfied with its then ending, in which Margaret quit her job. I was chatting with a friend, the horror writer Jessica Amanda Salmonson, and I mentioned my frustration to her, and described the story.

Jessica sniffed. "I bet Kafka did it better," she said. Jessica pulls no punches.

I was horrified. I hadn't even thought of Kafka. Of course Kafka did it better. I'd written this whole story, which had taken me at least a year, and all I'd done was rewrite "The Metamorphosis."

I must have looked totally stricken, because Jessica offered to read the story and help me out with the ending. I gave her the story, and she sat in my living room and read it. When she finished, she looked up at me and glared.

"This is *nothing* like Kafka!" she complained.

I was relieved. Whatever else was wrong with the story, at least it was nothing like Kafka.

Stable Strategies for Middle Management

Eileen Gunn

Our friend the insect has an external skeleton made of shiny brown chitin, a material that is particularly responsive to the demands of evolution. Just as bioengineering has sculpted our bodies into new forms, so evolution has changed the early insect's chewing mouthparts into her descendants' chisels, siphons, and stilettos, and has molded from the chitin special tools—pockets to carry pollen, combs to clean her compound eyes, notches on which she might fiddle a song.

—From the popular science program *Insect People!*

I AWOKE THIS morning to discover that bioengineering had made demands upon me during the night. My tongue had turned into a stiletto, and my left hand now contained a small chitinous comb, as if for cleaning a compound eye. Since I didn't have compound eyes, I thought that perhaps this presaged some change to come.

I dragged myself out of bed, wondering how I was going to drink my coffee through a stiletto. Was I now expected to kill my breakfast, and dispense with coffee entirely? I hoped I was not evolving into a creature whose survival depended on early-morning alertness. My circadian rhythms would no doubt keep pace with any physical changes, but my unevolved soul was repulsed at the thought of my waking cheerfully at dawn, ravenous for some wriggly little creature that had arisen even earlier.

I looked down at Greg, still asleep, the edge of our red and white quilt pulled up under his chin. His mouth had changed during the night too, and seemed to contain some sort of a long probe. Were we growing apart?

I reached down with my unchanged hand and touched his hair. It was still shiny brown, soft and thick, luxurious. But along his cheek, under his beard, I could feel patches of sclerotin, as the flexible chitin in his skin was slowly hardening to an impermeable armor.

He opened his eyes, staring blearily forward without moving his head. I could see him move his mouth cautiously, examining its internal changes. He turned his head and looked up at me, rubbing his hair slightly into my hand.

"Time to get up?" he asked. I nodded. "Oh God," he said. He said this every morning. It was like a prayer.

"I'll make coffee," I said. "Do you want some?"

He shook his head slowly. "Just a glass of apricot nectar," he said. He unrolled his long, rough tongue and looked at it, slightly cross-eyed. "This is real interesting, but it wasn't in the catalog. I'll be sipping lunch from flowers pretty soon. That ought to draw a second glance at Duke's."

"I thought account execs were expected to sip their lunches," I said.

"Not from the flower arrangements...." he said, still exploring the odd shape of his mouth. Then he looked up at me and reached up from under the covers. "Come here."

He smelled terribly attractive. Perhaps he was developing aphrodisiac scent glands. I climbed back under the covers and stretched my body against his. "How am I supposed to kiss you with a stiletto in my mouth?"

"There are other things to do. New equipment presents new possibilities." He pushed the covers back and ran his unchanged hands down my body from shoulder to thigh. "Let me know if my tongue is too rough."

It was not.

Fuzzy-minded, I got out of bed for the second time and drifted into the kitchen.

Measuring the coffee into the grinder, I realized that I was no longer interested in drinking it, although it was diverting for a moment to spear the beans with my stiletto. What was the damn thing for, anyhow? I wasn't sure I wanted to find out.

Putting the grinder aside, I poured a can of apricot nectar into a tulip glass. Shallow glasses were going to be a problem for Greg in the future, I thought. Not to mention solid food.

My particular problem, however, if I could figure out what I was supposed to eat for breakfast, was getting to the office in time for my 10 a.m. meeting. Maybe I'd just skip breakfast. I dressed quickly and dashed out the door before Greg was even out of bed.

Thirty minutes later, I was more or less awake and sitting in the small conference room with the new marketing manager, listening to him lay out his plan for the Model 2000 launch.

In signing up for his bioengineering program, Harry had chosen specialized primate adaptation, B-E Option No. 4. He had evolved into a textbook example: small and long-limbed, with forward-facing eyes for judging distances and long, grasping fingers to keep him from falling out of his tree.

He was dressed for success in a pin-striped three-piece suit that fit his simian proportions perfectly. I wondered what premium he paid for custom-made. Or did he patronize a ready-to-wear shop that catered especially to primates?

I listened as he leaped agilely from one ridiculous marketing premise to the next. Trying to borrow credibility from mathematics and engineering, he used wildly metaphoric bizspeak, "factoring in the need for pipeline throughput," "fine-tuning the media mix," without even cracking a smile.

I didn't like Harry much, but I envied him his ability to root through his subconscious and toss out one half-formed idea after another. I know he felt it reflected badly on me that I didn't join in and spew forth a random selection of promotional suggestions.

I didn't think much of his marketing plan, either. The advertising section was a textbook application of theory with no practical basis. I had two options: I could force him to accept a solution that would work, or I could yes him to death, making sure everybody understood it was his idea. I knew which path I'd take.

"Yeah, we can do that for you," I told him. "No problem." We'd see which of us would survive and which was hurtling to an evolutionary dead end.

Although Harry had won his point, he continued to talk. My attention wandered—I'd heard it all before. His voice was the hum of an air conditioner, a familiar, easily ignored background noise. I drowsed and new emotions stirred in me, yearnings to float through warm, moist air currents, to land on warm, bright surfaces, to engorge myself with warm, wet food.

Adrift in insect dreams, I became sharply aware of the bare skin of Harry's arm, between his gold-plated watchband and his rolled-up sleeve, as he manipulated papers on the conference room table. He smelled delicious, like a pepperoni pizza or a charcoal-broiled hamburger. I realized he probably wouldn't taste as good as he smelled. But I was hungry. My stiletto-like tongue was there for a purpose, and it wasn't to skewer cubes of tofu. I leaned over his arm and braced myself against the back of his hand, probing with my stylets to find a capillary.

Harry noticed what I was doing and swatted me sharply on the side of the head. I pulled away before he could hit me again.

"We were discussing the Model 2000 launch. Or have you forgotten?" he said, rubbing his arm.

"Sorry. I skipped breakfast this morning." I was embarrassed.

"Well, get your hormones adjusted, for chrissake." He was annoyed, and I couldn't really blame him. "Let's get back to the media allocation issue, if you can keep your mind on it. I've got another meeting at eleven in Building Two."

Inappropriate feeding behavior was not unusual in the company, and corporate etiquette sometimes allowed minor lapses to pass without pursuit. Of course, I could no longer hope that he would support me on moving some money out of the direct-mail budget....

During the remainder of the meeting, my glance kept drifting through the open door of the conference room, toward a large decorative plant in the hall, one of those oases of generic greenery that dot the corporate landscape. It didn't look succulent exactly—it obviously wasn't what I would have preferred to eat if I hadn't been so hungry—but I wondered if I swung both ways?

I grabbed a handful of the broad leaves as I left the room and carried them back to my office. With my tongue, I probed a vein in the thickest part of a leaf. It wasn't so bad. Tasted green. I sucked them dry and tossed the husks in the wastebasket.

I was still omnivorous, at least—female mosquitoes don't eat plants. So the process wasn't complete....

I got a cup of coffee, for company, from the kitchenette and sat in my office with the door closed and wondered what was happening to me. Was I turning into a mosquito? If so, what the hell kind of good was that supposed to do me? The company didn't want a whining loner, a bloodsucker.

There was a knock at the door, and my boss stuck his head in. I nodded and gestured him into my office. He sat down in the visitor's chair on the other side of my desk. From the look on his face, I could tell Harry had talked to him already.

Tom Samson was an older guy, pre-bioengineering. He was well versed in stimulus-response techniques, but had somehow never made it to the top job. I liked him, but then that was what he intended. Without sacrificing authority, he had pitched his appearance, his gestures, the tone of his voice, to the warm end of the spectrum. Even though I knew what he was doing, it worked.

He looked at me with what appeared to be sympathy, but was actually a practiced sign stimulus, intended to defuse any fight-or-flight response. "Is there something bothering you, Margaret?"

"Bothering me? I was hungry, that's all. I'm always short-tempered when I'm hungry." I found it difficult, but I made my mind go bland and forced myself to meet his eyes. A shifty gaze is a guilty gaze.

His expression changed to a more honest impatience. I stuck my tongue in my coffee and pretended to drink. It smelled burnt.

"Plus I'm just not human until I've had my coffee in the morning." My laugh sounded phony, even to me. Tom was obviously waiting for me to shut up.

"That's what I wanted to talk to you about, Margaret." He sat there, hunched over in a relaxed way, like a mountain gorilla, unthreatened by natural enemies. "I just talked to Harry Winthrop, and he said you were trying to suck his blood during a meeting on marketing strategy." He paused for a moment to check my reaction, but the neutral expression was fixed on my face and I said nothing. His face changed to project disappointment. "You know, when we noticed you were developing three distinct body segments, we had great hopes for you. But your actions just don't reflect the social and organizational development we expected."

He paused, and it was my turn to say something in my defense. "Most insects are solitary, you know. Perhaps the company erred in hoping for a termite or an ant. I'm not responsible for that."

"Now, Margaret," he said, his voice simulating genial reprimand. "This isn't the jungle, you know. When you signed those consent forms, you agreed to let the B-E staff mold you into a more useful corporate organism. But this isn't nature, this is man reshaping nature. It doesn't follow the old rules. You can truly be anything you want to be. But you have to cooperate."

"I'm doing the best I can," I said, cooperatively. "I'm putting in eighty hours a week."

"Margaret, the quality of your work is not an issue. It's your interactions with others that you have to work on. You have to learn to work as part of the group. I just cannot permit such backbiting to continue. I'll have Arthur get you an appointment this afternoon with the B-E counselor." Arthur was his secretary. He knew everything that happened in the department and mostly kept his mouth shut.

"I'd be a social insect if I could manage it," I muttered as Tom left my office. "But I've never known what to say to people in bars."

For lunch I met Greg and our friend David Detlor at a health-food restaurant that advertises fifty different kinds of fruit nectar. We'd never eaten there before, but Greg knew he'd love the place. It was already a favorite of David's, and he still has all his teeth, so I figured it would be OK with me.

David was there when I arrived, but not Greg. David works for the company too, in a different department. He, however, has proved remarkably resistant to corporate blandishment. Not only has he never undertaken B-E, he hasn't even bought a three-piece suit. Today he was wearing chewed-up blue jeans and a flashy Hawaiian shirt, of a type that was cool about ten years ago.

"Your boss lets you dress like that?" I asked.

"We have this agreement. I don't tell her she has to give me a job, and she doesn't tell me what to wear."

David's perspective on life is very different from mine. I don't think the difference between us is just that he's in R&D and I'm in Advertising—it's basic world-view. Where he sees the world as a bunch of really neat but optional puzzles put there for his enjoyment, I see it as...well, as a series of SATs.

"So what's new with you guys?" he asked, while we stood around waiting for a table.

"Greg's turning into a goddamn butterfly. He went out last week and bought a dozen Italian silk sweaters. It's not a corporate look."

"He's not a corporate *guy*, Margaret."

"Then why is he having all this B-E done if he's not even going to use it?"

"He's dressing up a little. He just wants to look nice. Like Michael Jackson, you know?"

I couldn't tell whether David was kidding me or not. Then he started telling me about his music, this barbershop quartet that he's involved in. He said his group was going to dress in black leather for the next show and sing Shel Silverstein's "Come to Me, My Masochistic Baby."

"It'll knock them on their tails," he said gleefully. "We've already got a great arrangement."

"Do you think it will win, David?" It seemed too weird to please the judges in that sort of a show.

Then Greg showed up. He was wearing a cobalt blue silk sweater with a copper green design on it. Italian. He was also wearing a pair of dangly earrings shaped like bright blue airplanes. We were shown to a table near a display of carved vegetables.

"This is great," said David. "Everybody wants to sit near the vegetables. It's where you sit to be *seen* in this place." He nodded to Greg. "I think it's your sweater."

"It's the butterfly in my personality," said Greg. "Restaurants never used to do stuff like this for me. I always got the table next to the espresso machine."

If Greg was going to go on about the joys of being a butterfly, I was going to change the subject.

"David, how come you still haven't signed up for B-E?" I asked. "The company pays half the cost, and they don't ask questions."

David screwed up his mouth, raised his hands to his face, and made small, twitching, insect gestures, as if grooming his nose and eyes. "I'm doing OK the way I am."

Greg chuckled at this, but I was serious. "You'll get ahead faster with a little adjustment, plus you're showing a good attitude, you know, if you do it."

"I'm getting ahead faster than I want to right now—it looks like I won't be able to take the three months off that I wanted this summer."

"Three months?" I was astonished. "Aren't you afraid you won't have a job to come back to?"

"I could live with that," said David calmly, opening his menu.

The waiter took our orders. We sat for a moment in a companionable silence, the self-congratulation that follows ordering high-fiber foodstuffs. Then I told them the story of my encounter with Harry Winthrop.

"There's something wrong with me," I said. "Why suck his blood? What good is that supposed to do me?"

"Well," said David, "you chose this schedule of treatments. You're in control of this. Where did you want it to go?"

"According to the catalog," I said, "the No. 2 Insect Option is supposed to make me into a successful competitor for a middle-management niche, with triggerable responses that can be useful in gaining entry to upper hierarchical levels. Unquote." Of course, that was just ad talk—I didn't really expect it to do all that. "That's what I want. I want to be in charge. I want to be the boss."

"Maybe you should go back to BioEngineering and try again," said Greg. "Sometimes the hormones don't do what you expect. Look at my tongue, for instance." He unfurled it gently and rolled it back into his mouth. "Though I'm sort of getting to like it." He sucked at his drink, making disgusting slurping sounds. He didn't need a straw.

"Don't bother with it, Margaret," said David quietly, taking his rosehip tea from the waiter. "Bioengineering is a waste of time and money and millions of years of evolution. If human beings were intended to be managers, we'd have evolved pin-striped body covering."

Kafkaesque

"That's cleverly put," I said, "but it's dead wrong."

The waiter brought our lunches, and we stopped talking as he put them in front of us. It seemed like the anticipatory silence of three very hungry people, but was in fact the polite silence of three people who have been brought up not to argue in front of disinterested bystanders. As soon as he left, we resumed the discussion.

"I mean it," David said. "The dubious survival benefits of management aside, bioengineering is a waste of effort. Harry Winthrop, for instance, doesn't really need B-E at all. Here he is, fresh out of business school, audibly buzzing with lust for a high-level management position. Basically he's just marking time until a presidency opens up somewhere. And what gives him the edge over you is his youth and inexperience, not some specialized primate adaptation."

"Well," I said with some asperity, "he's not constrained by a knowledge of what's failed in the past, that's for sure. But saying that doesn't solve my problem, David. Harry's signed up. I've signed up. The changes are under way and I don't have any choice."

I squeezed a huge glob of honey into my tea from a plastic bottle shaped like a teddy bear. I took a sip of the tea; it was minty and very sweet. "And now I'm turning into the wrong kind of insect. It's ruined my ability to deal with Product Marketing."

"Oh, give it a rest!" said Greg suddenly. "This is *so* boring. I don't want to hear any more talk about corporate hugger-mugger. Let's talk about something that's fun."

I had had enough of Greg's lepidopterate lack of concentration. "Something that's *fun?* I've invested all my time and most of my genetic material in this job. This is all the goddamn fun there is."

The honeyed tea made me feel hot. My stomach itched—I wondered if I was having an allergic reaction. I scratched, and not discreetly. My hand came out from under my shirt full of little waxy scales. What the hell was going on under there? I tasted one of the scales; it was wax all right. Worker bee changes? I couldn't help myself—I stuffed the wax into my mouth.

David was busying himself with his alfalfa sprouts, but Greg looked disgusted. "That's gross, Margaret." Greg made a face, sticking his tongue part way out. Talk about gross. "Can't you wait until after lunch?"

I was doing what came naturally, and did not dignify his statement with a response. There was a side dish of bee pollen on the table. I took a spoonful and mixed it with the wax, chewing noisily. I'd had a rough morning, and this constant bickering with Greg wasn't making the day more pleasant.

Besides, neither he nor David had any respect for my position in the company. Greg doesn't take my job seriously at all. And David simply does what he wants to do, regardless of whether it makes any money, for himself or anyone else. He was giving me a back-to-nature lecture, and it was far too late for that.

This whole lunch was a waste of time. I was tired of listening to them, and felt an intense urge to get back to work. A couple of quick stings distracted them both: I had the advantage of surprise. I ate some more honey and quickly waxed them over. They were soon hibernating side by side in two large octagonal cells.

I looked around the restaurant. People were rather nervously pretending not to have noticed. I called the waiter over and handed him my credit card. He signaled to several bus boys, who brought a covered cart and took Greg and David away. "They'll eat themselves out of that by Thursday afternoon," I told him. "Store them on their sides in a warm, dry place, away from direct heat." I left a large tip.

I walked back to the office, feeling a bit ashamed of myself. A couple days of hibernation weren't going to make Greg or David more sympathetic to my problems. And they'd be real mad when they got out.

I didn't used to do things like that. I used to be more patient, didn't I? More appreciative of the diverse spectrum of human possibility. More interested in sex and television.

This job was not doing much for me as a warm, personable human being. At the very least, it was turning me into an unpleasant lunch companion. Whatever had made me think I wanted to get into management anyway?

The money, maybe.

But that wasn't all. It was the challenges, the chance to do something new, to control the total effort, instead of just doing part of a project....

The money too, though. There were other ways to get money. Maybe I should just kick the supports out from under the damned job and start over again.

I saw myself sauntering into Tom's office, twirling his visitor's chair around and falling into it. The words "I quit" would force their way out, almost against my will. His face would show surprise—feigned, of course. By then I'd have to go through with it. Maybe I'd put my feet up on his desk. And then—

But was it possible to just quit, to go back to being the person I used to be? No, I wouldn't be able to do it. I'd never be a management virgin again.

I walked up to the employee entrance at the rear of the building. A suction device next to the door sniffed at me, recognized my scent, and clicked the door open. Inside, a group of new employees, trainees, were clustered near the door, while a personnel officer introduced them to the lock and let it familiarize itself with their hormones.

On the way down the hall, I passed Tom's office. The door was open. He was at his desk, bowed over some papers, and looked up as I went by.

"Ah, Margaret," he said. "Just the person I want to talk to. Come in for a minute, would you." He moved a large file folder onto the papers in front of him on his desk, and folded his hands on top of them. "So glad you were passing by." He nodded toward a large, comfortable chair. "Sit down."

"We're going to be doing a bit of restructuring in the department," he began, "and I'll need your input, so I want to fill you in now on what will be happening."

I was immediately suspicious. Whenever Tom said, "I'll need your input," he meant everything was decided already.

"We'll be reorganizing the whole division, of course," he continued, drawing little boxes on a blank piece of paper. He'd mentioned this at the department meeting last week.

"Your area subdivides functionally into two separate areas, wouldn't you say?"

"Well—"

"Yes," he said thoughtfully, nodding his head as though in agreement. "That would be the way to do it." He added a few lines and a few more boxes. From what I could see, it meant that Harry would do all the interesting stuff, and I'd sweep up afterwards.

"Looks to me as if you've cut the balls out of my area and put them over into Harry Winthrop's."

"Ah, but your area is still very important, my dear. That's why I don't have you actually reporting to Harry." He gave me a smile like a lie.

He had put me in a tidy little bind. After all, he was my boss. If he was going to take most of my area away from me, as it seemed he was, there wasn't much I could do to stop him. And I would be better off if we both pretended that I hadn't experienced any loss of status. That way I kept my title and my salary.

"Oh, I see," I said. "Right."

It dawned on me that this whole thing had been decided already, and that Harry Winthrop probably knew all about it. He'd probably even wangled a raise out of it. Tom had called me in here to make it look casual, to make it look as though I had something to say about it. I'd been set up.

This made me mad. There was no question of quitting now. I'd stick around and fight. My eyes blurred, unfocussed, refocussed again. Compound eyes! The promise of the small comb in my hand was fulfilled! I felt a deep chemical understanding of the ecological system I was now a part of. I knew where I fit in. And I knew what I was going to do. It was inevitable now, hardwired in at the DNA level.

The strength of this conviction triggered another change in the chitin, and for the first time I could actually feel the rearrangement of my mouth and nose, a numb tickling like inhaling seltzer water. The stiletto receded and mandibles jutted forth, rather like Katherine Hepburn. This time, form and function achieved an orgasmic synchronicity. As my jaw pushed forward, mantis-like, it also opened, and I pounced on Tom and bit his head off.

He leaped from his desk and danced headless about the office.

I felt in complete control of myself as I watched him and continued the conversation. "About the Model 2000 launch," I said. "If we factor in the demand for pipeline throughput and adjust the media mix just a bit, I think we can present a very tasty little package to Product Marketing by the end of the week."

Tom continued to strut spasmodically, making vulgar copulative motions. Was I responsible for evoking these mantid reactions? I was unaware of a sexual component in our relationship.

I got up from the visitor's chair and sat behind his desk, thinking about what had just happened. It goes without saying that I was surprised at my own actions. I mean, irritable is one thing, but biting people's heads off is quite another. But I have to admit that my second thought was, well, this certainly is a useful strategy, and should make a considerable difference in my ability to advance myself. Hell of a lot more useful than sucking people's blood.

Maybe there was something after all to Tom's talk about having the proper attitude.

And, of course, thinking of Tom, my third reaction was regret. He really had been a likeable guy, for the most part. But what's done is done, you know, and there's no use chewing on it after the fact.

I buzzed his assistant on the intercom. "Arthur," I said, "Mr. Samson and I have come to an evolutionary parting of the ways. Please have him re-engineered. And charge it to Personnel."

Now I feel an odd itching on my forearms and thighs. Notches on which I might fiddle a song?

J.P.K.

While this story diverges from "The Metamorphosis" most notably in its science fictional scaffolding and its triumphant protagonist, it shares a ruthless logic of Kafka's best work. And since Kafka was himself well-regarded in his chosen bureaucracy, he would certainly have gotten all the jokes.

J.K.

Gunn's insect-humans and their bureaucratic infighting, despite bioengineering, are no more credible than the mysteriously transformed Gregor Samsa. But Gunn's story reminds us that Gregor's first worry when he wakes to find himself changed in his bed into a gigantic insect is that he will be late for work.

DAMON KNIGHT:

This one presented itself to me as a vision, and all I could do was surround it with a suitable progression of events. Other people have explained it, but to me "The Handler" is just what it is.

—afterword to "The Handler" from *The Best of Damon Knight*

The Handler

Damon Knight

WHEN THE BIG man came in, there was a movement in the room like bird dogs pointing. The piano player quit pounding, the two singing drunks shut up, all the beautiful people with cocktails in their hands stopped talking and laughing.

"Pete!" the nearest woman shrilled, and he walked straight into the room, arms around two girls, hugging them tight. "How's my sweetheart? Susy, you look good enough to eat, but I had it for lunch. George, you pirate—" he let go both girls, grabbed a bald blushing little man and thumped him on the arm—"you were great, sweetheart, I mean it, really great. Now HEAR THIS!" he shouted, over all the voices that were clamoring Pete this, Pete that.

Somebody put a martini in his hand and he stood holding it, bronzed and tall in his dinner jacket, teeth gleaming white as his shirt cuffs. "We had a show!" he told them.

A shriek of agreement went up, a babble of did we have a *show* my God Pete listen a *show*—

He held up his hand. "It was a good show!"

Another shriek and babble.

"The sponsor kinda liked it—he just signed for another one in the fall!"

A shriek, a roar, people clapping, jumping up and down. The big man tried to say something else, but gave up, grinning, while men and women crowded up to him. They were all trying to shake his hand, talk in his ear, put their arms around him.

"I love ya *all!*" he shouted. "Now what do you say, let's live a little!"

The murmuring started again as people sorted themselves out. There was a clinking from the bar. "Jesus, Pete," a skinny pop-eyed little guy was saying, crouching in adoration, "when you dropped that fishbowl I thought I'd pee myself, honest to God—"

The big man let out a bark of happy laughter. "Yeah, I can still see the look on your face. And the fish, flopping all over the stage. So what can I do, I get down there on my knees—" the big man did so, bending over and staring at imaginary fish on the floor. "And I say, 'Well, fellows, back to the drawing board!'"

Screams of laughter as the big man stood up. The party was arranging itself around him in arcs of concentric circles, with people in the back standing on sofas and the piano bench so they could see. Somebody yelled, "Sing the goldfish song, Pete!"

Shouts of approval, please-do-Pete, the goldfish song.

"Okay, okay." Grinning, the big man sat on the arm of a chair and raised his glass. "And a vun, and a doo—vere's de moosic?" A scuffle at the piano bench. Somebody banged out a few chords. The big man made a comic face and sang, "Ohhh—how I wish…I was a little fish… and when I want some quail…I'd flap my little tail."

Laughter, the girls laughing louder than anybody and their red mouths farther open. One flushed blonde had her hand on the big man's knee, and another was sitting close behind him.

"But seriously—" the big man shouted. More laughter.

"No seriously," he said in a vibrant voice as the room quieted, "I want to tell you in all seriousness I couldn't have done it alone. And incidentally I see we have some foreigners, litvaks and other members of the press here tonight, so I want to introduce all the important people. First of all, George here, the three-fingered band leader—and there isn't a guy in the world could have done what he did this afternoon—

George, I love ya." He hugged the blushing little bald man.

"Next my real sweetheart, Ruthie, where are ya? Honey, you were the greatest, really perfect—I mean it, baby—" He kissed a dark girl in a red dress who cried a little and hid her face on his broad shoulder. "And Frank—" he reached down and grabbed the skinny pop-eyed guy by the sleeve. "What can I tell you? A sweetheart?" The skinny guy was blinking, all choked up; the big man thumped him on the back. "Sol and Ernie and Mack, my writers, Shakespeare should have been so lucky—" One by one, they came up to shake the big man's hand as he called their names; the women kissed him and cried. "My stand-in," the big man was calling out, and "my caddy," and "Now," he said, as the room quieted a little, people flushed and sore-throated with enthusiasm, "I want you to meet my handler."

The room fell silent. The big man looked thoughtful and startled, as if he had had a sudden pain. Then he stopped moving. He sat without breathing or blinking his eyes. After a moment there was a jerky motion behind him. The girl who was sitting on the arm of the chair got up and moved away. The big man's dinner jacket split open in the back, and a little man climbed out. He had a perspiring brown face under a shock of black hair. He was a very small man, almost a dwarf, stoop-shouldered and round-backed in a sweaty brown singlet and shorts. He climbed out of the cavity in the big man's body, and closed the dinner jacket carefully. The big man sat motionless and his face was doughy.

The little man got down, wetting his lips nervously. Hello, Harry, a few people said. "Hello," Harry called, waving his hand. He was about forty, with a big nose and big soft brown eyes. His voice was cracked and uncertain. "Well, we sure put on a show, didn't we?"

Sure did, Harry, they said politely. He wiped his brow with the back of his hand. "Hot in there," he explained, with an apologetic grin. Yes I guess it must be, Harry, they said. People around the outskirts of the crowd were beginning to turn away, form conversational groups; the hum of talk rose higher. "Say, Tim, I wonder if I could have something to drink," the little man said. "I don't like to leave him—you know—" He gestured toward the silent big man.

"Sure, Harry, what'll it be?"

"Oh—you know—a glass of beer?"

Tim brought him a beer in a pilsener glass and he drank it thirstily, his brown eyes darting nervously from side to side. A lot of people were sitting down now; one or two were at the door leaving.

"Well," the little man said to a passing girl, "Ruthie, that was quite a moment there, when the fishbowl busted, wasn't it?"

"Huh? Excuse me, honey, I didn't hear you." She bent nearer.

"Oh—well, it don't matter. Nothing."

She patted him on the shoulder once, and took her hand away. "Well excuse me, sweetie, I have to catch Robbins before he leaves." She went on toward the door.

The little man put his beer glass down and sat, twisting his knobby hands together. The bald man and the pop-eyed man were the only ones still sitting near him. An anxious smile flickered on his lips; he glanced at one face, then another. "Well," he began, "that's one show under our belts, huh, fellows, but I guess we got to start, you know, thinking about—"

"Listen, Harry," said the bald man seriously, leaning forward to touch him on the wrist, "why don't you get back inside?"

The little man looked at him for a moment with sad hound-dog eyes, then ducked his head, embarrassed. He stood up uncertainly, swallowed and said, "Well—" He climbed up on the chair behind the big man, opened the back of the dinner jacket and put his legs in one at a time. A few people were watching him, unsmiling. "Thought I'd take it easy awhile," he said weakly, "but I guess—" He reached in and gripped something with both hands, then swung himself inside. His brown, uncertain face disappeared.

The big man blinked suddenly and stood up. "Well *hey* there," he called, "what's a matter with this party anyway? Let's see some life, some action—" Faces were lighting up around him. People began to move in closer. "What I mean, let me hear that beat!"

The big man began clapping his hands rhythmically. The piano took it up. Other people began to clap. "What I mean, are we alive here or just waiting for the wagon to pick us up? How's that again, can't hear you!" A roar of pleasure as he cupped his hand to his ear. "Well come on, let me hear it!" A louder roar. Pete, Pete; a gabble of voices. "I got nothing against Harry," said the bald man earnestly in the middle of the noise, "I mean for a square he's a nice guy." "Know what you mean," said the pop-eyed man, "I mean like he doesn't *mean* it." "Sure," said the bald man, "but Jesus that sweaty undershirt and all…" The pop-eyed man shrugged. "What are you gonna do?" Then they both burst out laughing as the big man made a comic face, tongue lolling, eyes crossed. Pete, Pete, Pete; the room was really jumping; it was a great party, and everything was all right, far into the night.

J.K.

Knight never spoke of any connection between this story and Kafka's work, and I am not suggesting any direct connection. However, the completely offhand way the fantastic intrudes into this story, and the psychological overtones, the comedy, the way the story can be seen as arising out of the literalizing of a metaphor, all strike me as Kafkaesque.

J.P.K.

Knight makes use of the cinematic POV to help achieve the Kafka effect. Without access to the inner lives of the characters, all we can observe is the mysterious surface of this doppelgänger story, in which the metaphor is made literal.

JONATHAN LETHEM:

Carter and I, having conceived a collaboration (between us) on the premise of a collaboration between Kafka and Capra, became enslaved by a recursiveness that itself both generated the story and made constant mockery of our efforts, akin to two men standing in a bright light with pencils attempting to trace on a nearby white-painted wall the outline of one another's shadows. We fell into roles, likely inevitable by disposition, and then reinforced by the division of research assignments: I read studies of Capra and watched all the films, and so became the purveyor of details of Hollywood humiliation of émigré talent and a kind of rictus-grim sunniness; Carter delved into Kafka biographies and drew us ever deeper into finicky epistolary gloom and the Jewish Problem.

Two became one, however, in that intersection where the profoundest (the only profound) response to Capra's movies is to excavate their paranoid underside, while the Kafka devotee inevitably brandishes his not-so-secret vaudeville aspect. The two artists really were speaking to one another, at least when Carter or I lurched back into activity.

Time passed. Mistakes were made. At one point we found ourselves preempted by a short film that had been released, called *Franz Kafka's It's a Wonderful Life*, which threatened to do in five minutes what we'd begun as a willing agony of hours. The film was announced as a short program before a feature, playing, incredibly enough, at a theater near us. We went and paid for admissions on a weekday afternoon and found ourselves the only bodies in an entire theater. After the short—which was terrific, but still mercifully left us our prerogative—we exited, having no interest in the (title-now-forgotten) feature. Thus, Carter and I were responsible for its projection to a completely empty auditorium—Frank Capra's nightmare.

Receding Horizon

Jonathan Lethem and Carter Scholz

FROM DARKNESS, THE Statue of Liberty blazes onto the screen with a crashing fanfare of music. The arm bearing the sword rises up as if newly stretched aloft, and surrounding the figure are the glowing words COLUMBIA PICTURES. Frank Capra leans over to speak to the man on his right. "This one's for Jack."

3.VI.1924

Lieber Max!

We are settled. In the Holy Land's warm clear air, already I feel a new man. Yesterday we saw Dr Löwy, and he explained his cure. He uses the sputum of the bee moth, *Galleria mellonella*. They are plentiful in Palestine. They dote on honey. Löwy learned the technique from a Frenchman at the Pasteur Institute, Élie Metchnikov, who died in 1916. As he explains it, the substance breaks down the waxy armor of the tubercle bacillus. But Löwy is more than a man of science. His first words to me were: the difference between health and sickness is foremost a difference of imagination. So I knew I had a doctor I could trust. As to writing, my true sickness, I have cast it off as a penitent his hairshirt. Dora sustains me. Blessed be the day you introduced us.

Deiner, FK

Jack Dawson, screenwriter, 55; born July 4, 1883 in Prague, Czechoslovakia; died September 22, 1938, Cedars of Lebanon Hospital, Los Angeles, of pneumonia. Dawson, who emigrated to America in 1933 and legally changed his name from Kavka, rose rapidly in his profession under the patronage of director Frank Capra. Dawson shared writing credits on many Capra films, including "Mr. Deeds in the Big City" and "Meet Joe K."

4.VII.1935

Lieber Max!

After many anonymous months in the publicity department, I am now a screenwriter. The director Frank Capra, who won so many Oscars last year for "It Happened One Night," came to our office with a contest to name his next picture. I won fifty dollars with my title, "The Man Who Disappeared." As he was writing the check, you will not believe it, he recognized my name. (I have resolved to change it, to become fully American.) He had just bought at a fabulous price one of the few copies of *Das Urteil* to escape the burnings. He cannot read German, but my negligible volume, unread, shares an honored shelf at his Brentwood estate with a Shakespeare Fourth Folio, a first edition of *The Divine Comedy,* and a proof copy of *A Christmas Carol.*

I know this because he had me to dinner at his house. A strange evening. He was visibly disgusted by the way I chewed my food. He said he has just fired Robert Riskin, who wrote "It Happened One Night," and is looking for a new writer. According to Capra, Riskin's themes were too political, insufficiently "universal." He professed to have found a kindred spirit in me. I told him I needed a room and a vegetarian diet, nothing more.

The evening ended in near catastrophe. Capra collapsed and an ambulance was called. Next day he was out of danger, and I visited him in the hospital, attempting to buoy his spirits with tales of my own sickness. He was silent, and I grew increasingly ill at ease. He asked about my writing, and I said I was a coward, that I had withdrawn from it in order to save my life, that my work was an offense to God. He said nothing but regarded me intently.

Now he wants me to begin work with him as soon as possible. I am stunned by the rapidity with which one's fortunes change in America. Boundless opportunity! Though I came resigned to end my days as a faceless clerk, I find I am embarked again upon writing. Of a sort.

Joel 2:25, "And I will restore to you the years that the locust has eaten." But in what form?

Deiner, FK

The old druggist weeps as young George shows him his mistake. Still despondent from the death of his own son, he has erred in making a prescription for another child. George brandishes the vial with its death's-head emblem in a gesture almost threatening, while the druggist sobs out his gratitude. "How can I ever thank you, George. I'm an old fool! Why, if that prescription had gone out, it would have meant shame and disgrace and prison!" "And yet," George says, "sometimes a cure, or an inoculation, begins with a small amount of poison, isn't that so?"

Frank Capra shifts uneasily in his seat. Although the script has gone through many revisions, he is sure he has never heard that line before…

25.XI.1935

Lieber Max!

I have remade myself. A new life, a new name taken from the kavka, the jackdaw emblem that you will remember hung outside my father's store. I am still his son.

My first day on the set. Gaudy, vulgar, exciting. After a wrong turn on the lot, I found myself in a narrow street that might have been Prague. All the buildings were false fronts, mocking the reality of my past life. Rounding a corner, I found a camera pointed at me and heard the shouted command, "Cut!" I retreated to a sideline in embarrassment. There a couple of technicians were saying:

"What was Capra in the hospital for? He told me TB, that don't make sense."

"It was peritonitis. But that's no story Frank would tell on himself. Trouble with the gut, that's a peasant thing. TB, he thinks that's spiritual, an artist's disease."

"He thinks he's an artist so he fires Riskin? What a mistake. Frank's the schmaltz, Riskin's the acid."

"Why's he take up with a pisher like this Dawson?"

"Riskin wouldn't stand his crap any more."

On the set, Barbara Stanwyck. Like Milena, that stately dark vulnerability, that restrained fire. I could not keep from staring. I heard her say, "When you're desperate for money, you'll do a lot of things."

When he heard I was the new writer, George Bancroft told a joke. "You're not Polish, are you? Did you hear about the Polish starlet? She fucked the writer." Barbara looked coolly at us and I blushed like a boy of fifty-two.

JL to CS: It might be appropriate to include some of our notes to each other in the story itself, making it a metafiction. What do you think?

CS to JL: That makes me uneasy. Where do we stop? Calling the artifice into question requires further metamorphoses, and once you start the process, there's no burrow to hide in.

Max,

FC has changed the title from "The Man Who Disappeared" to "Mr. Deeds in the Big City." He wants to cut the trial scene, but I, I am convinced Deeds must prove himself in court. At stake is not the contested fortune, but the man's very existence. All around him people are trying to make him disappear, to replace him with their idea of him. He is in danger of ceasing to exist.

FC exhorts me to forget words, to think of the action, the image, the movement. He cannot see that this reality he carves out of light is a reality of surface, while my reality is not what moves, but what animates.

I am among mouse folk, Max. I am a singer, of a sort. They are tone deaf yet they seem to understand me and my faint piping. They give me no dispensation for my singing, no recognition, but I have a place in their hearts. Yet when I cease to sing, they will go on with their mouse lives as before and I will be forgotten.

Interior. Night. The Bailey dining room. George's father comes to the table, his heavy dressing gown swinging open as he walks. George thinks: my father is still a giant of a man.

His father sits, and pokes at the meal George has prepared. George speaks. "It's awful dark in here, Pop."

"Yes, dark enough," answers his father. "I prefer it that way."

"Y-you know, it's warm outside, Pop," says George, stuttering, a habit he knows his father despises, yet he cannot help himself. Indeed it is only with his father that he stutters.

His father lays down his fork. "Have you thought of what you're going to do after college?" George has been dreading this moment. With his brother gone, it was only a matter of time before his father brought up the family business. "I know it's only a hope," Bailey senior continues, "but you wouldn't consider coming into the asbestos works?"

"Oh, Pop, I couldn't face being cooped up in a shabby office..." At this, George understands that he has hurt his father. "I'm sorry, Pop, I didn't mean that remark, but this business of spending all of your life trying to save three cents on a length of pipe...I'd go crazy. I want to leave Progress Falls. I'm going to build things. I'm going to build skyscrapers a hundred stories high. I'm going to build a bridge a mile long!"

"George, there are many things in the business I'm not aware of, I won't say it's done behind my back, but I haven't an eye for so many things any longer."

"Anyway, you know I already turned down Sam Wainwright's offer to head up his plastics firm. I'm not cut out for business."

The elder Bailey glowers at him. "Oh yes. Sam Wainwright. You've told him about your engagement to Mary?"

"Well, sure, of course."

"Don't deceive me, George! Does this friend of yours Sam Wainwright really exist?"

Doubt flickers in George's eyes. He begins to answer, but his words are garbled, as if something has gone wrong with the sound equipment...

Max,

"Receding Horizon," the Ronald Colman epic, is permanently shelved. FC disregarded my advice to set it in Oklahoma, and went horribly over budget trying to re-create Tibet in a local icehouse. Harry Cohn declared the film "a consummate editing disaster" because of the proliferation of unrelated fragments towards the end. A late scene where Ronald Colman attempts to regain his lost paradise, which recedes from him at every step of his approach, especially infuriated Cohn.

My working title for the new film: "The Life and Death of Joe K." An innocent man, Gary Cooper, tries to survive in the midst of cynical manipulators. Innocent of the rising power of Norton and his motorcycle corps. Innocent of Barbara rifling her father's diaries for his speeches: the betrayal of intimacy into the public eye. "When you're desperate for money, you'll do a lot of things."

Finished writing the last scene in a kind of trance: suicide is the only redemption for Cooper.

CS to JL: You realize, don't you, that if we put ourselves into the story, those aren't our real selves? They're busily creating yet another alternate version of FK & FC, and possibly of themselves and their reality as well.

JL to CS: Lighten up! It's only a short story. You act as though the universe were at stake in every word.

CS to JL: But that's how I feel; more depends upon these acts of representation than we can know.

George thinks: this town is no place for any man unless he's willing to crawl to Potter. Even then one will be forced to wait a hundred years in the antechamber before being admitted to Potter's outer office, a room crowded with petitioners. There a secretary indifferently makes notations in a gigantic book, offering appointments to meet with Potter's personal assistant, who never appears in the office but who controls all access to Potter. At times George wonders whether Potter actually exists—but where did that absurd thought come from? George knows Potter, he has dealt with the man, and yet...

This scrap of film flutters to the floor of the cutting room and is lost among countless other scraps.

"Meet Joe K" is in the theaters. Tears of shame and pleasure mixed in my eyes at FC's changed ending. Regardless of its falsity, how affecting Cooper is! The betrayed intelligence that shines from his eyes. He knows he has not been redeemed, but damned to a life of pretense.

What is FC's reflex for the redemptive but a tragic attempt to make things come out right? He doesn't believe in it himself; doubt and skepticism live in his nerves, his haunted eyes. Yet despite his impositions, his unbearable confidences, I am drawn to him. As Barbara says, "he senses what you want to keep hidden." And the film will be a success. He tested five endings and chose the most popular.

As the final credits rolled, I felt an odd, almost narcotic relief. I was betrayed but not exposed. None of the film's surfaces and movements are the movements of my soul. This is no knife to be turned back upon me.

Exterior. Night. In a sort of baffled fury, George paces in front of the home where Mary Hatch lives alone with her mother. The town of Progress Falls has trapped him, the mocking laughter of the townsfolk when he spoke of traveling the world has chased him back to Mary's street. It is as though the greater world is an illusion, a receding horizon, whose only purpose is to establish more forcibly Progress Falls's inescapable reality. The town exists only to lead him back to this street, back to his pacing before this house.

He will not go in, he swears to himself. It would trap him forever, not just in Progress Falls, but in some abysmal predicament of which Progress Falls is merely the emblem. At that moment Mary leans from her window. She calls: "What are you doing, picketing?"

George starts in guilt. "Hello, Mary. I just happened to be passing."

"Yes, so I noticed. Have you made up your mind?"

"About what?"

"About coming in. Your mother just phoned and said you were on your way over to pay me a visit."

"But...I didn't tell anybody!" protests George. "I just went for a walk and happened to be..." But as he speaks his fingers are already fumbling the catch of the gate, they have made his decision for him, yet the catch won't release, and as he fumbles Mary's features become more anxious, and George almost prances with the strain of being caught between two worlds, and Frank Capra turns to ask how this outtake has made it into the rough cut…

Taking a deep breath, Odets entered Capra's office. The director's lips were pressed back in a pained smile belied by his heavy Sicilian brow. He's going to have me killed, thought Odets. This isn't a story conference, it's a rubout. That's what happened to Dawson—Capra had him done.

Capra tossed a sheaf of onionskin onto the desk between them.

"'The Judgment.' Jack thought this was his greatest work. And this is the best you can do? One page of notes?" Capra lifted the sheaf and read from the top page. "'Georg Aussenhof, a young merchant, is writing a letter to a friend. The friend has done what Georg always wanted to do: leave his home town for the big city. Friend has tried to encourage Georg to leave, but Georg is doing too well in his father's business. The father, however, is a monster. This drives Georg to suicide at a bridge.'

"'Evaluation: This material is hopeless for a movie. No fee is large enough for me to jump through these particular hoops. Find another writer.'" Capra dropped the manuscript and glared at Odets.

"I'm sorry, Frank. That's my honest opinion. I happen to think it's a good story, but it's completely internal. There's no movie there."

"Of course there's a movie there! I'm no writer, but I know genius when I see it!"

Odets saw with astonishment that Capra was stifling tears. "Damn it, I want to bring that sad little man's vision to the widest possible audience. But keep it true. Look, you're not thinking here. Why don't we turn it into a Christmas story?"

"Christmas?" Odets asked faintly.

"Dickens!" said Capra.

Odets thought it an odd response.

"Dickens!" said Capra again. "He was Jack's favorite writer!"

This seemed mildly unbelievable, and certainly irrelevant.

Capra punched at the single page of notes that Odets had produced in a week's labor. "Georg Aussenhof...what's that mean, anyway,
Aussenhof?"

Odets had looked it up. "It's the outer courtyard of a castle. What
the English call the bailey. Why, in London there's a court of law..."

"Fine. George Bailey, then. He thinks his life is worthless because
he's never left town?"

"That's about it," said Odets.

"Stay with me, Cliff. That's the point where he's driven to the bridge."

And me with him, thought Odets.

"A Christmas Carol."

Lord, thought Odets, he's around the bend. I'm a dead man.

"You've gotta do like the Ghost of Christmas did, pull him off that
bridge and show him what the town, what's the name of it?"

"I believe it's Prague," said Odets drily.

"Fine, call it Proggsville, or wait, Progress Falls, that's it. That's our
title: 'Miracle at Progress Falls.' The Ghost shows him what Progress
Falls would be like if he throws himself off that bridge. How many
people depend on him, and love him, his girl, his friends..."

Odets didn't interrupt. He was interested despite himself. Capra's
brand of integrity was not the worst in Hollywood, even though
Odets had already noted a few dodges and fades in the director's teary
encomium—Dawson had been over six feet, not a little man at all, and
Capra had shown no scruples about altering Dawson's great screenplay
"Meet Joe K" almost beyond recognition, copping out of the suicide
ending at the last moment. The result had been a travesty, an impossibly
uplifting ending to a tragic, bitter story.

But Odets had seen his own work similarly mutilated. It was par for
the course. If it was going to happen, let it happen at the hands of an
Oscar-winner like Capra. And at the best rates this town paid.

CS to JL: Odets? What kind of name is that?

JL to CS: Funny you should ask. I stumbled onto Odets in my
research. He was a celebrated dramatist in his day, and a guy who really
made the move we're ascribing to Kafka. He went to Hollywood and he
did write for Capra. What's odd is how completely he's disappeared from

literary history. It appears he championed some arcane philosophical system called Socialism.

The thing is, when I turned in this draft to the duty officer at Artistic Control, there was a red flag on my file. The next day the Odets research material was missing from the library. From the catalog, too.

Are we going to have trouble publishing this, Carter?

"Cliff, to help you realize Jack's vision, I'm giving you access to these papers of his. He left them to me. Notes, letters…"

"Who's Max?" said Odets, reading the salutation on the top sheet.

"That's Max Brod, his best friend. It's funny. I found out Brod was killed in 1933. The Nazis. Jack kept on writing to him anyway. There just wasn't anywhere to send the letters."

Odets studied the letter. The small, precise handwriting had the concentration of a real writer. Somehow this depressed Odets. A real writer doesn't end up working for a man who subverts his work.

"Cliff, I don't think you've heard how I met Jack."

Odets had. Three or four times, actually. But he was clearly going to hear it again. Capra thought Dawson had saved him not just from death, but from moral collapse as well. There was a moral economy in the world, and on this occasion Dawson had been its agent. Capra's version was as close to reality as this movie was to "The Judgment."

"He called me a coward, Cliff. He said, your talents aren't your own, they're a gift from God. When you don't use the gifts God blessed you with, you're an offense to God and humanity."

Capra glowered at Odets, as if to impress upon him the gravity of such an offense.

"Jack said he was through as a writer. Washed up. But he hated to see me go down the same way. That gave me the courage to rise from my sickbed and go back to work. I swore to myself that I'd make it up to him. And we made some pretty good films together, Jack and I. But now, Cliff, now I want you to show some courage. I want you to take another crack at this thing."

Do you remember those melodramas we saw decades ago at the Palast-kino, Max, you and Otto and I? "The Student of Prague"—the young student makes a deal with the devil, an Italian sorcerer. He trades his reflection for wealth and happiness. But the mirror-image takes on its own life and destroys his hopes. Is it too fanciful to see this tawdry tale in my relations with FC? Yet it is not FC who dooms me, it is FK asserting himself over Jack Dawson.

Or "The Golem"—the dull robot falls in love with his master's daughter, and her rejection rouses him to a rampage. When he falls from the parapet, his body shatters like clay. Myself and Barbara. She might as well be FC's daughter. Glimpse of the cold spaces between our worlds.

Alone in his office, Odets lit another cigarette and mimicked Dorothy Parker's fluting voice. "Cliff, the Dawson notes you so generously shared are intriguing, but I'm not sure, quite, what one can do with them. This, for instance: 'In the Oklahoma Open Air Theater, George recovers, through paradisal magic, his vocation, freedom, and integrity, even his parents and his homeland.' Is Frank making a musical?"

It had gone no better with Hammett. Nor Trumbo. West didn't even return his calls. He had gone through every name writer in town, even Aldous Huxley, merely because Capra wanted class. One was tied up, another was under contract, a third was drying out somewhere. Of those who had come in, none lasted a week. Capra wanted the impossible: a bitter minatory tale transformed into a fable of redemption.

Eventually Capra would be forced to bring in some real screenwriters, script doctors who knew what they were doing, who would excise the last trace of Dawson. Meanwhile Odets soldiered on alone. The conferences got grimmer. Capra was doing his godfather act again.

"Change it."

"It's very clear, Frank. The bad guy is George's father. See, says right here, 'Georgs Vater.'"

"Change it, Cliff. This is a Christmas flick, the bad guy can't be family. We need a Scrooge. Make him a competing businessman. Make up a name."

Odets sighed inwardly. Father, Vater, pater. "Potter," he said.

"Bingo," said Capra.

*

Uncle Willi, make that Billy, has misplaced an important file. A government agency requires the asbestos works to keep a close accounting of its procedures. This file has been lost. George is furious: "Do you know what this means, you old fool? It means shame and disgrace and prison! One of us is going to jail! Well, it's not going to be me!" George rushes out. In the gathering dusk, snow is falling. Across the town square is the courthouse, a structure that seems to rise to heaven, its every window blazing. The adjutants of the court perform close-order drill before the gates, under the floodlights.

This is no outtake, thinks Capra, but something stranger, as though some other reality, hiding between the frames, is asserting itself…

Every evening Odets dragged himself home from Columbia, drank a pint of Scotch, and stared at the walls, an unread book open in front of him. Every morning he drove back to the studio, tallying in his mind the interrupted projects of his own he would resume once he was done with Capra, even as he sensed that the potential world to which those works belonged, while he delayed in this one, relentlessly receded from him.

He dreamed of a library, vast and dim, in which Dawson's unwritten books could be found, alongside unwritten volumes by Parker, Fitzgerald, Hammett, Trumbo, Faulkner, himself. Odets crouched there, reading in an aisle; the heavy steps of booted guards could be heard at a distance. He could read and understand the pages, but they made no sense. It was as though the world had tilted away from an entire set of meanings. Like George Bailey, Odets felt estranged from a world as compromised, dull, threatening, and suffused with loss as Progress Falls. He awoke haunted by the unquiet ghosts of those unwritten books.

Odets had been around enough not to blame Hollywood. No writer needed outside help to procrastinate or to fail. Dawson himself had freely given up literature years before coming to America. But as Odets worked against the Dawson story it seemed to him that something more abstract, almost a cosmic principle, was at work, bestowing gifts merely to subvert them. George Bailey would never leave Progress Falls; nor, it seemed as the days dragged on, would Cliff Odets ever be free of this damned script.

Kafkaesque

Oddly, though, Odets was haunted less by his own unwritten work than by Dawson's, the outlines of which he vaguely glimpsed like the battlements of a castle in fog, looming darkly in Capra's world of determined optimism.

What had it cost the world that Dawson had written scripts instead of novels? He could not escape the feeling that the scripts were urgent warnings shouted in some arcane and forgotten language. Some days, the world Odets walked through seemed flimsy and insubstantial in the dim yet insistent light that Dawson's work cast.

What other world would have welcomed those unfinished works that Dawson alluded to in his letters to Max? Odets tried to imagine it, to imagine some other pair of writers in some other world, wrestling with this same material...

He was wasting time. He shook himself out of reverie and returned to his hopeless task.

JL to CS: Damn it, will you quit making this harder than it has to be? I thought we'd decided to drop Odets.

CS to JL: I don't see how, now that we've given him voice. Given the circumstances, I'm sure he'd be happier out of it—as would I, if you want the truth. But if we don't finish what we've started, in what red-flagged library carrel will we end up?

JL to CS: I'm worried more about where we'll end up if we do finish. When I handed in the last draft my AC duty officer said we were creating a penal colony for writers, torturing them on the racks of our prose. It sounded like a veiled threat to me.

CS to JL: I tried to warn you. A metafiction opens everything to question, even the ground of our own existence. It could be as hard to escape as Progress Falls.

Interior. Potter's office. George flinching under the lash of the patriarch's words. "You once called me a warped, frustrated old man. What are you but a warped, frustrated young man? A miserable little clerk crawling in here on your hands and knees begging for help, no better than a cockroach. You're worth more dead than alive. I'll tell you what I'm going to do, George. As a stockholder in the Bailey Asbestos

Works, I'm going to swear out a warrant for your arrest."

George feels he must sit down, but there is no chair. "B-but what have I done?"

"Why, we'll let the court decide that."

George turns to leave the office.

"Go ahead, George," says Potter. "You can't hide in a small town like this." The patriarch lifts the telephone, and says: "Bill, this is Potter." Then he covers the mouthpiece and speaks again to George: "So, now you know what more there is in the world beside yourself! An innocent child, yes, that you were, truly, but you're also a devilish human being! Yes, you are, George, don't try to deny it! And therefore, I sentence you to death by drowning!" George runs from the office, into the snowy streets of Progress Falls.

Capra turns to his assistant to complain, this was never in the script, but the seat is empty...

In Jack's dream, he is in Palestine. Dora is at his side. Outside, the desert is hot and brilliant. The sky is porcelain blue. A bowl of Jaffa oranges glows with its own light beneath the doctor's window.

"A clean bill of health. There is scarring from the lesions, of course, but the disease is arrested. You are cured, my friend." Dr Löwy, in a curious gesture, places his hand upon Jack's forehead.

Jack leaves the kibbutz where he has lived during his cure and moves to Jerusalem. He teaches law at Hebrew University. He writes articles and propaganda film scenarios for the Palestine ministry of information. The state of Palestine grows strong, and Jack is a valued citizen. From afar his lean German prose alerts European Jewry and its allies to the Nazi threat, and the pestiferous Hitler is crushed and humiliated in the 1933 election—but here the dream collapses. He cannot shut out the reality of Brod shot dead in a Prague alley, his sisters Elli, Valli, and Ottla hauled off to labor camps, the motorcycles roaring through the streets.

The bridge—! It is immense, a mile long, more! From the catwalk where George stands he cannot see the end of it, the roadway recedes and vanishes into falling snow. The bridge is so broad that even its far side is vague and distant. Unending traffic streams both ways in countless lanes, sending sickening vibrations through the soles of George's feet. The braided steel cable he clutches for balance is as thick as a man's thigh and vibrates as if all the machinery of the world were linked to it.

In desperation George cries, "Clarence! Get me back! I want to live again!"

"But, George, you've given all that up. You have no claim to live in Progress Falls. None at all. And yet..." Clarence stands, ear cocked to the falling snow. Abruptly he straightens. "Permission has been granted. Owing to certain auxiliary circumstances..." George doesn't wait. He is running from the bridge, up the snowy street, past a street sign: Aspetuck, Kitchawan, Katonah, Chappaqua. Which way? At home the sheriff and bank examiners are waiting. For a wild moment it seems that George might bolt to Aspetuck or Chappaqua, he appears to be on a racing horse, leaning against the wind, but the moment passes, and he is running home to the drafty old house on Sycamore Street, to accept his fate, to be beaten into an ecstatic submission by the love and regard of his fellows—yet at this moment the projector falters, so that frame by frame George's steps slow and his image flickers and the hope dawning in his face takes on a frozen alert look of concentration, as if he hears urgent but unintelligible voices from some other realm beyond even Clarence's ken.

In the darkness, Capra's voice rings out. "Damn it, what's going on here?" But even in the fading light from the projector, he can see that the screening room is empty but for himself...

CS to JL: An officer of the Directorate of Moral Economy called me this morning, wanting to know if this collaboration was your idea or mine. He suggested that we might have to file a Thematic Impact Statement.

JL to CS: Oh God. What have we got ourselves into?

CS to JL: The version of Kafka we've invented, those works he's failed to write, it's so strange, I almost feel they're seeping into our world...

JL to CS: You and your Kafka! We should have used Max Brod. At least people know who Brod is.

*

COL'S CAPRA XMAS CUT CANNED. Director Frank Capra, whose spendthrift rep has dogged him since his unreleasable epic "Receding Horizon," has put another nail in his own coffin with "Miracle at Progress Falls," insiders say. Capra's Christmas nod to deceased writer Jack Dawson is reportedly far over budget and as far from completion as his previous golden turkey. Eight high-priced scribes from Odets to Faulkner are said to have spilled ink on the project, to no avail. Columbia head Harry Cohn isn't talking, but he is steaming, as he prods Capra to salvage something from the expensive rough cut footage.
—*Hollywood Reporter,* July 5, 1946

We are shadowed, Max, by events that do not quite happen. An infinity of worlds exists alongside our own. I dream of worlds in which I have died, and you survived and yet betrayed my trust and exposed my unfinished work, my drafts, my inmost thoughts, to the world's scrutiny. Some nights I turn in bed to find Dora beside me, I feel her warmth for a moment before waking, alone. Some nights I hear my own voice calling across vastnesses, urgent but unintelligible.

When I went with Dora to Palestine, I told her: I love you enough to rid myself of anything that might trouble you; I will become another person. For over ten years I wrote nothing. But after her death, the return of the repressed was inevitable.

My disease also returns, Max, after all those years. A lost dog, abandoned on the street by its master, finds its way home at last, arrives grinning with matted fur, notched ears, bloodshot eyes, lolling tongue.

Dr Löwy is dead. The mark, the Shem, placed by his hand upon the golem's head awaits erasure.

My new doctor has not heard of the bee moth. Instead, he offers this course of treatment, from the third edition of Alexander's *The Collapse Theory of Pulmonary Tuberculosis.* Artificial pneumothorax: the intentional collapse of the afflicted lung by injecting gas between it and the thoracic wall; if this fails to collapse the lung, two holes are cut in the chest wall, for a thoracoscope and a cauterizing instrument; one searches for adhesions between lung and pleura, then burns them away, freeing the lung to permit a total collapse. Oleothorax: the pleural cavity is filled with oil rather than air. Extrapleural pneumolysis: the lung and both pleural layers are stripped from the rib cage; the phrenic nerve, controlling the diaphragm, may be crushed with forceps or reeled out through the chest, paralyzing the diaphragm and immobilizing the lung. Finally, one may simply remove a dozen or so ribs, breaking them from the spine and discarding them.

Were I still able, I would write the story of a patient obliged to a course of treatment that is in reality a penance for failing God. Bit by bit the body is taken away. Then the intellect, the personality, the soul, are broken off and discarded.

I am being erased. As if I had never written. All those torments and ecstasies belong to another world. At last! I am responsible for nothing.

It is a wonderful life.

JL to CS: My number just came up in the public safety lottery. I pulled Panopticon duty for two weeks. That's enough for me, I can take a hint; let's drop it. The pressure's giving me hives. Or maybe it's the material—the bridge between Kafka and Capra, Prague and Progress Falls, is too far for me. I'm jumping off.

CS to JL: Well, that's disappointing. Now I'll have to meet my Minimum Cultural Contribution Requirement with more of that ancient trunk novel I've been passing in. With the ozone hole officially declared a myth, it reads like science fiction now. Oh, I'll want back my copy of Kafka's *The Golem*.

JL to CS: You'll have to wait a few weeks. Keep your shutters closed.

*

After the disaster of the unreleased "Miracle At Progress Falls," Capra's career went into eclipse. He had become terminally afraid of any project or collaborator that might sidetrack him into questioning fundamental verities—a fatal fear in a profession based on collaboration. For the film's failure he variously blamed Jack Dawson, the eight writers who worked on the script, and James Stewart, cast as George only after Gary Cooper refused the role. Whatever the reason, "Miracle" marks one of the most precipitous declines in the American cinema. Capra in his later years was reduced to making promotional films for defense contractors, and working on an unpublished autobiography. He died in June Lake, California, in 1984. When the American Film Institute released a much-edited version after Capra's death as part of a "lost classics" series, their charity was more admired than their judgment.

—Michael D. Toman, *The American Cinema*

J.K.

Capra's George Bailey as Kafka's Georg Bendemann. It's quite remarkable to see the numerous clever parallels Lethem and Scholz find between Kafka's stories and the works of Frank Capra. The story brings to the surface the desperation and suicidal impulses, the lack of faith in people and institutions, the sense of the hero being stifled by an uncomprehending and incomprehensible society, that underlie Capra's "upbeat" cinema. Plus, by having Kafka change his name to Jack Dawson ("Jackdaw's son") Lethem and Scholz unwittingly anticipate the name of Leonardo DiCaprio's character in *Titanic*, the largest grossing movie of all time.

MAIROWITZ & CRUMB:

When he first came to Berlin, Kafka felt he had escaped from those phantoms which had forced him to write: "They keep looking for me but, for the moment, they can't find me." These were the same ghosts who "drank kisses" written in letters and who seemed to vampyrize his words and thought. Soon, he would ask Dora to burn many of his manuscripts.... All this while, his tuberculosis was crawling up from his lungs to his larynx and, in his last months, he could only communicate by written notes, and could scarcely eat. In April 1924, he was moved to a sanatorium near Vienna, but his condition continued to deteriorate until June.

Towards the end, he insisted that the doctor attending him give him morphine for the pain.

When Kafka regained consciousness for the last time, he apparently removed an icepack which had been placed on his neck, and threw it on the floor. Three days later, in his obituary, Milena Jesenská called him "a man condemned to regard the world with such blinding clarity that he found it unbearable and went to his death."

In June 1924, his "phantoms" saw to it—with their usual irony—that while dying of starvation he could be correcting the galley-proofs of an astonishing masterwork called "A Hunger Artist."

—David Mairowitz, from *R. Crumb's Kafka*

A Hunger Artist

David Mairowitz and **Robert Crumb**

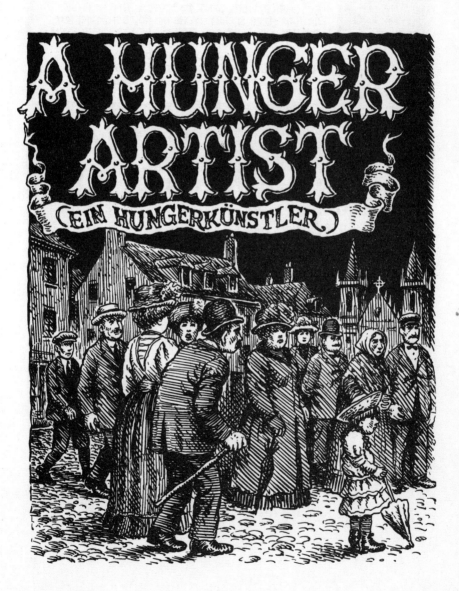

IN THE LAST FEW DECADES, THE INTEREST IN PROFESSIONAL HUNGER-ARTISTRY HAS GREATLY DIMINISHED. ONCE THE WHOLE TOWN CAME OUT TO SEE THE HUNGER-ARTIST. SOME EVEN BOUGHT SEASON TICKETS, AND AT NIGHT THE SCENE WAS BATHED IN THE LIGHT OF TORCHES.

GROUPS OF PROFESSIONAL WATCHERS, USUALLY BUTCHERS, WERE SENT TO WATCH HIM, IN CASE HE HAD SOME SECRET CACHE OF NOURISHMENT. BUT, DURING HIS FAST THE ARTISTE WOULD NEVER, EVEN UNDER COMPULSION, SWALLOW THE SMALLEST BIT OF FOOD; HIS PROFESSIONAL HONOR FORBADE IT. HE ALONE KNEW WHAT THE OTHERS DIDN'T: FASTING WAS THE EASIEST THING IN THE WORLD.

TICKETS

SEE THE HUNGER ARTIST

THE PERIOD OF FASTING WAS SET BY HIS IMPRESARIO AT FORTY DAYS MAXIMUM, BECAUSE AFTER THAT TIME THE PUBLIC BEGAN TO LOSE INTEREST. SO, ON THE FORTIETH DAY, WITH AN EXCITED CROWD FILLING THE ARENA AND A MILITARY BAND PLAYING, TWO YOUNG LADIES CAME TO LEAD THE HUNGER-ARTIST OUT OF HIS CAGE. WHEN THIS HAPPENED HE ALWAYS PUT UP SOME RESISTANCE...WHY STOP AFTER ONLY FORTY DAYS?!? WHY SHOULD THEY TAKE FROM HIM THE GLORY OF FASTING EVEN LONGER, OF SURPASSING EVEN HIMSELF TO REACH UNIMAGINABLE HEIGHTS, FOR HE SAW HIS ABILITY TO GO ON FASTING AS *UNLIMITED!*

A Hunger Artist

Kafkaesque

HE LIVED THIS WAY FOR MANY YEARS, HONORED BY ALL THE WORLD, YET TROUBLED IN HIS SOUL, DEEPLY FRUSTRATED THAT THEY WOULD NOT ALLOW HIS FASTING TO EXCEED FORTY DAYS. HE SPENT MOST OF HIS TIME IN A GLOOMY MOOD, AND WHEN SOME KIND-HEARTED PERSON WOULD TRY TO EXPLAIN THAT HIS DEPRESSION WAS THE RESULT OF THE FASTING, HE WOULD SOMETIMES FLY INTO A RAGE AND BEGIN RATTLING THE BARS OF HIS CAGE LIKE AN ANIMAL.

A Hunger Artist

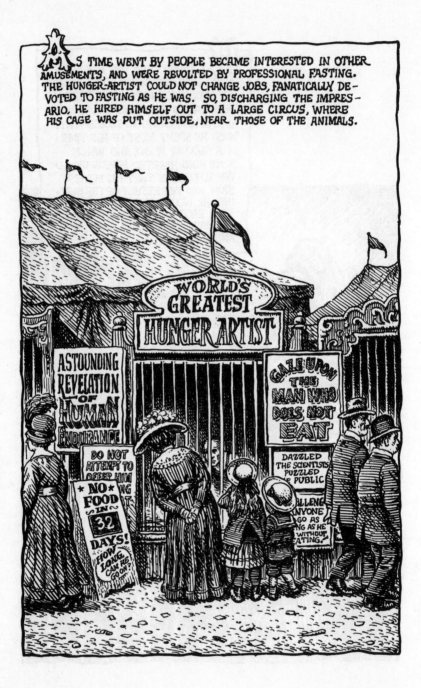

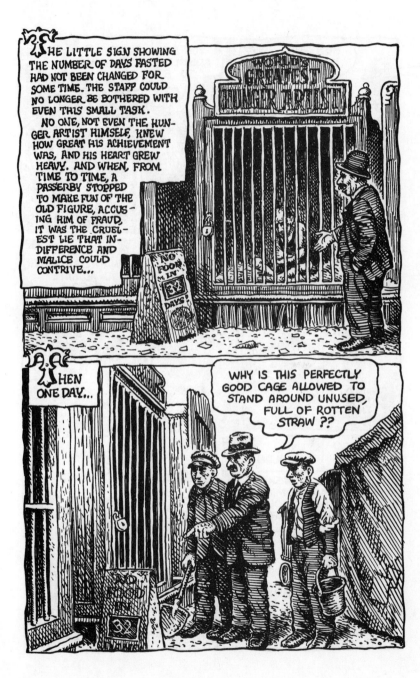

Kafkaesque

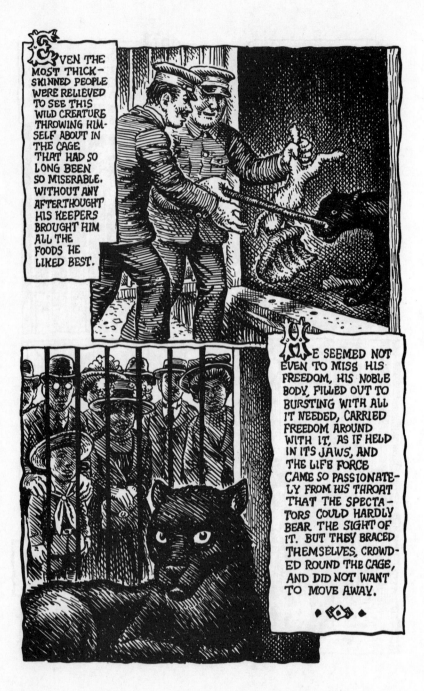

EVEN THE MOST THICK-SKINNED PEOPLE WERE RELIEVED TO SEE THIS WILD CREATURE THROWING HIMSELF ABOUT IN THE CAGE THAT HAD SO LONG BEEN SO MISERABLE. WITHOUT ANY AFTERTHOUGHT HIS KEEPERS BROUGHT HIM ALL THE FOODS HE LIKED BEST.

HE SEEMED NOT EVEN TO MISS HIS FREEDOM, HIS NOBLE BODY, FILLED OUT TO BURSTING WITH ALL IT NEEDED, CARRIED FREEDOM AROUND WITH IT, AS IF HELD IN ITS JAWS, AND THE LIFE FORCE CAME SO PASSIONATELY FROM HIS THROAT THAT THE SPECTATORS COULD HARDLY BEAR THE SIGHT OF IT. BUT THEY BRACED THEMSELVES, CROWDED ROUND THE CAGE, AND DID NOT WANT TO MOVE AWAY.

◆ ·◇· ◆

Kafkaesque

J.P.K.

In Kafka, the hunger artist is at pains not to show the effects that starvation is having on him. In Crumb, the hunger artist's stoicism is belied by the suffering etched on his face. Did we realize this from the text of the original story? We know that with his most famous story, Kafka insisted that there be no illustration of Gregor Samsa's metamorphosed form. "The insect itself cannot be depicted," he wrote. "It cannot even be shown from a distance." Does seeing the hunger artist's anguish change our reaction to the story?

J.K.

I get a strong sense of madness and physical corruption from Crumb's drawings. Kafka's fiction—"The Metamorphosis," "In the Penal Colony," "A Country Doctor," no less so than this story—is intensely aware of the body and its frailties.

Philip Roth:

Had he lived, perhaps he would have escaped with his good friend Max Brod, who found refuge in Palestine, a citizen of Israel until his death there in 1968. But *Kafka* escaping? It seems unlikely for one so fascinated by entrapment and careers that culminate in anguished death. Still, there is Karl Rossmann, his American greenhorn. Having imagined Karl's escape to America and his mixed luck there, could not Kafka have found a way to execute an escape for himself? The New School for Social Research in New York becoming *his* Great Nature Theater of Oklahoma? Or perhaps, through the influence of Thomas Mann, a position in the German department at Princeton… But then, had Kafka lived, it is not at all certain that the books of his which Mann celebrated from his refuge in New Jersey would ever have been published; eventually Kafka might either have destroyed those manuscripts that he had once bid Max Brod to dispose of at his death or, at the least, continued to keep them his secret. The Jewish refugee arriving in America in 1938 would not then have been Mann's "religious humorist" but a frail and bookish fifty-five-year-old bachelor, formerly a lawyer for a government insurance firm in Prague, retired on a pension in Berlin at the time of Hitler's rise to power—an author, yes, but of a few eccentric stories, mostly about animals, stories no one in America had ever heard of and only a handful in Europe had read; a homeless K., but without K.'s willfulness and purpose, a homeless Karl, but without Karl's youthful spirit and resilience; just a Jew lucky enough to have escaped with his life, in his possession a suitcase containing some clothes, some family photos, some Prague mementoes, and the manuscripts, still unpublished and in pieces, of *Amerika*, *The Trial*, *The Castle*, and (stranger things happen) three more fragmented novels, no less remarkable than the bizarre masterworks that he keeps to himself out of oedipal timidity, perfectionist madness, and insatiable longings for solitude and spiritual purity.

—from part 1 of "'I Always Wanted You to Admire My Fasting'; or, Looking at Kafka"

"I Always Wanted You to Admire My Fasting"; or, Looking at Kafka

Philip Roth

1942. I AM NINE; my Hebrew-school teacher, Dr. Kafka, is fifty-nine. To the little boys who must attend his "four-to-five" class each afternoon, he is known—in part because of his remote and melancholy foreignness, but largely because we vent on him our resentment at having to learn an ancient calligraphy at the very hour we should be out screaming our heads off on the ball field—he is known as Dr. Kishka. Named, I confess, by me. His sour breath, spiced with intestinal juices by five in the afternoon, makes the Yiddish word for "insides" particularly telling, I think. Cruel, yes, but in truth I would have cut out my tongue had I ever imagined the name would become legend. A coddled child, I do not yet think of myself as persuasive, or, quite yet, as a literary force in the world. My jokes don't hurt, how could they, I'm so adorable. And if you don't believe me, just ask my family and the teachers in my school. Already at nine, one foot in college, the other in the Catskills. Little borscht-belt comic that I am outside the classroom, I amuse my friends Schlossman and Ratner on the dark walk home from Hebrew school with an imitation of Kishka, his precise and finicky professorial manner, his German accent, his cough, his gloom. "Doctor

Kishka!" cries Schlossman, and hurls himself savagely against the news-stand that belongs to the candy-store owner whom Schlossman drives just a little crazier each night. "Doctor Franz—Doctor Franz—Doctor Franz—*Kishka!"* screams Ratner, and my chubby little friend who lives upstairs from me on nothing but chocolate milk and Mallomars does not stop laughing until, as is his wont (his mother has asked me "to keep an eye on him" for just this reason), he wets his pants. Schlossman takes the occasion of Ratner's humiliation to pull the little boy's paper out of his notebook and wave it in the air—it is the assignment Dr. Kafka has just returned to us, graded; we were told to make up an alphabet of our own, out of straight lines and curved lines and dots. "That is all an alphabet is," he had explained. "That is all Hebrew is. That is all English is. Straight lines and curved lines and dots." Ratner's alphabet, for which he received a C, looks like twenty-six skulls strung in a row. I received my A for a curlicued alphabet, inspired largely (as Dr. Kafka seems to have surmised, given his comment at the top of the page) by the number eight. Schlossman received an F for forgetting even to do it—and a lot he seems to care. He is content—he is *overjoyed*—with things as they are. Just waving a piece of paper in the air and screaming, "Kishka! Kishka!" makes him deliriously happy. We should all be so lucky.

At home, alone in the glow of my goose-necked "desk" lamp (plugged after dinner into an outlet in the kitchen, my study), the vision of our refugee teacher, sticklike in a fraying three-piece blue suit, is no longer very funny—particularly after the entire beginners' Hebrew class, of which I am the most studious member, takes the name Kishka to its heart. My guilt awakens redemptive fantasies of heroism, I have them often about the "Jews in Europe." I must save him. If not me, who? The demonic Schlossman? The babyish Ratner? And if not now, when? For I have learned in the ensuing weeks that Dr. Kafka lives in a room in the house of an elderly Jewish lady on the shabby lower stretch of Avon Avenue, where the trolley still runs and the poorest of Newark's Negroes shuffle meekly up and down the street, for all they seem to know, still back in Mississippi. A *room.* And *there!* My family's apartment is no palace, but it is ours at least, so long as we pay the $38.50 a month in rent; and though our neighbors are not rich, they refuse to be poor and they refuse to be meek. Tears of shame and sorrow in my eyes, I rush into the living room to tell my parents what I have heard (though not that I heard it during a quick game of "aces up" played a minute before class against the synagogue's rear wall—worse, played directly beneath a stained-glass window embossed with the names of the dead): "My Hebrew teacher lives in a *room*."

My parents go much further than I could imagine anybody going in the real world. Invite him to dinner, my mother says. *Here?* Of course here—Friday night; I'm sure he can stand a home-cooked meal, she says, and a little pleasant company. Meanwhile, my father gets on the phone to call my Aunt Rhoda, who lives with my grandmother and tends her and her potted plants in the apartment house at the corner of our street. For nearly two decades my father has been introducing my mother's "baby" sister, now forty, to the Jewish bachelors and widowers of north Jersey. No luck so far. Aunt Rhoda, an "interior decorator" in the dry-goods department of the Big Bear, a mammoth merchandise and produce market in industrial Elizabeth, wears falsies (this information by way of my older brother) and sheer frilly blouses, and family lore has it that she spends hours in the bathroom every day applying powder and sweeping her stiffish hair up into a dramatic pile on her head; but despite all this dash and display, she is, in my father's words, "still afraid of the facts of life." He, however, is undaunted, and administers therapy regularly and gratis: "Let 'em squeeze ya, Rhoda—it *feels* good!" I am his flesh and blood, I can reconcile myself to such scandalous talk in our kitchen—*but what will Dr. Kafka think?* Oh, but it's too late to do anything now. The massive machinery of matchmaking has been set in motion by my undiscourageable father, and the smooth engines of my proud homemaking mother's hospitality are already purring away. To throw my body into the works in an attempt to bring it all to a halt—well, I might as well try to bring down the New Jersey Bell Telephone Company by leaving our receiver off the hook. Only Dr. Kafka can save me now. But to my muttered invitation, he replies, with a formal bow that turns me scarlet—who has ever seen a person do such a thing outside of a movie house?—he replies that he would be *honored* to be my family's dinner guest. "My aunt," I rush to tell him, "will be there too." It appears that I have just said something mildly humorous; odd to see Dr. Kafka smile. Sighing, he says, "I will be delighted to meet her." Meet her? He's supposed to *marry* her. How do I warn him? And how do I warn Aunt Rhoda (a very great admirer of me and my marks) about his sour breath, his roomer's pallor, his Old World ways, so at odds with her up-to-dateness? My face feels as if it will ignite of its own—and spark the fire that will engulf the synagogue, Torah and all—when I see Dr. Kafka scrawl our address in his notebook, and beneath it, some words *in German*. "Good night, Dr. Kafka!" "Good night, and thank you, thank you." I turn to run, I go, but not fast enough: out on the street I hear Schlossman—that fiend!—announcing to my classmates, who are punching one another under the lamplight down from the synagogue steps (where a card game is also in progress, organized by the bar mitzvah boys): "Roth invited Kishka to his *house!* To *eat!*"

Does my father do a job on Kafka! Does he make a sales pitch for familial bliss! What it means to a man to have two fine boys and a wonderful wife! Can Dr. Kafka imagine what it's like? The thrill? The satisfaction? The pride? He tells our visitor of the network of relatives on his mother's side that are joined in a "family association" of over two hundred people located in seven states, including the state of Washington! Yes, relatives even in the Far West: here are their photographs, Dr. Kafka; this is a beautiful book we published entirely on our own for five dollars a copy, pictures of every member of the family, including infants, and a family history by "Uncle" Lichtblau, the eighty-five-year-old patriarch of the clan. This is our family newsletter, which is published twice a year and distributed nationwide to all the relatives. This, in the frame, is the menu from the banquet of the family association, held last year in a ballroom of the "Y" in Newark, in honor of my father's mother on her seventy-fifth birthday. My mother, Dr. Kafka learns, has served *six consecutive years* as the secretary-treasurer of the family association. My father has served a two-year term as president, as have each of his three brothers. We now have fourteen boys in the family in uniform. Philip writes a letter on V-mail stationery to five of his cousins in the army every single month. "Religiously," my mother puts in, smoothing my hair. "I firmly believe," says my father, "that the family is the cornerstone of everything."

Dr. Kafka, who has listened with close attention to my father's spiel, handling the various documents that have been passed to him with great delicacy and poring over them with a kind of rapt absorption that reminds me of myself over the watermarks of my stamps, now for the first time expresses himself on the subject of family; softly he says, "I agree," and inspects again the pages of our family book. "Alone," says my father, in conclusion, "alone, Dr. Kafka, is a stone." Dr. Kafka, setting the book gently down upon my mother's gleaming coffee table, allows with a nod that that is so. My mother's fingers are now turning in the curls behind my ears; not that I even know it at the time, or that she does. Being stroked is my life; stroking me, my father, and my brother is hers.

My brother goes off to a Boy Scout meeting, but only after my father has him stand in his neckerchief before Dr. Kafka and describe to him the skills he has mastered to earn each of his badges. I am invited to bring my stamp album into the living room and show Dr. Kafka my set of triangular stamps from Zanzibar. "Zanzibar!" says my father rapturously, as though I, not even ten, have already been there and back. My father accompanies Dr. Kafka and me into the "sun parlor," where my tropical fish swim in the aerated, heated, and hygienic paradise I have made for them with my weekly allowance and my Hanukkah *gelt*. I am encouraged to tell Dr. Kafka what I know about the temperament of the angelfish, the function of the catfish, and the family life of the black mollie. I know quite a bit. "All on his own he does that," my father says to Kafka. "He gives me a lecture on one of those fish, it's seventh heaven, Dr. Kafka." "I can imagine," Kafka replies.

Back in the living room my Aunt Rhoda suddenly launches into a rather recondite monologue on "Scotch plaids," intended, it would appear, for the edification of my mother alone. At least she looks fixedly at my mother while she delivers it. I have not yet seen her look directly at Dr. Kafka; she did not even turn his way at dinner when he asked how many employees there were at the Big Bear. "How would I know?" she had replied, and then continued right on conversing with my mother, about a butcher who would take care of her "under the counter" if she could find him nylons for his wife. It never occurs to me that she will not look at Dr. Kafka because she is shy—nobody that dolled up could, in my estimation, be shy. I can only think that she is outraged. *It's his breath. It's his accent. It's his age.*

I'm wrong—it turns out to be what Aunt Rhoda calls his "superiority complex." "Sitting there, sneering at us like that," says my aunt, somewhat superior now herself. "Sneering?" repeats my father, incredulous. "Sneering and laughing, yes!" says Aunt Rhoda. My mother shrugs. "*I* didn't think he was laughing." "Oh, don't worry, by himself there he was having a very good time—*at our expense.* I know the European-type man. Underneath they think they're all lords of the manor," Rhoda says. "You know something, Rhoda?" says my father, tilting his head and pointing a finger, "I think you fell in love." "With *him?* Are you *crazy?*" "He's too quiet for Rhoda," my mother says. "I think maybe he's a little bit of a wallflower. Rhoda is a very lively person, she needs lively people around her." "Wallflower? He's not a wallflower! He's a gentleman, that's all. And he's lonely," my father says assertively, glaring at my mother for going over his head like this *against* Kafka. My Aunt Rhoda is forty years old—it is not exactly a shipment of brand-new goods that he is trying to move. "He's a gentleman, he's an educated man, and I'll tell you something, he'd give his eyeteeth to have a nice home and a wife." "Well," says my Aunt Rhoda, "let him find one then, if he's so educated. Somebody who's his equal, who he doesn't have to look down his nose at with his big sad refugee eyes!" "Yep, she's in love," my father announces, squeezing Rhoda's knee in triumph. "With him?" she cries, jumping to her feet, taffeta crackling around her like a bonfire. "With *Kafka?*" she snorts. "I wouldn't give an old man like him the time of day!"

Dr. Kafka calls and takes my Aunt Rhoda to a movie. I am astonished, both that he calls and that she goes; it seems there is more desperation in life than I have come across yet in my fish tank. Dr. Kafka takes my Aunt Rhoda to a play performed at the "Y." Dr. Kafka eats Sunday dinner with my grandmother and my Aunt Rhoda and, at the end of the afternoon, accepts with that formal bow of his the mason jar of barley soup that my grandmother presses him to carry back to his room with him on the No. 8 bus. Apparently he was very taken with my grandmother's jungle of potted plants—and she, as a result, with him. Together they spoke in Yiddish about gardening. One Wednesday morning, only an hour after the store has opened for the day, Dr. Kafka shows up at the dry-goods department of the Big Bear; he tells Aunt Rhoda that he just wants to see where she works. That night he writes in his diary: "With the customers she is forthright and cheery, and so managerial about 'taste' that when I hear her explain to a chubby young bride why green and blue do not 'go,' I am myself ready to believe that Nature is in error and R. is correct."

One night, at ten, Dr. Kafka and Aunt Rhoda come by unexpectedly, and a small impromptu party is held in the kitchen—coffee and cake, even a thimbleful of whiskey all around, to celebrate the resumption of Aunt Rhoda's career on the stage. I have only heard tell of my aunt's theatrical ambitions. My brother says that when I was small she used to come to entertain the two of us on Sundays with her puppets—she was at that time employed by the W.P.A. to travel around New Jersey and put on marionette shows in schools and even in churches; Aunt Rhoda did all the voices and, with the help of a female assistant, manipulated the manikins on their strings. Simultaneously she had been a member of the Newark Collective Theater, a troupe organized primarily to go around to strike groups to perform *Waiting for Lefty*. Everybody in Newark (as I understood it) had had high hopes that Rhoda Pilchik would go on to Broadway—everybody except my grandmother. To me this period of history is as difficult to believe in as the era of the lake dwellers, which I am studying in school; people say it was once so, so I believe them, but nonetheless it is hard to grant such stories the status of the real, given the life I see around me.

Yet my father, a very avid realist, is in the kitchen, schnapps glass in hand, toasting Aunt Rhoda's success. She has been awarded one of the starring roles in the Russian masterpiece *The Three Sisters*, to be performed six weeks hence by the amateur group at the Newark "Y." Everything, announces Aunt Rhoda, everything she owes to Franz and his encouragement. One conversation—"One!" she cries gaily—and Dr. Kafka had apparently talked my grandmother out of her lifelong belief that actors are not serious human beings. And what an actor *he* is, in his own right, says Aunt Rhoda. How he had opened her eyes to the meaning of things, by reading her the famous Chekhov play—yes, read it to her from the opening line to the final curtain, all the parts, and actually left her in tears. Here Aunt Rhoda says, "Listen, listen—

this is the first line of the play—it's the key to everything. Listen—I just think about what it was like the night Pop passed away, how I wondered and wondered what would become of us, what would we all do—and, and, *listen*—"

"We're listening," laughs my father. So am *I* listening, from my bed.

Pause; she must have walked to the center of the kitchen linoleum. She says, sounding a little surprised, "'It's just a year ago today that father died.'"

"Shhh," warns my mother, "you'll give the little one nightmares."

I am not alone in finding my aunt a "changed person" during the weeks of rehearsal. My mother says this is just what she was like as a little girl. "Red cheeks, always those hot, red cheeks—and everything exciting, even taking a bath." "She'll calm down, don't worry," says my father, "and then he'll pop the question." "Knock on wood," says my mother. "Come on," says my father, "he knows what side his bread is buttered on—he sets foot in this house, he sees what a family is all about, and believe me, he's licking his chops. Just look at him when he sits in that club chair. This is his dream come true." "Rhoda says that in Berlin, before Hitler, he had a young girl friend, years and years it went on, and then she left him. For somebody else. She got tired of waiting." "Don't worry," says my father, "when the time comes I'll give him a little nudge. He ain't going to live forever, either, and he knows it."

Then one weekend, as a respite from the "strain" of nightly rehearsals—which Dr. Kafka regularly visits, watching in his hat and coat at the back of the auditorium until it is time to accompany Aunt Rhoda home—they take a trip to Atlantic City. Ever since he arrived on these shores Dr. Kafka has wanted to see the famous boardwalk and the horse that dives from the high board. But in Atlantic City something happens that I am not allowed to know about; any discussion of the subject conducted in my presence is in Yiddish. Dr. Kafka sends Aunt Rhoda four letters in three days. She comes to us for dinner and sits till midnight crying in our kitchen. She calls the "Y" on our phone to tell them (weeping) that her mother is still ill and she cannot come to rehearsal again—she may even have to drop out of the play. No, she can't, she can't, her mother is too ill, she herself is too upset! goodbye!

Then back to the kitchen table to cry. She wears no pink powder and no red lipstick, and her stiff brown hair, down, is thick and spiky as a new broom.

My brother and I listen from our bedroom, through the door that silently he has pushed ajar.

"Have you ever?" says Aunt Rhoda, weeping. "Have you *ever?*"

"Poor soul," says my mother.

"Who?" I whisper to my brother. "Aunt Rhoda or—"

"Shhhh!" he says. "Shut *up!*"

In the kitchen my father grunts. "Hmm. Hmm." I hear him getting up and walking around and sitting down again—and then grunting. I am listening so hard that I can hear the letters being folded and unfolded, stuck back into their envelopes, then removed to be puzzled over one more time.

"Well?" demands Aunt Rhoda. *"Well?"*

"Well what?" answers my father.

"Well, what do you want to say *now?"*

"He's *meshugeh,*" admits my father. "Something is wrong with him all right."

"But," sobs Aunt Rhoda, "no one would believe me when *I* said it!"

"Rhody, Rhody," croons my mother in that voice I know from those times that I have had to have stitches taken, or when I have awakened in tears, somehow on the floor beside my bed. "Rhody, don't be hysterical, darling. It's over, kitten, it's all over."

I reach across to my brother's twin bed and tug on the blanket. I don't think I've ever been so confused in my life, not even by death. The speed of things! Everything good undone in a moment! By what? *"What?"* I whisper. *"What is it?"*

My brother, the Boy Scout, smiles leeringly and, with a fierce hiss that is no answer and enough answer, addresses my bewilderment: "Sex!"

Years later, a junior at college, I receive an envelope from home containing Dr. Kafka's obituary, clipped from *The Jewish News,* the tabloid of Jewish affairs that is mailed each week to the homes of the Jews of Essex County. It is summer, the semester is over, but I have stayed on at school, alone in my room in the town, trying to write short stories. I am fed by a young English professor and his wife in exchange for baby-sitting; I tell the sympathetic couple, who are also loaning me the money for my rent, why it is I can't go home. My tearful fights with my father are all I can talk about at their dinner table. "Keep him away from me!" I scream at my mother. "But, darling," she asks me, "what is going on? What is this all about?"—the very same question with which I used to plague my older brother, asked now of me and out of the same bewilderment and innocence. "He *loves* you," she explains.

But that, of all things, seems to me precisely what is blocking my way. Others are crushed by paternal criticism—I find myself oppressed by his high opinion of me! Can it possibly be true (and can I possibly admit) that I am coming to hate him for loving me so? praising me so? But that makes no sense—the ingratitude! the stupidity! the contrariness! Being loved is so obviously a blessing, *the* blessing, praise such a rare bequest. Only listen late at night to my closest friends on the literary magazine and in the drama society—they tell horror stories of family life to rival *The Way of All Flesh,* they return shell-shocked from vacations, drift back to school as though from the wars. What they would give to be in my golden slippers! "What's going on?" my mother begs me to tell her; but how can I, when I myself don't fully believe that this is happening to us, or that I am the one who is making it happen. That they, who together cleared all obstructions from my path, should seem now to be my final obstruction! No wonder my rage must filter through a child's tears of shame, confusion, and loss. All that we have constructed together over the course of two century-long decades, and look how I must bring it down—in the name of this tyrannical need that I call my "independence"! My mother, keeping the lines of communication open, sends a note to me at school: "We miss you"—and encloses the brief obituary notice. Across the margin at the bottom of the clipping, she has written (in the same hand with which she wrote notes to my teachers and signed my report cards, in that very same handwriting that once eased my way in the world), "Remember poor Kafka, Aunt Rhoda's beau?"

"Dr. Franz Kafka," the notice reads, "a Hebrew teacher at the Talmud Torah of the Schley Street Synagogue from 1939 to 1948, died on June 3 in the Deborah Heart and Lung Center in Browns Mills, New Jersey. Dr. Kafka had been a patient there since 1950. He was 70 years old. Dr. Kafka was born in Prague, Czechoslovakia, and was a refugee from the Nazis. He leaves no survivors."

He also leaves no books: no *Trial,* no *Castle,* no Diaries. The dead man's papers are claimed by no one, and disappear—all except those four *"meshugeneh"* letters that are, to this day, as far as I know, still somewhere in among the memorabilia accumulated by my spinster aunt, along with a collection of Broadway Playbills, sales citations from the Big Bear, and transatlantic steamship stickers.

Thus all trace of Dr. Kafka disappears. Destiny being destiny, how could it be otherwise? Does the Land Surveyor reach the Castle? Does K. escape the judgment of the Court, or Georg Bendemann the judgment of his father? "'Well, clear this out now!' said the overseer, and they buried the hunger artist, straw and all." No, it simply is not in the cards for Kafka ever to become *the* Kafka—why, that would be stranger even than a man turning into an insect. No one would believe it, Kafka least of all.

J.P.K.

Roth cleverly reprises Kafka's courtship pattern with women in a way that helps us make sense of his actual relationships with Felice Bauer, Julie Wohryzek, Milena Jesenská, and Dora Dymant. When Roth's Kafka accepts "with that formal bow of his the mason jar of barley soup that my grandmother presses him to carry back to his room" we glimpse a Kafka that the hagiographers cannot see. Note also how the young Roth's ultimate, paradoxical rejection of his family's love echoes Dr. Kafka's rejection of Aunt Rhoda's. Does love create an intolerable obligation, an awareness of one's own inadequacy?

J.K.

It's interesting to compare the different life stories that Di Filippo, Scholz and Lethem, and Roth find their versions of Kafka pursuing in America. Though Roth's Kafka shares many traits with the real one, here he is metamorphosed into a Philip Roth character in a domestic urban Jewish social satire.

RUDY RUCKER:

I wrote this story near the start of my literary career, in the spring of 1980. My wife and I were in Heidelberg for two years—I had a grant to do research on infinity at the Mathematics Institute of the university. During this period I read and reread the Penguin Modern Classics edition of *The Diaries of Franz Kafka* several times, drinking in Kafka's vibes and chuckling over the crazy letters he'd write to his relatives and to the family of his lady friend.

One aspect of Kafka's writing that's perhaps not as well-known as it could be is that Kafka himself considered his stories to be funny. His friend Max Brod reports that Kafka once fell out of his chair from laughing so hard while reading aloud from one of his works, perhaps from *Die Verwandlung*, that is, "The Metamorphosis." Our puritanical and self-aggrandizing American culture tends to make out Kafka's work to be solemn and portentous. But it's funny in somewhat the same way as Donald Duck comics.

The humor comes across more clearly if you read Kafka's tales in the original German. He chooses tasty, funny, onomatopoeic words. I'll boldface two examples: The first paragraph of *Die Verwandlung* ends with a remark about how the protagonist Gregor's "*kläglich dünnen Beine* **flimmerten** *ihm hilflos vor den Augen*," that is, about how his "lamentably thin legs **wriggled** helplessly before his eyes." And then, two paragraphs on, Gregor closes his eyes so as not to see his, "**zappelnden** *Beinen*," that is, so as not to see his "**twitching** legs." *Flimmerten, zappelnden*—haw!

The physical setting for "The 57th Franz Kafka" was the house of my Heidelberg friend Imre Molnar, who lived on a very busy street that ran along the Nekar river. I remember noticing an old woman fruitlessly sweeping at the slush in front of the house next to Imre's. This was the spark for my story, and I tried to enliven it with Kafka's mad, antic humor—throwing in some gnarly horror as well.

My story's title comes from the fact that the story is set in 1981, which was fifty-seven years after Kafka's 1924 death. My story ended up in a literary journal, *The Little Magazine*, co-edited by David Hartwell, who'd later be my SF editor at Tor Books. And the story also appeared in my first collection, which took in fact took its title from my story, and appeared from Ace Books in 1983. Perhaps I nursed a fantasy that people would like my story collection so much that I would be considered a "new Franz Kafka" —certainly not the *first* "new Franz Kafka," but maybe the fifty-seventh.

The 57th Franz Kafka

Rudy Rucker

20 JANUARY 1981.

Pain again, deep in the left side of my face. At some point in the night I gave up pretending to sleep and sat by the window, staring down at the blind land-street and the deaf river.

The impossibility of connected thought. Several times I thought I heard the new body moving in the long basin.

It began snowing during the night. I opened both windows and hunched myself forward with my mouth open, drawing in deep, aching breaths. My hope: a perfect snowflake, if sucked down wholly and rapidly, might reach the black center of my lungs and freeze them solid. Imagine breathing water, breathing ice. Later, hearing the bells toll, I wept.

After Mema brought me my breakfast, she went out to clean away the melting snow. I stood well back from the window lest she see my cheers and gloating grimaces.

After clearing the sidewalk, she had not yet had enough of wielding her scrub-broom, and stepped, repeatedly and at great risk, into the heavy land-street traffic, trying to clear off *our half*. She has, in the years since I dissolved the marriage, become an automaton. I realize this with finality when I see her stare uncomprehendingly after the splashing motor-wagons, which again and again cover *our half* of the street, and splatter her apron and her thick legs with the grey, crystalline frosting.

The suppressed laughter hurts my chest. I begin to cough and have to sit down on my bed. Here I sit, words crawling off my pen-point.

There are only four more pages left in this, the last volume of my fifty-seventh series of diaries. I must write less.

23 January 1981.
Three days of fever. Straightening my wet bedclothes, Mema found my special pictures, the Fast-Night groupings, and took them away. *What if Felice were to see them?*

I have more pictures hidden in the attic, pictures I press to my ribs while I pour all my food out into the long basin. The new body is not so far along as I had hoped. There are still only the clotted fibers. It is strange that I could have thought otherwise.

25 January 1981.
Last night the worst yet. Dream: again Reb Pessin showing me the Book of Qlippoth, the secrets of immortality. A high buzzing, as of a tremendous propeller, drowns out his voice. The surprising weight of the little book. He makes a false gesture, and I spread out in space instead of time. A whole city where everyone wears my face, streets of women, the offices. A street-car conductor leaning over me, shaking with laughter, "If I were you…"

Awake before dawn. For the first time real fear that the new body will not be ready. But going into the attic with a candle, I see that all is well. Even the skin is finished.

26 January 1981.
Real sleep at last. Waking up, an unnatural feeling of lightness. So many memories are gone already, gone over.

I drank two cups of black tea with breakfast. Mema had to go back down to the kitchen for the second. When she brought it up, I had forgotten the first breakfast already, and asked her where it was. This is all as it should be. Soon I can begin again.

Yesterday, in a mood of wild exaltation, I mailed my remaining special pictures to Felice, first scribbling her real name on some of the women's faces.

Now, cheerful and whistling from my sound sleep and my two cups of tea, I take pen in hand and compose another letter to her father:

Honored Herr B!

I am not surprised that you have failed to answer my letters of 24.XII.80, 26.XII.80, and 15.I.81. You need not apologize! It is only right and natural that a man in your position must take thought, *in the interests of his daughter,* before moving to bind a marriage contract. The questions of my finances, age and health are undoubtedly your unspoken concerns.

As regards the question of age: I am forty-one, and *will remain so.* Although your daughter is now but twenty, she will in the course of time become sixty. Until that age, I vow to have and hold her as sole love-object. Frau Mema, my housekeeper and ex-wife, can attest to this.

My financial security is assured by certain interlocking fixed-interest annuities. I do not need to work, and I despise to do so. My *brutto* yearly income is in excess of fifteen thousand thalers... not a figure to conjure with, but surely adequate for your little mouse's needs.

The state of my health is a predictable matter. At present it is bad, and it will grow a bit worse. But next month, and in the summer, I will once again be fresh and strong. There can be no doubt of this.

Would a marriage date of February 30 be acceptable to you?

With high respect,

Franz K. LVII.

29 January 1981.

All evening, Mema watched television in the parlor, directly under my bedroom. The police were here yesterday, sent by Felice's father.

They did not dare come up to me, and spoke only to Mema. I stood naked at the head of the stairs, baring my teeth and trembling with a fierce joy each time I glimpsed their green, peaked caps. It struck me that the caps are living beings which *wear policemen*.

The excitement made me very weak, and all day I left the bed only to empty my cavities into the long basin. It is time to complete the task, to open my veins. Mema knows that today is the day, and under my feet she rocks and watches green, peaked caps move across the television screen.

30 January 1981.
LVIII is still waiting in the long basin behind the thin attic wall.

Last night I took candle and long knife and leaned over the basin, staring down through the thick, gathered fluids. The candle-wax dripped and sprung into little saucers, white disks that drifted down to rest on Franz LVIII's closed eyelids. His mouth is set in a smile, as always.

I am not frightened of death, not after fifty-six times. But when my new body walks, the green, peaked caps will take it away. Herr B. must pay for this.

I have resolved to make him murder me. The exquisite uncertainty of *how he will do it*. I feel like a virgin bride.

Mema has gone to the butcher to buy two kilograms of blood-sausage. Tonight I will chew the sausage up for LVIII. My true blood must belong to Herr B.

31 January 1981.
The blood-sausage was everything I had ever dreamed it to be. Thick and dark, with the texture of excrement, the congealed pigs' blood is stuffed into a greasy casing made of the animals' own small intestines.

Leaning over the long basin, chewing and spitting up, I felt a disgust purer and more complete than anything I have experienced since the time of the camps.

The sausage-casing is stamped with repeated pictures of a pig wearing a crown and making obeisances. I have stretched the casing enough to wrap it around my waist, like the little tailor who killed seven with one blow.

The chewing of the sausage took a long time, and I fell asleep in a sort of ecstasy, with my forehead resting on the rim of the long basin. I awakened to a touch of LVIII's hand, tugging petulantly at my hair. I started back, uncertain where I was, and heard the church tower toll three.

Filled with an implacable strength, I descended the stairs. Mema lay sleeping on her cot in the kitchen. I unplugged the phone and brought it upstairs. Then I crawled under my bed to muffle the sound, and dialed Felice's number over and over.

The shining love-words dripped off my lips that still glistened with blood-sausage. My tongue felt slender, magically flexible, as if it could pierce the phone wires and the shell of her ear. After my second call, her father answered, and I gibbered like a golem, ever-new inspirations striking me with each call. I continued calling for two hours. They answered less and less often, and finally not at all. Now I have left my phone off the hook to keep theirs ringing.

Franz K. LVIII is sloshing about in the long basin, impatient for the final spark. The dawn strikes through my window and gilds this page, the last of this volume. Now, before Mema awakes, I must go to pound on Felice's door, a long knife in my hand.

J.P.K.

When he came up with the wonderful grace note of the living caps wearing policemen, Rucker was filtering Kafka through his own gonzo sensibility. Kafka was a prodigious journal keeper, and casting this story as a series of entries adds verisimilitude to a story that lurks at the edge of credibility.

J.K.

Rucker's number 57 shares the first Kafka's acute sensitivity to his body's decay. Kafka was a vegetarian, eating mostly vegetables, nuts, and fruit, and number 57's consuming the blood sausage conveys the horror (and perhaps the thrill of the forbidden) Kafka felt at eating meat, which he once described as leaving him "feeling my abused and punished body in the bed like an alien, disgusting filth."

Carter Scholz:

I wrote this story in order to complete a small volume Jonathan and I had decided upon. It started because Jonathan Lethem lived near me then, and we had lunch pretty often. One noon he showed me a page from his notebook: KAFKA/CAPRA, it said, nothing else. He said, there's a story in there somewhere. I agreed and went home and wrote the first few pages. We traded pages back and forth and after some time we had "Receding Horizon," first published by Bryan Cholfin in *Crank!* 5.

I'd already written one story based upon Kafka ("Blumfeld, An Elderly Bachelor," published in *Crank!* 1), and so had Jonathan ("The Notebooks of Bob K"). After "Receding Horizon" he suggested that we each write one more, and offer the package to Bill Schafer at Subterranean Press. I wrote "The Amount to Carry" and he wrote "K For Fake."

The book of five stories, *Kafka Americana*, came out from Subterranean in 2000 in a limited edition and was reprinted a year later by W. W. Norton. "The Amount to Carry" became the title story of my 2002 collection from PicadorUSA at the urging of my editor, Tim Bent.

As artists, my three protagonists could hardly have had less in common, yet all three worked as insurance executives, competent and highly respected in their day jobs. The hotel owes something to Gilbert Sorrentino's *Splendide-Hôtel*, his rumination on Rimbaud (who therefore makes an uncredited cameo appearance).

The Amount to Carry

Carter Scholz

*Et la Splendide-Hôtel fut bâti dans le chaos de glaces et de nuit du
pôle.*
   —Rimbaud

THE LEGAL SECRETARY of the Workman's Accident Insurance Institute
for the Kingdom of Bohemia in Prague enters the atrium of the hotel.
Slender, sickly, his tall frame seems bowed under the weight of his title.
But his dark darting eyes, in a boyish face as pale as milk, take in the
scene eagerly.

What a fantastic place! The dream of a visionary American, the
hotel has been under construction since the end of the War. A bro-
chure lists its many firsts: an observatory, a radio station, a resident
orchestra (Arnold Schönberg conducting), an indoor health spa, bank
kiosks open day and night for currency exchange. From the atrium an
escalator carries guests to the mezzanine, where a strange aeroplane is
suspended, naked as a bicycle, like something designed by da Vinci
or a Cro-Magnon, nothing like the machines the secretary saw at the
Brescia air show, years ago.

The secretary likes hotels. He loses himself in their depths, their
receding corridors, the chiming of lifts, the jangle of telephones, the
thump of pneumatic tubes. It is the freedom of anonymity, with roast
duck and dumplings on the side.

A placard in the lobby proclaims in four languages, "Conference of International Insurance Executives—Registration." Europe has gone mad for conferences. More placards welcome professional and amateur groups diverse as rocketeers, philosophers, alpinists, and the Catholic Total Abstinence Union. So many conferences are underway that the crowd seems formed of smaller crowds, intersecting, breaking apart, and reforming on their ways to meetings, meals, or diversions, jostling like bemused fowl.

The falsity of public places. Their implacable reality.

Hotels he likes, but not conferences. His first was eight years ago. Terrified beyond stage fright, he spoke on accident prevention in the workplace. He felt sure that the men listening would fall on him and tear him apart when they understood what he was saying. But he was wrong. They recognized that with safer conditions fewer claims would be filed. With a lawyer's cunning the secretary had put altruism before them as self-interest. He felt such relief as he left the stage that he was unable to stay for the other talks. Uncontrollable laughter welled up in him as he bolted for the door.

That was 1913, the year his first book was published. Now, at thirty-eight, he is becoming known for his writing, but finds himself miserably unable to write. Summoned to the castle but kept at the gate. And his time grows short. Last month at Matliary he underwent another hopeless treatment. It rained the whole time. At the end of his stay the weather cleared, and he hiked in the mountains. On his return, Prague seemed more oppressive than the sanatorium. Some dybbuk of the perverse made him volunteer for the conference.

The secretary pauses at a display of models. Marvels of America, of engineering. New York City! Finely carved ships are afloat in a harbor of blue sand. Pasteboard cliffs rise from the sand, buildings and spires surmount the island. In the harbor stands a crowned green female, Liberty, tall as a building, holding aloft a sword.

Beyond a glass terrace is the hotel's deer park, an immense enclosed courtyard. On its grass peacocks stride, tails dragging. One turns to face him. The iridescent blue of its chest. The pitiless black stones of its eyes.

The sideboard in his suite holds fresh flowers, a bottle of champagne, a bowl of oranges, a telephone. From his window he sees a lake and thinks of Palestine.

The gentleman from Hartford pauses at the cigar stand. A wooden Indian shades his eyes against the sun of an imaginary prairie. The gentleman purchases a panatela. Bold type on a magazine arrests his eye: *de stijl*. Opening it he reads, The object of this magazine will be to contribute to the development of a new consciousness of beauty. On the facing page is a photograph of this very hotel. Beauty. Is that what surrounds him? He looks from the photo of the lobby into the lobby. He adds the magazine and a *Paris Herald* to his purchase, receiving in change a bright 1920 American dime. His wife Elsie regards him sidelong from its face.

Crowds rush to their morning appointments. Mr. Stevens is free until lunch. In truth, his presence here is unnecessary to his agency's business, but he has developed a knack of absences from home and from his wife.

His attention is taken by a scale model of the hotel itself, accurate even to the construction scaffolding over the entrance. Through a tiny window of the tiny penthouse he sees two figures studying blueprints unfurled between them.

In *de stijl*, Stevens reads: Like the young century itself, the hotel is a vortex of energies and styles. It thrusts upward, sprawls sideways, even sends an arm into the lake, where a floating walkway winds through a houseboat colony designed by Frank Lloyd Wright, fresh from his triumphant Imperial Hotel in Tokyo. Many architects have been engaged, Gropius and Le Corbusier, de Klerk and Mendelsohn; they draw up plans, begin work, are dismissed or quit; so the hotel itself remains more an idea than a thing, a series of sketches of itself, a diffracted view not unlike M. Duchamp's notorious *Nude* in the New York Armory Show of some years ago. The hotel is a sort of manifesto-in-progress to a multiple futurism, as though the very idea of the modern is too energetic and protean to find a single unified expression.

It occurs to Stevens that the hotel is unreal. Reality is an exercise of the most august imagination. This place is a hodgepodge. It gives him a sense of his own unreality. Then again, the real world seen by an imaginative man may very well seem like an imaginative construction.

He folds the magazine and looks for a place to smoke in peace.

The senior partner of Ives & Myrick awakes right early. The morning light is somehow wrong. And where is Harmony, his wife? Outside, birds sing their dawn chorus, hitting all the notes between the notes. He remembers the two pianos in the Sunday school room of Central Presbyterian. One piano had fallen a quartertone flat of the other. He tried out chords on the two of them at once, right hand on one, left hand on the other. Notes between notes—an infinity of notes! Again and again he struck those splendid new chords. Out of tune—what an idea! Can nature be out of tune?

Now he remembers. The conference. It should be Mike Myrick here. He's better at this hail-fellow-well-met stuff. But Mike said Ives should go. Do you a world of good, Charlie. Write some music on the boat. Give Harmony some time off from you. Ives had been laid up for three months after his second heart attack. It wore Harmony out, caring for him. Mike's right, she deserves a vacation from him.

These memory lapses worry him. He's forty-seven years old, he calls in sick a lot, he's not pulling his weight. His job, his future, how long can he keep it up? Shy Charlie, who's never sold a policy in his life, has come to this conference to prove the point—to himself, he guesses—that he's still an asset to the agency, and no loafer.

Out of bed, then. On the desk is the latest draft of his essay, "The Amount to Carry," condensed for his luncheon talk. Just the key points. It is at once a mathematical formula for estate planning and a practical guide to making the sale. Sell to the masses! Get into the lives of the people! I can answer scientifically the one essential question. Do you know what that is?

In the last twelve years Ives & Myrick has taken in two hundred million dollars. Two millions of that have gone to Ives. By any measure he's a rich man, but still he dreads retirement. The end of his usefulness, of his strength. So he's making provisions. Much of his income now comes from renewal commissions. Normally the selling agent gets a nice piece of change every time a policy is renewed, but that takes years, and the younger men are impatient, so they've been selling their commissions to him at a discount. A little irregular, perhaps, but they're happy to take the money!

A man has to provide for his family. They adopted Edie five years ago, and her parents are still asking for help. It amounts to buying the child. But isn't Edie better off now? When Harmony lost their baby, she and Charlie wept nightlong. For a month she lay in hospital. Sick with despair and worry, Charlie set to music a Keats poem:

> The spirit is too weak;
> mortality weighs heavily upon me
> like unwilling sleep,
> and each imagined pinnacle and steep
> tells me I must die,
> like a sick eagle looking towards the sky.

From that day he knew that they must carry one another. It scared him, then, for two people to so depend.

The money's for his music too. It cost him $2,000 last year to print the "Concord" Sonata. And it will cost a sight more to bring out the songs. But the only way the lily boys and the Rollos will ever hear this music is if he prints it himself. He mailed 700 copies of the "Concord" to names culled from *Who's Who* and the *Musical Courier*'s subscription list. Gave offense to several musical pussies. All those nice Mus Docks and ladybirds falling over in a faint at the sight of his manly dissonances.

In open rehearsal last spring the respected conductor Paul Eisler, holding a nice baton, led his New Symphony through Ives's "Decoration Day." Musicians dropped out one by one, till by the last measure a violinist in the back row was the sole survivor. There is a limit to musicianship, said Eisler coldly, handing the score back to him.

A limit to someone's, anyway.

But this fuss with revisions and printers is hollow. The truth is he hasn't written any new music since his illness—since the War, really. If music is through with him, he guesses he can take it, he's written enough. But how do you get it heard? Isn't it enough to write it? Do you have to carry it on your back into the town square?

Wilson dead and the League of Nations with him. That weak sister Harding in the White House.

He's getting into one of his black moods that Harmony so hates, and he'd better not, not with his talk ahead of him. He remembers seeing a piano in a parlor off the main lobby. Playing it might put him right.

When K was hired in 1908, the Institute was a scandal, not unlike the life insurance companies in New York a few years before, though it was a scandal of Bohemian incompetence rather than American greed. For twenty years the institute had run at a loss. K's hiring coincided with a sweeping reform; he was made to put a cash value on various injuries: lost limbs, fingers, hands, toes, eyes, and other maimings. He adjusted premiums, which had been constant, to correspond to levels of risk in specific occupations. In the course of travel to verify claims, he found himself examining production methods and machinery. Once he redesigned a mechanical planer.

Even the most cautious worker is drawn into the cutting space when the cutter slips or the lumber is thrown back, which happens often.... Accidents usually take off several finger joints or whole fingers.

How modest these people are. Instead of storming the institute and smashing the place to bits, they come and plead.

Stevens locates an armchair. At one end of the bronze-trimmed parlor stands a potted palm, in which a mechanical bird twitters silently. The dime is still in his hand. Surely she is beautiful: Elsie in a Phrygian cap, the Roman symbol of a freed slave. The master carving by Adolph Weinman, twelve inches across, is on their mantelpiece in Hartford. Does Stevens oppress her? Does Weinman think so, is that the message of the cap? Its wings tempt confusion with Mercury, Hermes, messenger, god of merchants and thieves, patron of eloquence and fraud. Holder of the caduceus, whose touch makes gold. On the reverse, a bundle of sticks, Roman fasces. He tucks the coin into a vest pocket, feeling his ample flesh yield beneath the cloth. That monster, the body.

He unfolds the *Herald*. Victor Emmanuel III is losing power to blackshirted anarchists called *fascisti*. The Paris Peace Conference demands 132 billion gold marks in reparations from Germany, prompting a violent protest from the new chairman of the National Socialist German Workers' Party's—some berber with a Chaplin-Hardy mustache. European politics is *opera buffa,* when not *bruta.* Stevens turns with relief to the arts section. New Beethoven biography by Thayer. New music festival in Donaueschingen. Caruso still being mourned. Play by Karel Capek, *R.U.R.,* opens in Prague. Review of Van Vechten's new book.

Lately Van Vechten suggested Stevens assemble a book of poems. He promised to give it to Alfred Knopf. Surely it's time for his first book, whatever friction it causes with Elsie. Stevens is forty-two.

At the Arensbergs' once, Elsie said, I like Mr. Stevens's writing when it is not affected. But it is so often affected. No, what she liked was being his sole reader. When he sent poems out she resented it.

He unrings the panatela, rolling it between his fingers as he turns titles in his mind. Supreme Fiction. The Grand Poem: Preliminary Minutiæ. How little it would take to turn poets into the only true comedians.

As he's about to light up, a sobersided balding type sits at the piano. New York suit, Yankee set to his jaw. After a moment he starts to play plain chords, as from a harmonium in a country church. Stevens thinks he knows the hymn from his Lutheran childhood, but then there are wrong notes and false harmonies, played not with the hesitations and corrections of an amateur, but with steady confidence. A pianist himself, Stevens listens closely. At an anacrusis, the treble disjoints from the bass and goes its own way, in another key and another time. His listening mind is both enchanted and repelled. Music then is feeling, not sound.

A tall thin Jew with jug ears and a piercing gaze, *echt mitteleuropisch,* has paused in the doorway to hear the Yankee's fantasia.

—Doch, dass kenn' ich, he says.

The Yankee starts, but says nothing.

—That, that music you play. In München war's, seit zehn Jahren. Max Brod hab' ich am Konzert begleiten. Mahler dirigiert. Diese Melodien, genau so.

—Huh? says the Yankee.

—Something about a concert, Stevens interjects from his chair, startling Ives again. —He says he's heard that song before. At a concert in Munich ten years ago. Conducted by Mahler.

—Gustav Mahler?

—Ja ja, Gustav Mahler. Erinnere mich ganz klar, ganz am Schluss kommen die Glocken, gegen etwas vollkommen anders in die Streicher. Unheimlich war's.

—He says a bell part, against strings at the end, in, apparently, two different keys?

—Yes! That's it! Glocken and Streicher! The Yankee's German is atrocious.

—Glocken, agrees the Jew. —Ganz unheimlich.

—An uncanny effect, says Stevens.

—But that's my Third Symphony! How could he have heard it? It's never been performed. Wait now. Tams, my copyist, he once told me that Mahler came looking for American scores. This was in 'ten, when Mahler conducted the New York Phil. Tams said he took my Third. I never believed it, I thought Tams lost the score and made up a tale. But by God, it must be true!

The Yankee, excited now and voluble, rises from the piano bench, extending a hand.

—Charles Ives, Ives & Myrick Agency, New York. Life insurance.

—Franz Kafka. Of Workman's Accident Insurance Institute in Praha. I am very pleased to meet you.

—Cough…?

—Kafka.

Stevens, having unwisely involved himself, cannot now politely withdraw to the solitary pleasure of his cigar.

—Stevens, Hartford Casualty. Surety bonds.

—Hartford? says Ives. —We used to have an office in Hartford. Are you a Yale man?

—Harvard 'o1.

—Yale '98, says Ives, defensively.

—Do you live in New York, Mr. Ives?

—New York and Redding.

—Reading! Pennsylvania?

—Redding Connecticut.

—Oh, Redding. I'm from Reading Pennsylvania.

—I thought you said Hartford.

—I was born in Reading. As was my wife.

—My wife Harmony's a Hartford girl. Her father is the Reverend Joe Twitchell. He's the man that married and buried Mark Twain.

—I've heard of Twain, says Stevens drily.

—A great American writer, says Kafka.

—Are you married, Mr. Kavka? asks Ives.

—Married…no. An elderly…bachelor, do you say? With a bad habit of, ah, Verlobungen? Engagements?

Ives appears shocked by this display of loose European mores, and Stevens hastens to change the subject.

—Mr. Ives, do you happen to know Edgard Varèse?

—Who?

—A composer. He moved to Greenwich Village from Paris. He founded the New Symphony a few years ago.

Ives narrows his eyes. —Never heard of him. Some Bohemian city slicker, I guess.

—Bohemian? asks Kafka.

—Meaning an artistic type, says Stevens. —La vie bohême. Are you artistic, Herr Kafka?

The faint smile on Kafka's face vanishes. Dismay fills his serious dark eyes.

—Oh, not in the least.

Ives strides briskly to the luncheon. He's keyed up, excited, raring to go. He took to the hotel at once, its brash mix of styles, chrome and ormolu, like a clamor of Beethoven, church hymns, and camp marches. He passes the scale model of Manhattan, so finely made he can almost pick out the Ives & Myrick office on Liberty Street. But what is this? South and east of Central Park are two unfamiliar needletopped skyscrapers, even taller than the Woolworth Building. The downtown building is where the Waldorf-Astoria should be. Surely that's not right, yet something about them projects a natural authority. As he puzzles, he hears a shout.

—Fire!

People turn. Ives smells smoke. A clerk steps forward.

—Please! No cause for concern! There is always a fire somewhere in the hotel. We have the most modern sprinkler and containment systems. Everything is under control.

And indeed, the smoke has dispersed. Alarm yields to sheepishness as guests return to their occupations.

At luncheon, Stevens is seated across from Kafka. Kafka slides his *veau cordon bleu,* fatted calf, to one side of the plate and diligently chews some green beans. Stevens is looking on with, he realizes as Kafka's penetrating gaze meets his, the jaundiced eye that Oliver Hardy turns on Stan Laurel. Stevens touches his ginger mustache and looks away.

—Life insurance is doing its part in the progress of the greater life values, Ives is saying.

Stevens, on his third glass of Haut-Medoc, cocks an eyebrow at the podium. Can Ives believe this stuff? Has he forgotten the Armstrong Act? Just fifteen years ago, the life insurance business was so corrupt that even the New York legislature couldn't ignore it. Sales commissions were fifty, eighty, one hundred percent of the premiums. Executive parties were bacchanals. Mutual president Richard McCurdy, before his indictment, called life insurance "a great benevolent missionary institution." His own benevolence, before he was indicted, enriched his family by fifteen millions. The state shut down half the agencies and sent any number of executives into forced retirement. Come to think of it, that's probably how young Ives got his start, stepping into that vacuum.

As a surety claims attorney, Stevens is inclined to finical doubt. Defaults, breaches, and frauds are his profession. He is a rabbi of the ways and means by which people fail their commitments, and how they excuse themselves. He feels that the attempt to secure one's interests against chance and fate is noble but vain. Insurance is a communal project but a capitalist enterprise, a compassionate ideal ruled by the equations of actuaries. In the risk pool, it appears that the fortunate succor the misfortunate, but that is a salesman's fiction; the pool is more precisely like a mass of gas molecules in Herr Boltzmann's kinetic theory. The position of the individual is unimportant. We are dust in the wind. What can we insure?

Kafka is still chewing.

But insurance is only the prelude to Ives's fugue: now he is off onto nation-wide town meetings, referenda, the will of the people, the majority! Quotations from Shakespeare, Lamb, Emerson, Thoreau. He's lost his audience.

From a tablemate, Stevens hears, —Deny a claim for a year and most people give up.

Stevens feels a fleeting pang for Ives's pure, unreal belief. The poet chides himself: Have it your way. The world is ugly, and the people are sad.

The final belief is to believe in a fiction which you know to be a fiction, because there is nothing else.

Hotel of the future. Once a grand hotel in the Continental style, it has been made completely new. Even the location has changed. With over a thousand rooms and more added every day, twenty ballrooms, a retail arcade, an underground parking garage, automatic elevators, and a mooring mast for aircraft, it is the hotel of the future.

Tradition. Yet tradition is not forgotten. Arthur, the original owner, now in his late sixties, has been kept on as concierge. Take him aside, offer him a bowl of haschisch, and he may tell you tales of old Java, of gunrunning in Ethiopia. His ravaged face, wooden leg, and clinking moneybelt are reminders of a more colorful, dangerous, and perhaps more actual world.

Below. Some say, if you pass muster with Arthur, he may press a key into your palm, and whisper directions to the labyrinthine cellars. There your every whim can be indulged.

Apparatus. Others swear that the cellars are not like that at all, but are filled with machinery, row upon row of brass rods and cogwheels, brightly lit by hanging electric globes, churning with a peculiar clacking noise and a smell of oiled metal. A small rack of needles, like a harrow, pivots to hold for a moment a punched card, until a hiss of compressed air shoots it down a runnel and another card is grasped. The apparatus is said to control all the hotel's workings, from the warmth of the hothouses to the accounting of bills. It is a remarkable piece of apparatus, not so different from the Hollerith tabulating machines that have lately made themselves essential to the insurance industry. The apparatus is based on designs by the late Charles Babbage of England, William Seward Burroughs, Herr Odhmer of Sweden, and the Americans Thomas Watson and Vannevar Bush. But no one fully understands it, for it is self-modifying. Some say that elements of reason and intelligence, of life itself, have accrued to it.

Work in progress. As with the apparatus, it is hard to know what in the hotel is finished and what is in progress. The raw concrete walls of the natatorium may be a bold statement of modernity, or may await a marble cladding. The genius of the hotel may be precisely this ambiguity, this unwillingness to declare itself.

Transnational. The owner calls the hotel a machine for living away from home. The master plan calls for groundbreakings in six continents, every hotel different, yet with the same level of service. Even Antarctica, that chaos of ice and polar night, will one day fly the hotel's flag. Home, the owner believes, is an obsolete fiction.

After his talk, Ives is depressed and uncertain. His exhilarations are often followed by a crash. He doubts that he put over any of it, apart from the business formulas. Yet surely, after the War, after the Spanish influenza that swept the globe, all men must see that their common good is one.

The fabric of existence weaves itself whole. His music and his business are not separate; his talk was as pure an expression of his belief and will as any of his music. He's given it his best, and now he has no interest for the rest of the proceedings. He's ready to go home. The hotel, which delighted him, now oppresses him. It seems endless. He leaves behind the meeting rooms overfull with conventioneers, passes vacant ballrooms with distant ceilings, he walks down deserted corridors where the repeating patterns of carpet, the drift of dust in afternoon sun, are desolate with melancholy, ennui, loss. It begins to frighten him, this vast, unfathomable place. He is overcome with a sense of futility. He thinks of his father's band playing gavottes at the battle of Chancellorsville.

Turning a corner, he spots the one-legged concierge, limping and clanking down the hall. The old rogue comes up to Ives.

—I carry about in my belt 16,000 francs in gold. It weighs over eight kilos and gives me dysentery.

—Why do you carry it? asks Ives.

—For my art! To insure my liberty. Soon I will have enough!

—I see. Can you tell me which way to the main lobby?

Scornfully the ancient laughs. —You see nothing. That way.

The elevator lurches to a halt between floors.

There are numbers between numbers, thinks Stevens. Between the integers are fractions, and between those the irrationals, and so on to the dust of never-quite-continuity. If numerical continuity is an illusion, perhaps temporal continuity is as well. Perhaps there are dark moments between our flickers of consciousness, as between the frames of a movie. The Nude of Duchamp descends her staircase in discrete steps. Where is she between steps? Perhaps here at the hotel. At this moment, stuck between floors, where am I?

Stevens presses the button for ROOF. The elevator begins to move sideways.

Past its glass doors windows slide by, offering views of the city, shrunk to insignificance, by height. The car seems to be traveling along the circumference of a tower. After a quarter circuit, the outer windows cease, and shortly the car resumes ascent.

Its doors open to verdancy. The rooftop garden is a maze, a forest, an artificial world. A hothouse opens onto a short arcade that corners into an arbor. Lemon thyme grows between the cobbles and he crushes fragrance from it as he walks. In his more virile youth, he often hiked thirty miles in a day up the Hudson from New York, or ferried to New Jersey to ramble through the open country near Hackensack, Englewood, HoHoKus. Slowly he finds a geography in the paths, steps, and terraces. It is indeed a world. Small signs, like lexical weeds, mark frontiers. From SOUTH AMERICA and its spiked succulents with their starburst flowers of yellow and pink and blue he enters MEXICO. On the path is a fallen *tomato verde*. The enclosing lantern, which the fruit has not quite grown to fill, is purple at the stem and papery, but at the tip has decayed to a tough, brittle lace of veins, like an autumn leaf. Inside the small green fruit is split. His fingers come away gummy.

Abruptly, past espaliered pears, there is the roofedge, cantilevered into air. Light scatters through the atoms of the air: blue. Not even sky is continuous.

Distant snowcapped peaks shelve off into sky. He remembers with sharp yearning his camping and hunting trip in British Columbia with Peckham and their rough guides. Twenty years ago. Another lost paradise.

His elate melancholy follows the ups and downs of the distant range: however long he lives, how much and well he writes, no poetry can compass this world, the actual.

K decides to walk abroad in the city, but the hotel baffles his efforts to leave it. Curving corridors lead past ballrooms and parlors, but never reach the atrium. After ten minutes, K stops at a desk in an arcade.

—Bitte, wie geht man hinaus?

—And why do you want to go out?

Though the desk clerk has clearly understood K's question, he answers in English, and with another question. K is annoyed, but perseveres in German.

—Ich will spazieren.

—You can walk in the hotel. Try the lake ramp, the deer park, the rooftop gardens. Here is a map.

—Danke nein.

K turns down corridors at random. At the end of one he sees sunlight. Although the exit door is marked CLOSED UNDER CONSTRUCTION it is unlocked. He transgresses and finds himself in a small grotto, perhaps a corner of the deer park. Around him the hotel walls rise sixteen floors to a cantilevered roof.

He is in a graveyard of worn stones. His fingers move right to left over the nearest, reading. Beautiful eldest, rest in peace, Anshel Mor Henach. 5694 Sivan 3.

The gentleman from Hartford has dined alone. Susceptible with wine he follows the chance of shifting crowds through the lobby.

—Faites vôtres jeux, mesdames messieurs.

The casino's Doric columns remind Stevens of the Hartford office. A temple to probability, and the profit to be had from it.

Dice chatter, balls racket round their polished course, cards slap and sigh on baize. In his good ear rings the bright syrinx of hazard. In the bad one, the dull hoo-hoo of drums. Chance and fate, high flute and groaning bass.

—Un coup de dés jamais n'abolira le hasard.

Stevens bets. The wheel rumbles, the ball rattles.

In the spa, K glimpses himself in a full-length mirror. Hollow cheeks, sunken stomach, spindly legs, ribs like a charcoal sketch of famine. Other nude bodies, ghostly in steam, pass in a line. In modesty he turns away, but he sees then uniformed men, like guards in some Strafkolonie, herding the others through doors. The flesh of their bodies is as haggard as their faces. The men are all circumcised. Then come the women. Faces downcast, but some turn to him.

—Ottla! Elli! Valli!

Is there no end to this? Another woman turns her imploring face to him.

—Milena!

The doors close, and he is alone but for two guards murmuring in German, the angelic tongue of Goethe and Kleist. K is invisible to them. Their gleaming leather boots, their gray uniforms, the stark black and white device on their red armbands, show none of the Prussian love of pomp. This is something new. Yet it is the old story.

Enough, then! Let it be done! Let every child of Israel be run through the Harrow and tattooed with the name of his crime: *Jude*. All but K the invisible, the impervious. Instead of him they have taken Milena, not even a Jew, for the crime of having loved him.

The vision passes. K dresses, slowly apprehending that the hotel is not style, but a force as implacable as history. He has lived through one world war and will not see another. But unlike Ives with his one-world utopianism, unlike Stevens in the protected precincts of his being, K knows that another war is coming.

Style is optional, history is not.

In his room that night, Ives tries to compose.

Six years past, in the Adirondacks, he had a vision of earth, mountains, and sky as music. In the predawn it seemed that he was high above the earth, Keene Valley stretched below him, mist lying in its sinuous watercourse and the lights of the town burning within it like coals in smoke. The last stars were fading, and the horizon held bands of rose, orange, and indigo. The greening forests took on color and depth, the fallow fields, the curdling mist. He imagined several orchestras, huge conclaves of singing men and women, placed in valleys, on hillsides, on mountain tops. The universe in tones, or a Universe Symphony.

The plan still terrifies him. He's made notes and sketches, but the real work hasn't begun. He doubts he can do it. The vision is remote now, a fading memory, impalpable as his childhood. He sits, he sketches, he notes. Even at this hour from some far part of the hotel the sound of construction is unceasing. Danbury and Redding seem another world. He no longer knows how things go together.

Pulmonary edema due to arteriosclerotic and hypertensive heart disease with probable myocardial infarction.

He sees an old man outside the house in Redding. An airplane buzzes overhead, and the old man shakes his cane at it. The hillsides and valleys roll away into the haze of distance. It's all there, the old man thinks. If only I could have done it.

Sleepless, K sits writing to Max, to Klopstock, to his sisters Elli and Ottla. He starts and tears up another letter to Milena. What is left to say?

His windows are black as a peacock's eyes. Memory is a pyre that burns forever. Felice, Grete, Milena, how shamefully he has treated them.

The life one lives and the stories one tells about it are never the same. Every moment has a secret narrative, so intertwined with those of other moments that finding the truth about anything becomes a labor of Zeno. An endless maze of connecting tunnels, branching and intersecting without end.

He sips at a glass of water, swallows with difficulty.

Laryngologische Klinik
Pat.-Nr. 135
Name: Dr Kafka Franz
Diagnose: Tbc. laryngis
Pat. ist völlig appetitlos u. fühlt sich sehr schwach.
Pupillen normal, reagieren prompt.

Pat. ist leicht heiser.
Hinterwand infiltriert.
Taschenbänder gerötet.
Haemsputum.

What is it, to write? I want rather to live.

He will give Milena all his diaries. Let her see what he is, let her take him entire. Is this contrition? Or a sly way of freeing himself from his burden? Or is it, at last, the only marriage he can make?

A curious small voice addresses the secretary: *It was late in the evening when K arrived. The village was deep in snow.* He holds the pen unmoving.

A faint squeaking comes from the floor. Near the head of the bed is a mousehole, from which a small gray head peers. A pink nose winks at him.

—Guten Abend, Fräulein Maus. What a pretty voice, what a singer you are! Won't you come in? Come, here is a nice warm slipper for you to sleep in.

He edges his foot forward, slipper on his toe. Whiskers twitch and the mouse is gone, running in the tiny corridor behind the baseboard, through all the secret passages of the hotel, unwatched, unsuspected, secure.

It is late. The model Manhattan is now a cordillera of skyscrapers. At the island's southmost tip rise a pair of silver towers, blunt as commerce. Stevens feels old, past meridian. His own worldliness reproves him. He understands nothing of the cold wind and polar night in which he moves. But he knows that he will live through awful silences to old age.

There is no insurance. There is no liberty. Elsie is his wife, despite his yes her no. He must be better to her.

The airplane has come and gone. The Redding air is still. He listens to the silence: his blood thrums, a jackdaw cries, wind rustles an oak. Universe symphony. And Edith calls, running towards him:

—Daddy! Carry me!

He catches her up and lifts her to his shoulders. Her thin legs dangle down.

—Carry me! she commands again, and he starts towards the house, where Harmony has stepped onto the porch. She sees them, and the moment is so full that he pauses, misses his step, then quickly recovers, walking forward as Harmony calls in concern:

—Charlie! Your heart!

From uneasy dreams the secretary awakens transformed. A coverlet recedes before him like the Alps. He holds out his hands, seeing spindly shanks, thin gray fur, grasping claws. There comes a heavy knock at the door. He scampers across the bed, his claws grasping the fabric as he goes down the side and under the bed. Cowering there, nose twitching, chest heaving, tail wrapped round his shivering flanks, he sees the enormous legs of the maid moving about the room. She is sweeping with a broom as big as a house. Crumbs fly past him like stones; in a storm of dust he sneezes and trembles.

Near the head of the bed he spies the dark hole in the baseboard, and without a moment's thought he dashes for it. The maid exclaims, the shadow of the broom descends, he is squeaking in terror, running, and then he is in his burrow, in the darkness, in the walls of the hotel, carrying nothing, but wearing, as it were, the whole world.

J.K.

Kafka retired from the Workers' Accident Insurance Company, because of his failing health, on July 1, 1922, but in the previous few years he had taken several long leaves of absence due to his deteriorating health. So the events in this story would have to have taken place sometime before 1922. Charles Ives was nine years older than Kafka, and Wallace Stevens was four years older.

J.P.K.

In the fantastic hotel of the future, three great artists who never met greet and misunderstand one another. The more you know about the real Kafka, Wallace Stevens, and Charles Ives, the more Scholz's vision will take hold in your imagination.

TAMAR YELLIN:

For many years I could not read Kafka. I would get to the bottom of the first page of *The Castle* and my brain would seize. Then something clicked inside me and I became obsessed with him.

I believe reading Kafka to be a deeply personal experience. You can accept what others tell you Kafka means or you can interpret him for yourself. His enigmatic work lends itself to almost infinite interpretation. For me, Kafka came at a time when I felt I had inexcusably renounced all the things one is supposed to do in life in order to write. The freedom I seemed to have was crushed by a paralysing sense of responsibility (the word is key in Kafka's world view) and my resultant guilt was its own punishment. The Kafka I read presented life as a trial in which we are guilty from the start and the sentence is always death. He spoke to me.

This is not expressed in the story which is included in this collection, but in my other Kafka story, "A Letter from Josef K," in which the protagonist writes from what it becomes clear is a self-inflicted prison. This is a K who does not die "like a dog" (at least not yet) but lives voluntarily under a life sentence.

The Kafka in the present story is a more benign manifestation: an old man living out his afterlife on the Yorkshire moors. He represents the ironic side of my Kafka infatuation. Once again he is an alter ego, but this time he is Kafka the outsider, the alien, the Jew. This was a breakthrough story for me as a young writer. In writing it I came to realize that my sense of dislocation was inextricable from my creativity.

Kafka in Brontëland

Tamar Yellin

My PARENTS BELONGED to the lost generation, and when I was growing up their drawers were full of old letters, stopped watches, bits of broken history: a Hebrew prayer book, an unblessed mezuzah, nine views of Budapest between the wars. I drew pictures on the prayer book, mislaid the mezuzah, swapped the postcards for Peruvian stamps; and when my parents were dead and I was fully grown I looked at the hoard and saw it was nothing but junk. Then I hired a skip and threw the lot—watches, pictures, letters and prayers—onto the heap of forgotten things, and came up here to start a new clean life; but I rattled the cans of the past behind me willy-nilly.

There is a man in the village, they call him Mr. Kafka. I do not know if that is his real name. He does not often speak to people. He is very old. Every day he walks down the village in the company of an elderly and asthmatic wire-haired terrier.

He does not speak to people. But he smiles occasionally: a faint and distant, somewhat dreamy smile. In this respect, but in no other, he resembles a little the Kafka of the photographs.

Derek the builder says that he is Dutch. Kafka is a Dutch name. No, no, I tell him, it is Czech, it is the Czech for jackdaw. It is like the writer Kafka, who was born in Prague. Who? The writer. Kafka the writer. The one who wrote *The Trial*.

Well, you never know, says Derek. And he tells me a story of how people die and come back to life. How young Philip Shackleton, who used to work at the quarry over Dimples Hill, fell into the crusher one day and disappeared. "Never found his body. Just traces of blood in the stones. Next year he turns up in Torremolinos."

The main question, however, is whether there are beams behind my cottage ceiling. Derek taps the plasterboard with his implement.

"Yes, I should think you've got a nice set of beams under there. Pine. Shall I go whoops with the crowbar?"

I say we had better wait a little.

When he has gone I dart across to the Fleece for a box of matches. Mr. Kafka is sitting in the corner over a pint of dark beer. He wears a dirty mackintosh and a buff-coloured hat like James Joyce, and he stares into his beer as though time has ended for him. I consider making conversation, but I haven't the courage.

When I was a girl I wanted to be Emily Brontë, but this summer I am reading Kafka with all the new enthusiasm of an adolescent. I walk the moors with a book, utterly entranced. I have fallen in love with him. Sometimes I imagine that I am him.

These literary obsessions are hardly innocent. My urge to be Emily, for instance, has altered my entire life. That is why I am here, alone in Brontëland. I grew up determined to live in passionate isolation. Only recently did I realise I had been misled: that she never spent a single day of her life alone in Haworth parsonage.

And now I have chosen to fall in love with Kafka. Kafka, child of the city. Kafka the outcast, Kafka the Jew. He wasn't inspired by spaces, he didn't belong in the hills. He didn't care for weather. He would have hated it here.

Emily Brontë called these mountains heaven. Today they are referred to as the white highlands. Down in the valley, in the poor town, live the Asians, Pakistanis, Muslims from Karachi and Lahore.

Derek tells me about the first time he ever laid eyes on a Black man. "I just stared." It was in the next village. "Nothing so exceptional now." "Yes," nods Hilda. "You don't see that many here still; but they're creeping up the valley road."

Hilda is a Baptist, Derek a Wesleyan; or it might be the other way round. They are always sparring. When she hears that I play the piano, she lends me a copy of *The Methodist Hymn Book*. "You're not the only Jew round here, you know. Mr. Simons who runs the off-licence, I think he's half-Jewish."

I ask about Mr. Kafka. Kafka, I say uncertainly, is a Jewish name.

"I thought he was Polish. Isn't he Polish, Derek?"

"Dutch," says Derek, with conviction. He lights his pipe. "Some sort of a writer fellow, so I've heard."

Then he tells a story about the Irish navvies who helped to build the reservoir. One of them, who was in love with the same lass as his neighbour, took the brake off one of the carts one day and ran him over, and they carried him up to the village, dead. "They said it was an accident," he concludes, "but you ask Ian Ogden and he'll always tell you, murder was committed in this village."

The Greenwoods and the Shackletons all have Irish blood. Derek's great-grandfather was a Sussex landlord. Hilda's used to make boots for Branwell Brontë.

Twice a week I ride down from the white highlands to the black town. In fact it is more of a grey colour. It has a shopping centre, a cenotaph and a community college. I am learning Urdu.

Ap ka nam kiya hai?

Mera nam Judith hai.

On Tuesdays I teach English to a young woman from Lahore. She is recently married: at the moment she seems to spend most of her time rearranging the furniture in the lounge. Every time I visit we sit somewhere else.

As a matter of fact her English is rather more advanced than my Urdu. She has a degree in psychology. I decide we will read *Alice in Wonderland* together.

Mrs. Rahim has lovely tendrils of hair at the nape of her neck, and I spend much of the lesson watching her play with them. I also stare at a framed picture of the Ka'ba done in hologram. The mad dream of Wonderland, taken at such protracted length, makes no sense whatever: we might as well be reading Japanese.

Mr. Rahim pops his head around the door: a cheerful face, a white kurta. He is carrying a live chicken by the legs. Shortly afterwards I hear him killing it in the kitchen.

As I leave the house at five the children are making their way to mosque to learn Koran: boys in white prayer caps, solemn little girls in long habits. I remember that a Jew should not live more than half a mile from a synagogue, to prevent the desecration of the sabbath; nor can he pray the services alone. Ten men are required for a congregation; though they do say that a Jewish woman is a congregation in herself.

It is getting dark, and all the shops, the Sangha Spice Mart, Javed Brothers, the Alruddin Sweet Palace, are lit up like Christmas. I am filled with nostalgia for something I never had.

Today I read the following lines in my *Introduction to Kafka*:

More than any other writer, Kafka describes the predicament of the secular alienated Jew. Yet his work, so personal on one level, remains anonymously universal. He has no Jewish axe to grind. Nowhere in any of his fictions does Kafka mention the words Jewish, or Jew.

This seems to me remarkable. Can it be so? I resolve to make a thorough survey. There must be the odd Jew somewhere that my commentator has missed.

I cannot escape the impression that this is a pat on the back for Kafka. Yet they seem rather a sad conjuring trick, these disappearing Jews. A bit like that author who composed an entire novel without using the letter e.

The Brontë sisters did not recoil from mentioning Jews. I know all their references by heart. *Villette* has an "old Jew broker" who "glances up suspiciously from under his frost-white eyelashes" while he seals letters in a bottle; but at least he does a satisfactory job. Charlotte describes her employers, "proud as peacocks and wealthy as Jews," but I have never liked Charlotte much. There is a "self-righteous Pharisee" in

Wuthering Heights, and in some ways I am grateful Emily did not live to finish that second novel.

The Brontës, of course, are often praised for the universality of their work. Especially *Wuthering Heights*, which is extremely popular in Japan. All of which goes to disprove our professor's thesis: in order to be universal you don't have to leave out the Jews.

I may change my mind about ripping down the ceiling in my cottage. It is a perfectly good ceiling, after all. A little low, perhaps—it gives the room a constricted feeling—but it covers a multitude of problems. Exposed plumbing, trailing cables, not to mention the dust, the spiders. And there may not even be any beams behind it.

"Can you assure me categorically that the beams are there?"

"Put it this way, I'm ninety-nine percent certain." Then Derek tells me how once, when he was pulling down a ceiling at Egton Bridge, he found a time capsule hidden in the joists. "One of those old tin money boxes with a lock. But it wasn't mine, so I gave it to the owner and he broke it open." What did they find? "A bit of a newspaper, five d. and a picture of a naked lady."

I say we will hold off on the ceiling for the time being. I ask him to tell me more about Mr. Kafka. Has he lived in the village long?

"I can't rightly say. Have you seen his place? That cottage on back lane with the green door: looks like a milking shed. The one with thistles growing out of the doorstep." In winter the thinnest trail of smoke came from the chimney. Sometimes the children played round there, but their parents didn't like it. Sometimes the old man tried to give them sweets.

No doubt the council were trying to get him rehoused. But, though he was a foreigner, he had Yorkshire tenacity: he wasn't moving for anyone.

I stop asking questions about Mr. Kafka. I am suddenly embarrassed, as though by taking a special interest I have linked myself to him. It is a kinship I would prefer not to acknowledge.

Not long before she got married, Mrs. Rahim's father died. She nursed him herself for three months before the wedding. When he died she felt a great peace in her heart, as though she could sense him entering the gates of paradise.

Even so, he was always very close. Sometimes she was certain she could hear him talking in the next room. When she opened the door there was nobody there, but the room was filled with a feeling of warmth and love.

We are talking about death, and we are not making much progress with *Alice in Wonderland*. Death is less perplexing: we share many certainties regarding it.

"I think they are still here: I think they are listening," says Mrs. Rahim. "My father suffered very much. But he is happy now."

Mrs. Rahim reaches for her big torn handbag and brings out a man's wallet, worn, old-fashioned, foreign-looking. It is stuffed with papers covered in tiny handwriting. She clasps the wallet between her palms and holds it to her nose: sniffs deeply as though it is some redolent flower.

"I always keep it with me. It is like him."

I have a cold. She makes me milky tea boiled with cardamom, ginger and sugar. She slips a dozen bangles up my arm. Later, in an aura of almost sacred comradeship, we look at the Koran, which she carries to the table wrapped in a silver cloth.

She cannot touch it, she explains, because she is menstruating. Nevertheless I turn the pages for her reverently as she reads. She reads beautifully. I dare not tell her I am menstruating too.

"Kafka. K-a-f-k-a. Kafka."

"What sort of a name is that, then? Is it Russian?"

"No, it's Czech."

"Have you tried under foreign titles? I don't think we have any books in Czech."

"He wrote in German, actually. But he's been translated."

"Oh, look, it's here, Jean: someone must have put it back in the wrong place."

A robust copy of *The Trial*, wrapped in institutional plastic: they leave me to it. Avidly I check the date stamps and the opening page.

Why do I do this? It's a symptom of the literary obsessive: merely the desire to see the cherished works in as many editions as possible. As though one could open them up and discover new words, new revelations. I myself possess four different copies of *Wuthering Heights*. With Kafka, it is something else. I need to see which translation it is. This I can tell immediately, from the first sentence. "Someone must have traduced Josef K., for without having done anything wrong he was arrested one fine morning." I don't like "traduced." It's an immediate stumbling block. A lot of people don't know what it means. "Someone must have been telling lies about Josef K., for without having done anything wrong he was arrested one fine morning." That's better. Comprehensible. This copy is a traduced.

I didn't expect the people of Brontëland would have much call for a book like *The Trial*. There would be a few lonely borrowings, half-hearted attempts, defeated best intentions. But I get a surprise. The label is a forest of date-stamps, repeated and regular, going back years: there are even a couple of old labels pasted beneath with their columns filled. I pick up *The Castle*. That will be different, I think: everybody reads *The Trial*. *The Castle* is, if anything, just as popular. There is a kind of frenzy in the frequent date-stamps which suggests, even, a profound need for Kafka in Brontëland.

It could all have been the same borrower, of course.

I leave the library with a strange reverence. It is as though the town and its cenotaph carry a peculiar secret, which I have stumbled on in the pages of a book. I see them for a moment with different eyes.

Having soaped my arm to remove Mrs. Rahim's obstinate bangles, Hilda has lent me another book, *John Wesley in Yorkshire*. I thank her politely. I have not yet learnt any of the pieces in the *Methodist Hymn Book*.

My front door is open. Derek strides in, a big rangy man, and without a word he buries his pickaxe in my smooth white ceiling. It smashes up like papier-mâché. He grins a long sideways grin.

"By heck, I hope I'm right about this."

He heaves at the plasterboard with all his strength and it comes crackling down, along with a shower of dirt and beetles which covers us both.

My beams are there. My revelation. The double crossbeam, backbone of the house: the ribwork of joists between. One has a blackened bite taken out of it where the oil lantern used to be. All are hung with a drapery of webs. Not so beautiful just now, perhaps: but when I have scrubbed them and scraped them, sanded and stained them, varnished them three times with tender loving care, they will be magnificent.

Derek stoops and picks out something from the heap of dirt: a piece of metal wrapped in a strip of cloth. "Old stays," he mutters. He raises his eyes to the ceiling. "Lady of the house must have been dressing herself up there," he says, "and dropped 'em through the floorboards. An heirloom for you."

He hands it ceremoniously to me. I use it as a bookmark.

When he has left I go for a walk on the moors. The sun is setting: lights are coming on in the valley. Someone is walking towards me down the moorland track.

It is Mr. Kafka. He is following his slow dog down the hill to the village. He has nearly finished his walk, and his head is bent, contemplatively.

I wonder whether to acknowledge him. I am afraid to disturb his silence. He does not often speak to people. Sometimes he nods a greeting to those he knows.

As we pass each other my voice chokes in my throat, I can say nothing; but I manage a smile. Our eyes meet; he smiles back at me.

It seems a smile of recognition, and for the briefest moment he resembles once more the Kafka of the photographs.

J.P.K.

The narrator announces her intention to throw her past—including her Jewishness—onto the "heap of forgotten things" and start anew. It's never that simple. As her own past refuses to stay forgotten, she begins to wonder about Kafka's complicated relationship to his Jewish upbringing. Was he trying to escape it to become the mysterious Kafka she keeps encountering? Maybe, but no matter how you cover it up, the past, like the ancient beams in the story, remains. They are "the backbone of the house."

Acknowledgments

For suggestions, comments, advice and moral support, we thank the following people:

Wilton Barnhardt
John Boston
Richard Butner
Jetse de Vries
Dr. Ruth V. Gross
Kij Johnson
Barry Malzberg
Edward Morris
David Pringle
Lewis Shiner
Jeff VanderMeer
Gordon Van Gelder
Scott Wolven